To Rusty Baetz, for the culinary advice and Nancy Carper, for answering my questions about immigration.

To Suzette Vandewiele and Sharon DeVita, without whose loving support I never would have done it.

PATTY COPELAND

Love of reading led Patty Copeland to join a local writers' workshop and Chicago North RWA. That led to stringing for a local newspaper and writing a business column for three years. She also started writing non-fiction articles for local and national magazines and her first romance. Patty was recently president of a local professional women's group and uses her writing and PR experience to support other women in business. Though now a single parent, she still believes in happy endings. Correspondence is welcome: P.O. Box 1585, Barrington, IL 60011-158.

AUTHOR'S NOTE

Immigration laws have changed giving some provisions for the spouse of a deceased citizen. Any stretching of those laws is purely my invention.

ONE

"Charlie, stop that! Your tongue feels like sandpaper."

Ted froze. Cool March air whipped around him as he entered the back of his building and held the edge of the door in his hand. Ahead of him stairs rose to his law offices. Behind the door he now held open and across a small entryway, another door led to what was supposed to be vacant ground floor space. Or at least it had been vacant when he left on his trip. Ted cocked his head and listened to an unfamiliar, yet unmistakable feminine voice coming from that direction.

"That tickles, Charlie," the voice went on. "Would you quit! I don't have time to fool around right now."

What the hell was going on? Ted wondered with a frown. Who on earth was Charlie and what was he doing in his office building at this hour of the morning? Theodore Camden Carlyle, head of Carlyle and Linden, intended to find out. Still frowning, he closed the back door with a snap, prepared to escort the unknown woman and her paramour off his premises. Pronto.

He glanced across the small entry hall to an open doorway. A trim female posterior, lifted to the heavens, greeted him, causing his frown to deepen.

"Charlie," the muffled female voice scolded, "stop it!" A huge, taffy-colored cat sat licking a woman's decidely slim ankle.

Dumbfounded, Ted grinned. So much for his vivid imagination. The woman was on her hands and knees searching under a shelf, and the cat was obviously Charlie. As he stepped closer to investigate, the cat turned its inquiring gaze on him and began to growl.

"What's the matter with you? And where's the cold air coming from?" the woman demanded. She didn't budge. Not bothering to lift her head, she said, "Charlie, if you've moved those kittens again . . ."

Annie Marie Rafferty shivered and called out, "Close the door!" Muttering under her breath, Annie turned around on her hands and knees. Her words died as she took in the dark gray covered legs blocking her view. Uh-oh. Unless Charlie had taken to wearing pin-striped suits, she had a visitor. It seemed to take forever for her gaze to travel up the length of the man's suit-clad body, enveloped in an expensive cashmere coat.

Annie's gaze continued upward, and her mouth dropped open in admiration. He had the bluest eyes she'd ever seen—much bluer than any of her cousins, aunts, and uncles. Her gaze traveled to the man's bright gold hair before coming back to scrutinize his suntanned features. Suntan. Three-piece suit. Cashmere coat. Scowling face. As the thought clicked into place, Annie sprang to her feet. This was not the first impression she wanted to make on her landlord.

"Oh, you must be Mr. Carlyle. Welcome back. I hope you had a nice vacation. I'm your new tenant." Sticking out her hand, she waited until the man's firm grasp met hers before continuing, "I'm Anne Rafferty. Annie to my friends. I'm sorry. I didn't mean to snap at you about the door, but the kittens are newborns." Her landlord glanced behind him at the cardboard carton at his feet.

Annie finally quit pumping his hand and glanced down at the cat. "Charlie, stop that," she scowled before turning back to Ted. "I don't know why Charlie's growling at you. She doesn't normally do that. At least, I don't think so," she said with a frown. "She's a new addition to the family. One of my little nieces found her loitering in the alley. When I realized she was expecting"—Annie flashed him a smile—"I couldn't turn her out."

"Glad to meet you," Ted said when he could get a word in. He retracted his hand and rubbed the back of his head, looking from the small dark-haired woman in front of him to the still-growling cat almost behind him. After a moment, he relaxed and said to his puzzled tenant, "Ah, I think I know what the problem is. Permit me." He drew Annie toward him. "I'm blocking her way."

A shock ran through Annie at his touch. Rattled at her reaction to her new landlord, Annie talked even faster than normal. "Why, for heaven's sake. Charlie's never done that before. Of course, the kittens are only a day old, but there've been dozens of people in and out of here since then."

Ted looked down at his new tenant. Used to tall women, this one seemed so little next to him. Her dark winged brows were knit in confusion, and her mobile lips which had smiled at him so widely a moment ago were pressed together in concentration as she watched the cat. Her lips quirked up in a grin before spreading into a wide smile once more. She turned her face up to his, and Ted noticed a tiny dimple in her right cheek. He marveled at the woman's creamy complexion. Beautiful, he thought. Just beautiful. Under his intense scrutiny, she lowered her lids as a blush swept her cheeks. He'd had a quick flash of grayish blue, though, before her heavy fringe of lashes swept down.

The cat pranced by with one of her kittens, and Ted's brows rose. "Charlie?" he said, clearly confused.

Annie laughed. "Well, my niece had already named him—her—before we discovered that he—I mean, she—wasn't just well fed, but expecting."

Shoving back the sides of his overcoat, Téd stuck his hands in his pants pockets and looked at the cat again. "If you wanted to give the animal a home, don't you think someplace other than an office building would have been a little more appropriate?"

"It's no more inappropriate than our place with no one home all day."

"Cats are solitary animals. And haven't you ever heard of litter boxes? That should solve the problem."

Annie's Irish temper began to simmer at his know-it-all attitude. "Look, at first I was worried about Charlie expecting and being alone. What if she developed problems? I've been here twelve to fifteen hours a day lately. It seemed more sensible for her to stay here where I could keep an eye on her. Once the kittens arrived, I was faced with the same problem. Besides, I always feed her outside on the porch, and she never goes into the restaurant. In fact, she never even goes into the kitch—"

"Restaurant?" Ted looked at her as if she'd just announced she was a leprechaun. "What restaurant?" he repeated with a frown, glancing around in confusion.

Annie sighed, pushing her hair out of her eyes. "My restaurant," she said with forced patience. "Here." His reaction to her words almost made Annie laugh. She'd always heard of the expression "turned as white as a sheet," but this was the first time she'd ever seen it happen. "Didn't you know?" she asked in surprise.

"Restaurant," he repeated dully. "Here in my office building. With my law offices." When he'd left to attend to business, first on the East Coast, then in Europe for two weeks before he took a week's vacation, the ground floor space had been vacant. His partner had told him he would take care of renting it.

Preparing for a fight, Annie said, "I signed a contract with your partner. You can check it with Jim if you like."

Ted glanced around again. He'd never dreamed that Jim would rent the empty space to a restaurant. He looked back at Annie. "But the smells, the noise." He turned defensive at Annie's expression of mounting outrage. "The confusion."

"My restaurant doesn't smell! I mean, it won't. We have a perfectly adequate exhaust system." Annie felt her color rising with the volume of her voice. Taking a deep breath to calm herself, she added, "As for noise, it's not a bar. We will sell wine and beer, but only to diners. We won't in the least resemble any of the singles' hot spots," she assured him, visions of the noisy Near North's singles' bars running through her mind.

Annie had felt lucky to find space on the fringe of the River North area, assuring plenty of foot traffic to contribute to her business. Perched on the north branch of the Chicago River, the area had evolved from dilapidated warehouses and second-rate hotels into art galleries and avant-garde furniture stores, with boutiques and other businesses following to create a trendy quarter. An additional bonus for Annie was that the space, which had last housed an art supply store and school, had obviously been a restaurant in a prior life because they had found electrical and plumbing outlets in place. All they'd had to do was update existing wiring and pipes to meet current city codes.

"And I might remind you," she pointed out, gathering steam once more, "that a large part of our clientele will come from this neighborhood, which you *obviously* approve of since you own this building!"

"You have a point there," Ted agreed, rubbing the back of his head. Everything she said made perfect sense. So why did he feel so uncomfortable?

Drat the man. She was on a roll, and he had taken the

wind out of her sails by agreeing with her. Annie looked at him suspiciously and noted that he seemed only partially mollified. Aha, she thought, here it comes. Wasn't there always a "but"?

"However," he added, "why this building? Wouldn't you rather be in the midst of things? I should think that would make the most sense, from a business point of view."

"It would," she informed him dryly, "if I could afford the astronomical rents they're demanding. That and the fact that this building was ideal for my purposes and circumstances." Annie explained about her original lease falling through after she'd already ordered her kitchen equipment. Begging dealers to hold shipment, a frenzied search of near north locations had turned up this space. "So you see, it was like it was meant to be."

"Meant to be," he repeated, obviously not convinced.

Annie looked at him carefully. From his attire, she could see he was obviously successful; from his demeanor, she could tell he was all business. Just what she needed: a stick-in-the-mud landlord with a balance sheet for a brain.

"Well, it seems a moot point," he said with a trace of casual arrogance. "As long as your exhaust system is effective, I'll obviously have to make the best of it, Miss . . ."

"Rafferty," Annie supplied as her eyes narrowed. Make the best of it, huh? Determined to make him change his mind about the restaurant, she said, "Come on, I'll give you a quick tour." Looking back over her shoulder, her step slowed as she realized that Ted Carlyle wasn't following her. Instead he had taken out a small pocket notebook and was writing something. "Are you coming?" she asked in exasperation, wondering what he was writing.

"Hmmm?" Ted looked up. "Oh, yes. I was just making a note before I forget. What were you saying?" Putting away his pad, he followed her.

Annie shook off her curiosity. "You're just in time for

our grand opening. It's next week. We weren't sure we could get everything ready in time, but with the whole family pitching in I think we'll make it by Monday.''

Coming to a stop past stocked shelves and the walk-in refrigerator, Annie beamed as she indicated the bustling kitchen. From the pristine white walls to the gleaming chrome worktables to the red quarry-tile floor, every inch of the new kitchen had been installed by her family or family friends who owed them favors. Even now, some electrician friends of her cousin Kerry worked at finishing the wiring for the dishwasher. She watched in amusement as her Uncle Tully followed a plumber around, anxious that every requirement be met. She could probably look forward to a contingent of uncles arriving in a few days to follow after the health, fire, and building inspectors.

A smile still lingered from the image of her zealous uncles trailing the forthcoming inspectors when, out of the corner of her eye, Annie saw that her landlord had taken out his notebook and was writing in it again. "Look here," she said, facing him with determination, "just what are you writing in there?"

Ted Carlyle looked up, clearly startled. "Why?"

"Because if it has something to do with me or the restaurant, I think I should know about it."

"Why?"

"Why?" Annie echoed, dumbfounded. She wasn't used to attorneys who answered every question with another question.

Rarely did anyone question Ted, let alone a petite bundle who was, after all, his tenant. He found her perplexing and didn't know why. Studying her slight form under the concealing apron, he thought she looked so harmless, too. "What possible interest could it be to you what I write?"

"It's very disconcerting to find you scribbling every time I turn around. And rude, too," she added, staring at him intently.

Rude? No one had ever called Theodore Camden Carlyle rude before. He slid the notebook and pen into an inside pocket of his jacket and forced a slight smile. "In this particular case, you're right. It does concern you. You said the restaurant was opening in a week, and I simply made a note so I wouldn't forget. Am I forgiven?" He looked at her with raised brows.

Though his smile held a touch of condescension, Annie felt slightly foolish. She shrugged and wondered why she was making such an issue of the incident. She must be more tired that she thought. It *had* been a hectic month. And it would be better, she reminded herself, to be in her landlord's good graces than squaring off with him over every peculiarity of his personality. After all, was his habit of scribbling notes any different than Aunt Nola waking from a sound sleep every morning at 3 A.M. to get up, write herself a note, and post it on the refrigerator? In vain had Annie repeated that a pad beside her aunt's bed would accomplish the same thing. Her good humor restored, Annie smiled and shook her head. Besides, she should be pleased. At least Ted Carlyle cared enough about the opening to make a note of the date.

She stepped back, automatically pulling him with her, as Morgana and Rowena, two more cousins, huffed past her with laden arms. She should be helping them unload the supplies of condiments, but she couldn't help showing off her pride and joy.

"Isn't it wonderful?" Not giving Ted a chance to reply, she pulled him along after her, past some of her aunts who were unpacking boxes, past more cousins who were lining shelves with dishes and glasses, past the electricians and plumber, and out of the kitchen proper into a serving area.

"This is where we'll have the coffee pots set up," she explained, trailing one hand along the satiny, bleached perfection of the wooden countertop, "and over here, as you can see, are the soda dispensers. We're also going to have espresso. That is," Annie's voice slowed for the first time, "if the machine arrives in time. Oh well," she continued more cheerfully, "people will probably be understanding for the first few days until we work out the kinks. And here is the dining area."

She never tired of looking at the result of several weeks' intensive work. Golden, bleached wood floors and bright white walls lightened the interior, while artistically arranged wooden wine racks and plants enhanced the seating area with its tables clothed in white. Her colors of teal and rose were represented in the blue-green napkins and a silk sprig of wild roses that would be slipped into every vase of real carnations. She had had a wonderful time tracking down the paintings and photographs of food and wine that warmed the pristine walls, again playing off her favorite colors. Since family and friends knew she was going to use huge plants to create alcoves of privacy, they had inundated her with early opening-day gifts of tree-size plants such as schefflera, ficus, and dracaenas, as well as smaller ones.

Ted could hear the pride in Annie's voice. She obviously had worked very hard to accomplish so much in such a short time. He had tried to hide his initial dismay at learning his new tenant was a restaurant, but she was like a prosecuting attorney who reasoned away every objection he raised. His objections were still valid, but as he'd told her, it was a little late to be making them. He had to admit that the interior was warm and inviting. He tried to concentrate on her deliciously husky, cheerful voice, which had a funny way of ending sentences on an up note. Very intriguing, he thought, turning to ask about the name of the restaurant.

"It's Apple Annie's."

Smiling, Annie watched her landlord's reaction beneath lowered lids. After a brief moment, his careful, blank expression became one of amusement if twitching lips (*decidedly nicely shaped ones*), raised sandy brows, and wide blue, blue eyes crinkled at the corners meant anything. Most strangers, when told the name of her new restaurant, looked at her in bewilderment.

"Does it have anything to do with *A Pocketful of Miracles?*" he asked.

"Well . . . not directly." Ever honest, Annie tried to explain. You see, my mother died when I was about twelve—"

"Oh, I'm sorry. I—"

"It's all right. Aunt Nola came to stay and help Papa and me take care of Lynn, Celia, and Kit—"

"Who?"

"My sisters and brother." Annie frowned at the confusion on her landlord's face. If he kept interrupting her every second, she'd never get the explanation out. "Anyway, as I was saying, *or as I was trying to say,*" Annie emphasized as Ted opened his mouth again, "my mother had this thing about apples. You know, 'An apple a day . . .' " She glanced at his bewildered eyes and rushed on. "I just continued the pattern she had set. When I started catering, I—"

"Catering?"

Ignoring the latest interruption, she continued, "slipped a couple of apples into every basket. It was just an oddity the family accepted until a customer started calling me Apple Annie. Guess he must have seen the movie. Anyway, the nickname stuck. I decided to rename my catering business and when it came time to choose a name for the restaurant, the family was adamant that the name would be appropriate for this area. All these artsy people. Sort of catchy, don't you think?" Not a trace of a smile lightened her new landlord's expression, and Annie groaned inwardly.

Oh, darn, the impression she had formed of this man

sight unseen must be right after all. She had hoped for a minute when he showed appreciation for her nickname that she was wrong. After all, she reminded herself, what did she expect of a man who had a girlfriend like Veronica? Old Theodore must really be the uptight, buttoned-down, stick-in-the-mud lawyer she'd first imagined.

His brows contracted in a frown, Ted asked, "You started catering when you were twelve?"

"What?"

"I said, 'You started catering—' "

"No, I heard you. Whatever gave you that idea?"

"You did. You said—"

"No, I didn't."

"No?" Looking slightly aggrieved, Ted said, "Let's start over again. When—"

"Didn't you hear anything I said? I didn't start catering until I was sixteen and not in a serious way until I was almost seventeen." Drat the man; now he had her interrupting everything *he* said. It must be catching. *"And,"* she added hastily as he opened his mouth again, "that was just to supplement my regular job. The business didn't really take off for almost two years."

"What about your father? What was he doing all this time?" Ted asked in disapproval. His frown faltered as the pride died out of Annie's expression to be replaced by one tinged with sadness.

Annie straightened. "I decided to tackle the catering business seriously when Papa stopped a bullet. A policeman's pension doesn't stretch very far when you have to worry about college tuition for three."

The wind went out of Ted's sails as he realized he had misjudged this woman. "Family," he said. "Surely you had some family."

"Oh, yes." Humor replaced the sorrow in her eyes. Ted leaned toward Annie. There was something about this woman that drew him like a magnet and for some reason he was willing to follow his soul's fancy. He blinked and focused on her dimple to bring his errant thoughts back in line.

"I have plenty of family. In fact"—Annie laughed—"if you're short a few aunts or uncles, I can lend you some of mine." She gave a rueful grin and shook her head. "Unfortunately, Irish families tend to run to the large size, and when Papa died my aunts and uncles had their hands full with their own lives. My sisters and brother and I managed quite well," she said in haste as he opened his mouth to insert a question. "And there was no shortage of love or protection, I assure you. In fact, I've been trying for years to convince all my relatives that I really am dry behind the ears now."

Her grin really was quite infectious, Ted thought as he felt his own twitching lips stretch to match hers. Not only was she brave, but she was independent and quite obviously did not want his sympathy. Now, if he could just manage to get a comment in once in a while between her monologues . . .

He tucked his hands in his pockets and rocked back on his heels. "I take it that all those people we passed in the kitchen are related to you?" He couldn't imagine having that many relatives, let alone having them all in one room.

"Most of them," Annie admitted. "I'll introduce you on the way out." Annie turned on her heel, clearly expecting him to follow. "I warn you, though," she said over her shoulder at her usual machine-gun speed, "you're going to be thoroughly confused."

Going to be confused, Ted thought in amusement. He needed a court transcript just to keep track of her convoluted explanations.

Ten minutes later, Annie ushered Ted out and listened for a moment as he made his way up the back stairs to his offices. She turned to the penetrating gaze of her Aunt Nola.

"Somehow he doesn't resemble the dry old stick you'd said he'd be." As usual, her aunt didn't mince words.

Annie's quick glance took in the older woman's rumpled appearance and other less obvious signs of tiredness. "As you've told me innumerable times before presenting blind-date material, 'Looks can be deceiving.' "

"Come on, Aunt Nola," she said, putting an arm around the older woman's shoulders, "you've been up since dawn. I'm taking you home, like it or not. The others and I can finish quite well without your help. Home and feet up for you. Just as soon as I have a word with Uncle Tully about the exhaust system."

After dropping her aunt off at their Near North brownstone with admonitions to rest, Annie decided to check personally with one of their produce suppliers on South Water Street. With their opening so near, she couldn't afford any slip-ups in delivery schedules.

On the return drive to the restaurant through mid-morning traffic, she replayed the scene in her mind from the moment she had first seen her landlord. She stalled at the memory of his blue eyes. Even her cousins Guy and Brian couldn't top him, and they were famous in the family for the legions of girls trailing them after one glance from periwinkle blue eyes surrounded by long, dark lashes. She snorted in disgust. Why couldn't her branch of the family be blessed with extraordinary blue eyes rather than ordinary pale ones? Well, maybe not so ordinary since hers tended to be blue green if she wore the right colors. But that didn't count. Not compared to Theodore Camden Carlyle's blue, blue eyes.

With a start, Annie realized she had allowed herself to be trapped in the traffic waiting at the Orleans Street bridge as it was raised to accommodate a sailboat. Now she'd be stuck for at least another ten minutes while the boat went through on its path from the Chicago River to

Lake Michigan. Nuts! The others were going to wonder what was keeping her.

At the thought of the legions of relatives waiting for her, Annie almost lost heart. If she knew her family, every single one of them was going to ask her what she thought of Ted Carlyle.

She closed her eyes. What did she think? He certainly was attractive enough. Not overly handsome, just average—except for those eyes. She hesitated a moment, remembering how he'd smiled at the mention of Apple Annie's. His face had taken on life where previously it was politely blank or frowning disapproval. The smile hadn't lasted long though, so old Theodore probably *was* the stick-in-the-mud his constant reference to business indicated.

Having met only his partner, Jim Linden, Annie had had high hopes that Ted Carlyle, who was on vacation at the time she signed her lease, would also be compatible. Her run-in with Veronica had dispelled that hope. Jim had introduced them and after only a few words with her, Annie decided she didn't like the woman. She'd met that type before: reserved to the point of chilliness and unemotional. Veronica had cut off Jim's explanation about Annie's lease and pointedly left a personal message for Ted. Her proprietary attitude indicated she might be engaged to Ted Carlyle, but since Veronica wore gloves Annie couldn't tell if she also wore a ring. Annie decided right then that he must be a stuffed shirt to be interested in such an ice queen.

Good, Annie thought as traffic began to inch forward, old Theodore and Veronica deserved each other. One disapproving, the other boring. And that's what she'd tell the family.

Ted entered his office after climbing the rear flight of stairs, his head in a whirl with the memory of voices and colors. As he gazed at the familiar pale gray carpeting, charcoal upholstered furniture, and gray- charcoal- and black-plaid drapes, the clean lines and colors of his office soothed an incipient headache induced by the chaotic noise and exotic warmth of the restaurant below.

Thank goodness he had had the good sense to let Veronica decorate the suite of offices. She knew what she was doing. Competence was one of the things he admired about her. It was only one of the myriad details his mother set forth regularly as a benefit of making Veronica his wife. After careful thought, he was almost ready to take the plunge and ask her to marry him.

Ted sat at his desk and propped his head in his hands. Anne Rafferty had said he would be confused, and she was right. He scanned the names he had made note of while climbing the rear stairs. Moira, Morgana, Norah, Nola, Rowena, Linette, Delia, Fionna, Fenella, Cameron, Casey. The only person who stood out clearly in Ted's memory at the moment was Uncle Tully, probably as much because he fit the stereotype of an Irish policeman as because his name was so different from the others. And, Annie had said, the group he'd met today barely scratched the surface.

Now, there was a contradiction. Obviously she was smart. She had turned a catering business into such a success she was opening a restaurant. Yet the woman couldn't answer a simple question . . . simply. He grinned. One minute into her story, she'd had him in knots trying to untangle the different skeins of her tale.

Yes, Annie did raise conflicting emotions in him. One moment he wanted to cradle her small body next to his protectively; the next he wanted to wring her neck; then before he knew it, he was laughing at something she said. He couldn't deny she was damned attractive, though. Even her colorful clothes seemed right somehow. All he remembered clearly was a riot of hues topped by an apron and an intriguing dimple that made him smile as he thought of it.

A restaurant for a tenant. And an Irish restaurant at that. He groaned as he conjured up the scent of boiled cabbage and corned beef filtering into the gracious air of his office as he discussed cases with clients. What was Veronica going to say?

Ted rubbed his eyes and stared at his desk. His calendar came into fuzzy focus. He blinked rapidly to clear his vision, but the numbers stubbornly stayed in the same pattern.

One week, Annie had said, till the restaurant opened. Ted groaned again, checking the note he'd made earlier. Not only did he have a restaurant for a tenant, an Irish restaurant, but it was going to open on St. Patrick's Day.

If there was any holiday more wildly celebrated in Chicago, Ted had yet to hear about it. He knew it was a cowardly thought, but he longed to be able to get back on a plane and fly to the islands again.

TWO

Ted reread the third paragraph of the page in front of him one more time. The constant tapping noise finally broke his concentration altogether, and he realized that someone was at the rear door of his offices.

When his secretary, Mrs. Marshall, didn't materialize in the back hall to solve this latest disturbance, Ted glanced at his watch and sighed in frustration. Lunchtime already and he hadn't finished going over his case notes for his appearance in court this afternoon.

The staccato beat went on. Reluctantly, he rose and strode through his office, across the short hallway to the rear entrance. Annoyed at the disruption, he wrenched open the door. Ted's gaze dropped from his six foot two inch height down to the diminutive form of Miss Rafferty's aunt.

"Oh, my. You startled me."

What was her last name again? Sullivan, Donovan, Kerr, Rafferty? For the life of him, he couldn't pick her name from the deluge of Irish relatives he had met on Monday.

"I'm sorry. I thought the pounding—uh, noise—was

23

coming from below." Confronted with this rosy-cheeked, twinkling-eyed older version of Annie, Ted held his temper in check. After all, it wasn't her fault his office routine had been disrupted half a dozen times this week by either the noise from work going on below or someone needing an extension cord, the telephone, or God knows what else. "What can I do for you?"

"Well, dear boy, it's rather what I can do for you." She patted his cheek, then bent down by his door and picked up a tray he hadn't noticed. "It's lunchtime, you know. I saw your secretary on her way out and in passing the time of day, she mentioned you were working through lunch. So I thought it would only be neighborly if I brought something up for you."

She bustled through his hall, the pungent aroma of some kind of fish chowder following her progress. Ted trailed after her. Peeking through the open door to his office, she made a beeline for Ted's desk and set the tray squarely on top of his papers. "Here we are. Now, you just sit down and eat this soup while it's hot."

"Mrs.—"

"Now, there's to be no formality, dear boy. You just call me Aunt Nola like the others. Well, come on." She waved him toward his chair impatiently. "Don't let it get cold."

She beamed at him, a fine network of lines deepening with her smile. Her once-dark hair was fully threaded with silver, but age hadn't bent her slim back, nor had it dimmed the sparkle in her eyes or her creamy complexion. If heredity followed its own laws, Annie would look like this someday.

Bemused, Ted sat down and sniffed appreciatively at the steaming soup. His stomach rumbled as he picked up a spoon and stirred, increasing the fragrant steam drifting toward him. Pieces of some kind of fish surfaced in the savory soup. It smelled wonderful. It was times like this when he was really hungry that he regretted his decision to become a vegetarian. Not that he was doing such a hot job of it. He hadn't lasted two days in Europe before he succumbed to the desire for meat. The thought of the paper-thin slices of veal and the tantalizing scent of herbs steaming into his nostrils had him practically slavering. At the same time, he wondered if there was an ulterior motive for feeding him. He stirred the soup a little more and thought perhaps it wouldn't do any harm just to sample it. That way he wouldn't hurt Aunt Nola's feelings.

His delight in the subtle flavors must have been evident on his face because she said, "Delicious, isn't it? I swear, that Annie can cook anything. It's scallop and snapper, in case you can't figure out what it is. And over here"—she leaned over and lifted the cover from a dish Ted hadn't yet noticed—"is Chinese dumplings with black bean sauce. The other stuff on the plate is mango and saffron rice. I know the soup doesn't exactly go with Chinese food, but Annie is experimenting. And anyway, it all ends up the same place, doesn't it?"

Before Aunt Nola lowered the cover, Ted stared with longing at the small, delicate dough casings nestled in Chinese vegetables. He knew inside he would find minced meat and vegetables. These days he could eat all the Chinese food he wanted, as long as it was only vegetables or fish. His mouth watered at the thought of dipping the meaty morsels into black bean sauce. If it was half as good as this chowder, Annie's reputation as a chef was assured. He frowned at the contradiction. What kind of Irish restaurant served Chinese food? He turned to ask Aunt Nola about the menu and realized she was still in full spate. Now he knew where Annie had picked up her penchant for nonstop monologues.

"—shouldn't bother you after those interruptions this morning, but I told her you wouldn't consider it a bother if I was giving you lunch. After all," Aunt Nola paused as she stood back and took a good look at him, "you look like you need to put on a few pounds. It's not healthy to be too thin.

"I know what we'll do," she said, coming closer again and patting him on the shoulder. "You can sample all these dishes Annie keeps coming up with." She leaned close, confiding, "I don't like to tell Annie, but at my age all these exotic dishes just give me heartburn. You'd be doing me a big favor if you'd be the official taster for a change and give my stomach a rest." She rubbed the general area of her abdomen under a concealing apron similar to Annie's.

Ted stiffened his resolve. "I'd like to, Aunt Nola, but I'm a vegetarian." Finished with the chowder, he sniffed appreciatively at the Chinese dumplings. "I'm afraid all I'm allowed to eat is fish and vegetables, you see."

"What, a big strapping man like you?" He nodded, and she looked appalled, as if he'd confessed to belonging to some strange cult. "Seems like a sin somehow. And a waste of food. Not that I don't know the concoctions are good," she said, turning away to gaze absently around his office. "That Annie is a wonder. Whatever she sets out to do, you can be sure it's a done thing. She isn't afraid to tackle anything. That's what's worrying, though. I mean, what if one of these days she takes on something she can't handle? Then where will she be? There's no stopping her though. Trying to restrain that girl is like trying to keep a lid on a broken pressure cooker." Aunt Nola's voice drifted off as she wandered around.

"Don't you think," she said with a decided frown, "that your office is a little plain? I don't mean to be insulting, but a touch of color would put some life into this place."

Ted, taking a last bite of the delicious vegetables and rice, almost choked at her bluntness. He tried to swallow quickly so he could reply that he was quite happy with his office the way it was.

"The color scheme is supposed to be monochromatic," a cool voice said from the doorway.

Ted looked up, saw Veronica, and *did* choke on his food. He hastily took a sip from the glass of water on the tray while Aunt Nola came around behind him and began to pound on his back.

"Veronica," he rasped out when he could. Clearing his throat, Ted looked at his about to be fiancée uncertainly. Her cool, blonde beauty usually appealed to his sense of aesthetics; right now she looked extremely frosty. "What are you doing here?"

"I came by to take you to lunch, but I can see I'm a little late." Veronica stepped smoothly into his office, peeling one long leather glove from her hand. She shrugged at her fur coat and pointedly waited for Ted to assist her out of it. He jumped to his feet to help her. "Thank you, darling."

When Veronica turned and surveyed the older woman with a pale, arched brow, he hastily made introductions. "Veronica, this is Aunt Nola—I mean, Mrs.—"

Ted felt a rush of gratitude as Aunt Nola quickly came to his rescue with, "I'm Nola Donovan, but everyone calls me Aunt Nola." She stepped forward, prepared to shake hands with Veronica.

Veronica appeared not to see the movement as she continued to remove her remaining glove and absently pull the two through one hand. She stepped away, turning to gaze at the office interior. Ted knew she had lavished many hours on the design and felt almost as much pride as she at its clean lines, uncluttered appearance, and the harmonious blend of tones.

"It's not everyone who can appreciate the aesthetics of style," Veronica said. Giving a last glimpse around as if to make sure everything was still in its place, she turned to Aunt Nola. "This is a business office, you know, and an attorney's office at that. The monochrome scheme presents a certain . . . decorum."

"Oh, it does that all right," Aunt Nola agreed.

By her turned-down mouth, Ted could see that Annie's aunt clearly thought it dull. But Veronica's choice of pale gray, charcoal, and black was so . . . so sane and subtle compared to the riot of colors that apparently Annie and her aunt seemed to prefer.

"Veronica," he said hastily, "Aunt—I mean, Mrs. Donovan is the aunt of my new tenant. It's to be a restaurant, you know."

"Really. And what kind of restaurant is it to be?" Veronica's languid question was directed at Aunt Nola.

"Well, there you got me. I don't rightly know what you call it, but Annie said the food's to be hearty, plentiful, and all different kinds of it. She says people are tired of big plates with one little slice of meat and two spears of asparagus drowned in mango chutney or some other funny sauce. Or those tiny vegetarian salads, even the pasta ones, that wouldn't fill up a flea. She said this is a hearty city and people here have hearty appetites, even the artsy . . . ones." Eyeing Veronica's thin frame, Annie's aunt faltered, clearly unsure if she had just insulted her. "Probably from starving themselves in a garret somewhere," Aunt Nola muttered.

Before she could start off again, Ted quickly inserted, "I can hardly wait for the restaurant to open, Veronica. Lunch was delicious."

"Oh, what did you have?"

"Uh, soup and some delicious Chinese vegetables." Waving a hand toward his desk top and the remains of his meal, he said, "If this was any indication of A—Miss Rafferty's ability, I think the restaurant will be a success."

"How . . . reassuring." Veronica glanced at Ted's desk as Aunt Nola removed the tray from atop scattered papers.

"I can see you're buried in work as usual, darling. I might as well be on my way.

"I wonder, though," she said, pulling on her gloves, "if I could ask you to come down with me. It was the most extraordinary thing, but there's a cat in the entryway and it actually *growled* at me when I came in. For a moment there, I thought the beast was going to attack me."

Ted smothered a smile at Aunt Nola's snort, but he could understand Veronica's concern. When he had received the same treatment two mornings running, he decided that fearing attack every time he came and went to his own office was ridiculous. With no one around to watch on Wednesday, he had hunkered down beside Charlie and her litter and talked soothingly until the cat stopped growling and went about the business of washing a kitten. Eventually he extended one hand and lightly stroked Charlie in time to the beat of her tongue as she washed yet another kitten. This morning there hadn't been a peep out of her when he greeted her and her litter.

"It's simply a matter of Charlie getting to know you," he reassured Veronica. Ignoring her incredulous look, he took the tray from Aunt Nola's hands and said he would escort both ladies downstairs.

From her office immediately behind the restaurant's refrigerator and storage shelves, Annie eyed Aunt Nola as she passed. By the looks of the tray, old Theodore hadn't turned down the offer of free food. She ignored his rumbling baritone which carried easily through the open back door and tried to concentrate on the rows of figures on the paper before her. When it became obvious that Veronica was with him, she gave up all pretense and blatantly eavesdropped.

"Honestly, darling, the way you act anyone would think you're attached to the beast. And besides," Veronica continued, "why on earth is a cat even in the same building with a restaurant. Isn't there some law against that?"

"Don't be silly. In the old days, I imagine most restaurants kept them as mousers."

"That doesn't say much for the cleanliness of the restaurants, does it? No, I won't fondle the beast. Who knows what diseases cats have."

Annie stalked out of her office, fury propelling her. Each word spoken in that woman's clear, carefully modulated, and sterile voice set her teeth on edge. If she called Charlie a beast once more . . . The cat's now familiar deep growling interrupted Annie's thoughts and she smiled in satisfaction. Good, Charlie didn't like them either.

Her surprise was total when she stepped around her open back door into the hall and confronted Veronica scowling in distaste as Charlie wound her way around Ted's ankles.

Ted looked up at her with a smug smile. "I've won the battle over territory, it seems. Now we just have to get Charlie used to Veronica."

We don't have to do any such thing, Annie thought. Let Veronica fend for herself.

Before she could voice her lack of concern for Veronica's feelings, the ice queen spoke for herself, pointedly pulling herself out of range as Ted made to touch her. "I told you, darling. There's no way to know what diseases the little beast is harboring."

"The little *beast* is not harboring any diseases," Annie snapped. "When I learned she was expecting, I took her to a vet. He gave her a clean bill of health."

Veronica eyed her with what Annie was coming to think of as a perpetual habit: raised, arched brows. Someone should tell her that if she kept wrinkling her forehead like that, she was going to need a face lift by the time she was forty.

After a moment of cool assessment, Veronica said,

"You're to be congratulated on your warm heart, but don't you think a shelter would have been a more appropriate home than a restaurant?" Veronica's words might have sounded like faint praise, but her sardonic expression and cold eyes clearly said she thought Annie an idiot.

Annie nodded agreeably. "I did consider a shelter, of course. The only problem is they have more animals than they can handle. Did you realize they put about twenty-five animals to sleep each week?"

"And a good thing, too. I can't see why the loss of one more—" Veronica broke off, gingerly leaned over, and counted Charlie's litter. "I don't see why the loss of five more would make the slightest difference. It certainly would be much healthier than cluttering up a restaurant with the little . . . animals."

Veronica's switch from beasts to animals was obviously in reaction to the wrath Annie felt simmering inside her. Aunt Nola always said she was a poor poker player, with her face too clearly revealing her thoughts. Annie struggled to find adequate words to put the animal-hating *beast* in her place. She probably believed in legislated euthanasia for people who had outlived their usefulness, too, Annie fumed.

Before she could open her mouth to tell Veronica exactly what she thought of her, Ted unceremoniously took the blonde beauty by the elbow. "I thought you said you had to be on your way," he reminded her, opening the hall door and gently easing her outside. Before he stepped through, he turned back to Annie.

"Veronica is obviously not an animal lover," he said with an apologetic shrug of his wide shoulders. "But I might remind you that her sentiments pretty much reflect what I said about the cat." He hesitated a moment, then added with a slight smile, "By the way, thanks for lunch. I think you're a terrific chef." With a wink, he was gone.

Annie stood mesmerized, her clenched fists relaxing at

her sides. The change in Ted Carlyle's face when he smiled and winked at her was unbelievable. She had been ready to jump down his throat before he took the wind out of her sails again by switching topics. At least, she reminded herself, he'd had the grace not to agree with Veronica in front of her. Maybe the man was human after all.

Though what he saw in that—Annie searched for a scathing description—mannequin called Veronica, she couldn't understand. The woman didn't have a feeling bone in her body. Why would a man want a woman like that? Used to the forthright earthiness of her male relatives, Annie was confused by Ted's choice and even more so at the thought of what it had to do with her anyway.

Aunt Nola poked her head around the door. "That woman gone?"

"Yes, and just in time, too." Annie told her about Veronica's animal elimination proclivities.

Aunt Nola dismissed her with a sniff. "I hope Charlie does more than growl at her. It would serve her right to have a chunk taken out of that disdaining hide."

On the Sunday evening before the restaurant's opening, Annie stepped away from the refrigerator after storing dishes prepared for a catering job the next day. As the door snapped shut, she looked at her watch for the first time in hours, surprised to find it was after 9:30. She put her hands to the small of her back and leaned backward to relieve her aching muscles. A groan escaped, not so much from the effort, but from the thought of the forthcoming scold from Aunt Nola. She'd promised to try to be home early tonight. After all, tomorrow was their big day, the official opening of Apple Annie's.

Oh, well, at least the worst was over now. The inspectors had given her a green light, all the necessary equipment had arrived—including the espresso machine—the produce and meat had arrived on schedule, she'd finished preparing mounds of chicken tarragon for the luncheon they were scheduled to cater tomorrow, and the kitchen was all cleaned up and ready for business.

Annie hitched herself up on one of the tall stools next to the wooden chopping table and glanced around her gleaming kitchen with pride. She had looked forward to working in her kitchen by herself for the first time so much that she had talked Aunt Nola into leaving after her aunt formed tomorrow's croissants and put them in the proofing oven. It had been a matter of minutes to switch them into the baking oven later, and between boiling chicken and chopping celery for the salad and preparing pineapple, berries, and melons for the fruit tray for tomorrow's luncheon, time had flown.

The muted strains of a popular movie theme seeped into her consciousness from the kitchen speaker of the sound system her cousin Kerry and his electrician friend had installed. Otherwise the silence was complete; even the furnace blower was off for the time being. Annie sat and luxuriated in the silence, something so rare in her life. This was what she needed, a few minutes alone to regroup for the strenuous week ahead.

Conflicting thoughts warred back and forth in her head. She sighed, feeling disloyal even thinking about how overwhelmed she had been by her family lately. Annie reminded herself yet again that she was lucky to have such a large, loving family. What would she, Lynn, Celia, and Kit have done without Aunt Nola and all the others over the years? The problem was, a lifetime of habit had so ingrained certain actions and reactions with her family that now the mold was hard to break.

Take the restaurant, for instance. No . . . perhaps it went further back than that. Back to when she had first started catering. Having put herself through secretarial school, Annie was looking for other ways to make money, to put Celia and Lynn through college. She might have had to give up her dream of college and art school, but that didn't mean she couldn't make sure the girls and Kit realized their dreams when the time came.

The catering had started innocently enough by her offering to help a neighbor who found herself facing a high school graduation party for her eldest with her two younger children sick. Annie was so used to helping cook for her hordes of relatives that cooking for twelve seemed like a snap and an easy way to earn some extra money. Word flew around the neighborhood about how innovative she'd been in carving a watermelon like a basket and filling it with a multitude of fruits, plus how delicious the lasagna and dessert had been. By the time she was nineteen and had been catering for two years, she was making enough to quit her job as a secretary to work at catering full-time.

And every step of the way, she'd had to work harder convincing her family that she could handle things, than at the jobs themselves. Cooking and doing basic preparations one night, rushing home from work the next to assemble and pack up everything for a catering job, falling into bed about midnight, and getting up the next morning at seven had not exhausted her. She'd never lost sight of her goal of the college fund, and the challenge of being ever creative sustained her. Before she'd made her decision to go into catering full-time, she had done research on the number of women's clubs in the area, as well as canvassed local businesses to see about catering luncheons and dinners for special meetings. She had talked to an accountant and an attorney and made her plans, then she'd tackled the family.

Annie smiled to herself, remembering that breaking the news to the family about the catering business had been more difficult than persuading them about the restaurant. Oh, well, by that time they'd had eight years to get used to the idea she knew what she was talking about. And once they accepted the idea, the family had gone all out to help her. The restaurant, which she saw as particularly hers, had become a family project. Practically every aunt, uncle, and cousin had become involved one way or another, either by working themselves or roping in friends of theirs who owed them favors for specialized services like the wiring, plumbing, and replacing the floors. It wasn't that Annie couldn't afford to pay to have those services performed; she could. Only in the face of the family's enthusiasm, she didn't have the heart to tell them hands off. If she didn't love them so much . . .

Love. The thought caused Annie's forehead to crease as she remembered the last goal she had set for herself at seventeen: someday she would have a marriage as happy as that of her parents. The face of her husband-to-be had always remained nebulous, even when she was lost in the throes of puppy love. At no time over the last ten years had anyone made such an impression on her that she dreamed about him. And a good thing, too. Every man she met was scared off within a month by an overprotective brother, cousins, and uncles, not to mention sisters, female cousins, and aunts!

Annie laughed softly and slid off the stool. Turning off the sound system and overhead lights, she told herself there was plenty of time for a social life. Maybe in a year or two when the restaurant was on its feet. Leaving on the lone overhead light by the back door, she had just reached her office and was turning off the lights there when she heard a door close above, then steps on the stairs. Good. She hadn't seen her persnickety landlord for several days, and she had some news that would lay his worries to rest about her *smelly* restaurant. She gathered her jacket and purse and opened the rear door of the restaurant.

Ted Carlyle was just reaching for the outside doorknob

when the sound of a latch clicking in the silence made him turn in surprise toward the restaurant entrance. Annie stood framed in the doorway, her dusky, rioting curls haloed by the light above. Even in the dim light, she appeared vibrant and alive with color. Her usual apron was missing, he noted as he took in an ample bust under a fuchsia turtleneck sweater.

He noticed the coat bunched under one arm and said, "Let me help you with that." Putting down his briefcase, he reached for the winter jacket, forcing Annie to turn her back to him as she inserted her arms. As far as he could tell in the available light before he had to raise the coat up over her shoulders, her blue slacks fitted snugly over nicely rounded hips. This was the first real look he'd had at Annie's figure since she was usually enveloped in the ever-present apron. "Isn't it rather late for you to be working?"

She flipped her ponytail over her coat collar as she turned, releasing a faint scent of sweetness. Her grin was mischievous as she said, "You sound just like Aunt Nola." Fishing for and finding gloves in a coat pocket, she looked back up. "But, yes, it is rather late. At least it is since we're not open until tomorrow, as I expect Aunt Nola will remind me once I get home. Let me lock up, then I have some news for you."

Ted waited patiently while she searched through her pocketbook before she remembered she had left the keys in a coat pocket for convenience. She locked the door then knelt to say good night to Charlie and her litter.

"Doesn't she have to go out?"

"No, I fed her and let her out earlier this evening. She's all set for the night. We'll be here practically at dawn tomorrow." Annie stroked the cat once more, then rose and faced him in the small hall.

"I thought I would put your mind at rest about our exhaust system. After your comment, I talked to the electrician and had him install a bigger fan in the kitchen. He assured me that the one we had was adequate, but I insisted on a more powerful model.''

Ted frowned. She made him sound like the Simon Legree of landlords. "I hope you didn't have to go to a lot of extra expense, but I appreciate your thoughtfulness." Feeling defensive, he decided to shift tactics. "Tell me something. Aunt Nola described the type of food you were going to be serving and mentioned something about not wanting to have tiny vegetarian plates. Does that mean you won't be having healthful food at all?''

"Why ever would you think such a harebrained thing? And besides, *all* my food is healthful!"

"Now, don't get on your high horse, I just—''

"High horse, indeed! What kind of cook would I be if I didn't serve good, healthful food?''

Ted smothered a grin. It was almost worth picking a fight with Annie to see the sparks fly from those magnetic blue eyes of hers. "Let me rephrase the question. What I meant to ask was, are you going to serve vegetarian plates?''

"Well, I'm certainly not going to serve those dainty salads and fill up the plate with bean sprouts and all that nonsense that leaves a body hungry after an hour.''

"Well, what are you going to serve?''

"It might interest you to know, *Mr. Carlyle*"—Annie leaned forward and pushed one gloved finger into his overcoat-covered chest, emphasizing each word—"that I'm a certified nutritionist. I have my degree, earned I might add by sandwiching school in between catering jobs, hanging in my office if you care to see it.'' She snatched back her hand as he covered it with one of his own, then gazed at him intently, her mouth open slightly as if to speak. Ted fought the impulse to lean down and kiss her soft, parted lips. He must have made a slight movement for Annie blinked and said, "As—as I said, *all* my food is healthful. I plan to serve nourishing meals."

"Yes, but are you going to serve meals for vegetarians?" Ted pushed for clarification since it was safer to concentrate on their conversation rather than his thoughts.

"Which ones? The lacto-ovarians or those who eat nonwarm-blooded animals?"

"Lacto what?"

"I thought Aunt Nola said you were a vegetarian." She raised a skeptical eyebrow. "I must say you don't sound very knowledgeable. Lacto-ovarians are people who only eat eggs, dairy products, and vegetables. No fish at all. That's the nonwarm-blooded animal, in case you haven't figured it out." Annie looked at him doubtfully.

Ted absently rubbed the back of his head. Giving a rueful grin, he said, "You might say I've come to it late. But you're right, I don't know all that much about it . . . except that it's supposed to be good for you. I only wish it were more filling."

"Aha, that's my point exactly! Food can be filling and still be good for you. Which I plan to prove when the restaurant opens."

"If that's true, I'll be forever in your debt. Between my growling stomach and Aunt Nola tempting me with some of your creations, I'm about to go out of my mind or turn green from eating so much salad."

Annie giggled, then tossed back her head and laughed out loud. Sobering at last, a smile lingered as she said, "That's too bad of Aunt Nola. Once she gets an idea in her head it's hard to change her mind, but I'll have a talk with her.

"And speaking of Aunt Nola, if I'm not home soon she'll send out a posse for me. Good night." Turning at the bottom of the porch steps as he locked the outside door, she added, "Try the restaurant and see what I mean about the food before you make any more snap decisions."

Ted watched Annie walk to her car, debating on whether to argue her last statement or not. *He* didn't make snap decisions, ever. As he gave up the thought of prolonging their conversation, he sighed in the cold night air, and a plume of frosty smoke drifted past him as he made his way to his own car. Starting it, he waited until Annie pulled out into the alley on her way home before doing the same. He was humming and tapping his gloved hands on the steering wheel in time to the car radio when he realized that he'd enjoyed the argument with Annie. She hadn't reacted at all like his mother and Veronica did when they were miffed about something.

A strange lady, Annie. A puzzle he would enjoy trying to figure out.

THREE

"To you, Annie darlin', and to success." Sprawled at the table, Uncle Tully toasted her with his favorite ale, his brogue thickening with every additional glass he downed. He peered at her intently. "Ah, Annie, me girl, you look just like your sainted mother. Duke, doesn't she look like her mother?"

"Aye, that she does," agreed another of her favorite uncles as he sat up straighter and placed his hands on the table. Annie knew his gestures preceded his proposing a toast of his own.

Shooting to her feet, she said, "Thank you, Uncle Tully and you, too, Uncle Duke." If she didn't put an end to the toasting now, every one of her relatives and friends present would feel compelled to make a toast also. They'd been all over that earlier in the evening with champagne. And if it happened again, they'd be *under* the table rather than sitting at the remains of an expansive meal. "In fact, I want to thank all of you for making tonight's opening so memorable. I love you. And now, because we have to be here so early tomorrow, it's last call for drinks while we clean up."

Annie ignored the groans and, leaning over, began to stack dishes. Her cousins Maureen, Rowena, and Kendra who had been waiting tables earlier rose to help. Her sisters, Lynn and Celia, looked at each other and struggled to their feet, nudging Kit to join them.

He leaned back in his chair, patting his stomach. "I can't move," he told them. "I haven't eaten this much since Annie last cooked dinner at home."

"Well, I like that!" Celia glared at him. "If you want any dinner in the future, you can fix it yourself."

Kit grinned and said, "I won't have to. We'll all be eating here. Remember?"

"Even at home you're expected to help out," Aunt Nola reminded him. "Grab yourself a tray."

Groaning exaggeratedly, Kit collected glasses while his cousins helped clear the long double row of tables that had been pushed together after the regular customers departed. The aunts and uncles were left to enjoy their drinks and the latest family news with friends who still remained.

In the kitchen, Annie organized the dishwashing crew. When the last of the male cousins returned to the dining room, the talk became more feminine and she enjoyed listening to the women prattle about their dates and latest boyfriends as they cleaned the various pots and pans.

"Who are you seeing, Annie?" one of her cousins asked.

"No one," her sister Celia answered for her. "How could she when she spends every waking moment in this restaurant or supervising catering jobs somewhere?"

"Maybe now that the restaurant is open, you can get your life organized to include some free time," Fionna, an older cousin, sympathized.

"From what I hear," Kendra said, "she may not have far to look. Moira mentioned a smashing-looking landlord. Is he single?"

At the mention of Ted, Annie felt a telltale warmth stealing into her cheeks and kept her back turned longer than necessary to replace some plates on a shelf. She didn't even have to think to know when she had become self-conscious about him. Last night had been very revealing.

"Well, don't keep us in suspense, Annie." "What's this?" "Come on, give!" several cousins said at once.

"There's not much to tell," she said reluctantly, turning to confront about ten curious faces. With their expectant looks, she knew they wouldn't settle for anything less than a blow-by-blow description of Ted and his character. Irritated at being pressed when she had some newfound and revealing thoughts about him gave her an idea. And it wasn't all that far from the truth, unfortunately. "I told Aunt Nola before I met him that he must be a stuffed shirt, and I really haven't seen any reason to change my mind."

"What?" "Oh, come on, Annie." "Who cares? What does he look like?"

Annie clapped her hands over her ears until the chorus of voices died down. Looking defiant, she said, "Yes, he looks like a Greek god with heavenly blue eyes, and he's tall and well built, and he's also arrogant and strictly business.

"All he's been concerned about is whether the restaurant would be smelly and create noise. He has absolutely *no* imagination at all. And he's not too happy about Charlie and her litter being in the back hallway. Also," she added as an afterthought, "he may not be married, but there *is* a woman in his life." The disappointed faces reflected her own inner feelings, Annie noted with surprise.

"Is that the blonde I saw one day?" Moira asked. At Annie's nod, her cousin added, "Umm. Some competition."

"I'd place my bet on Annie any day," Celia fired back

loyally, "compared to that stiff piece of plastic Aunt Nola described."

Her youngest sister, Lynn, put an arm around Annie's shoulder. "If he's that stupid, he's not good enough for you anyway. You're always telling *me* there are plenty of fish in the sea, so you'll have to take your own advice and continue fishing."

"Who said I wanted him?" demanded Annie. "Did I sound like I was interested in him?" Working up her indignation, she added, "And on top of everything else, he's trying to tell me what to serve in the restaurant. Just because *he's* a vegetarian!"

With that parting shot, Annie spun on her heel and disappeared into the restaurant to close out the cash register. Her last words had revived last night's scene in her mind and her resulting discomfort.

She had been enjoying herself in the midst of a roaring good argument when Ted had reached for her hand, then occupied in pushing a finger into his chest to emphasize her point. In a flash, she'd perceived him as something other than just her landlord. He was a man, and a very good-looking man at that. Her breath had caught momentarily, mesmerized by his blue eyes and the smile tugging at those finely etched lips that suddenly seemed too close for comfort.

She'd snatched back her hand, but it was too late to retrieve her errant thoughts, as she discovered later when trying to go to sleep. Her pillow had received several good whacks before she was comfortable enough for fatigue to claim her.

Annie banged the open drawer of the cash register as she lost count of the one-dollar bills and had to start over again. Back in her thoughts, she admitted a sense of disappointment that Ted had failed to show up today for lunch or dinner. So much for his precious reminder in that blasted notebook he carried around with him! And anyway, he probably would have found fault with all the noise if he couldn't have found anything else to complain about. She should be glad he hadn't had a chance to spoil the day for her.

The turnout at lunch and dinner had been very respectable for opening day, she thought. Especially dinner, but that was because most of her family had shown up as well as a lot of their friends alerted to the event. By eight o'clock most of the casual diners had gone, leaving family and friends to pull their tables together. Annie had broken out the champagne and the toasts began. She smiled, thinking that at least they hadn't had to worry about someone calling the police. They were already here. What with Uncle Tully and his friends, there were about a half dozen now sitting in the restaurant. The noise level had risen considerably and though not as raucous as the singles' places, Annie was suddenly grateful Ted was nowhere in evidence. She sighed, realizing she'd lost count again.

"Annie," her cousin Kendra called, "there's someone to see you."

Putting aside the stack of bills, Annie turned and looked around, but saw no one. Puzzled, she glanced at Kendra.

"In the kitchen. At the door, to be precise. He said he didn't want to interrupt a family party and just wanted a minute of your time."

Curious, Annie replaced the money in the register and closed the drawer. She followed her cousin back to the kitchen where Kendra stopped and waved her hand toward the rear entrance.

Ted Carlyle was the last person she expected to see. He stood by the door looking distinctly uncomfortable at being the center of attention of the bevy of women in the kitchen. That was a change. He usually walked around like he owned the place. Annie bit back a smile, realizing the foolishness of her last thought. He *did* own the place.

She tried to keep a straight face as she walked toward

him, relishing the thought that something could make the urbane Mr. Carlyle ill at ease. She also tried to ignore the impact of his tuxedo-clad figure on her jangling nerve endings. He looked like a model from an ad she had seen recently for a ritzy European casino. She had admired the slick magazine composition aesthetically, but Ted's living, breathing person made her want to do more than just look. She wondered what it would feel like to run her fingers through his perfectly combed hair, what he would look like when a little mussed instead of the perfectly groomed person she always saw.

Reaching him at last, she said with forced brightness, "I'm afraid you're a little late for dinner."

"Yes, I know. I'm sorry. I had meant to come very early this evening, but I was stuck in court all day, which delayed me all down the line. Then I had to attend a charity thing this evening— Well, never mind. You're not interested in all that. Look," he said, glancing at her female relatives gathered in a huddle at one end of the kitchen, "would you mind stepping out into the hall for a moment? I'd like to speak to you, but I could just as well do without the audience."

A trace of his old arrogance had returned by the time he finished, and Annie followed his glance to the far end of the kitchen. Her sisters and cousins might have thought they were being discreet, but they weren't fooling her for a moment. They were hanging on every word exchanged between her and Ted. And apparently they hadn't fooled him either.

"All right," she agreed.

Ted pushed the door open wider and allowed her to go through first. He closed it behind him, and Annie looked up at him in surprise. The episode of Veronica and Charlie surfaced in her memory, and she thought he wanted her alone to reprimand her about something. She tried to think what unwritten rule she might have broken this time. At least he hadn't chosen to bawl her out in front of everyone.

Stiffening her spine, Annie folded her arms and faced him squarely. She would give as good as she got. Her chin tilted as she said, "Well?"

He confounded her by looking sheepish. "I've . . . got something for you. Just a minute." Ted brushed by her, and Annie was warmed by his touch as he put his hands on her arms to move her slightly to one side. He bent over the foot of the stairs and turned, holding a long, narrow, ribbon-tied box in his hands. "Here. Happy opening."

Dumbfounded, Annie glanced from the box to Ted's face, back to the box, and her gaze finally came to rest on him again. "Th-thank you," she managed at last, taking the box from his hands. "That's very thoughtful of you."

Ted rubbed the back of his head, then shoved his hands into the pockets of his tuxedo. "It—I was shopping for a birthday gift for my mother when I saw this. It reminded me of you."

Annie looked down at the box in her hands and winced as she took in the front of her dirty apron. Good grief, how did he perceive her when all he ever saw her in was an apron, usually one stained with whatever particular dishes she had concocted that day? Next to his impeccable appearance, she felt sloppy and unkempt.

"Go ahead, open it." When Annie glanced up at Ted, the look on his face reminded her of Kit when he was eight years old giving Aunt Nola a tiny ship he had carved for Christmas: eager, yet afraid the gift might not measure up.

She pried the ribbon off one corner of the box saying, "It really was very thoughtful of you to do this." The ribbon dangled from Annie's fingers as she lifted the top from the box and laid back several layers of tissue. Whatever it was lay smothered in more layers of paper. Shifting the lid to beneath the box, she reached in and lifted out a swathed object. Its weight surprised her.

"Let me hold this for you," Ted said, taking the box, "then you can unwrap it."

Annie sat on the stairs, putting the tissue-wrapped object in her lap before gently peeling back the layers of paper. Her fingers encountered cool, smooth ceramic as she continued to pull away padding. She recognized the familiar blue, gray, and white colors of a Lladro figurine.

"Ohh," she breathed in pleased surprise, her hands busy stripping away the last of the paper. The statue was of a young girl, one leg cocked at the knee as if she were dancing or running, her bunched skirts caught up in both hands. But it was the head covered with dark curls that fascinated Annie. The girl was looking back over one shoulder, an expression of impish delight on her delicately tinted face. "It's exquisite," she said, running her hand over the flawless folds of the girl's dress.

"You like it, then?" Ted leaned down, his gaze swinging between her and the statue.

Annie didn't miss the uncertainty in his voice. Touched, she stared up at him, seeing behind the stiff business mask to his warmth and kindness. To have given her such a treasure . . . A rush of feeling engulfed Annie, and her practical nature warred with her emotional side. Her emotions won. "Oh, yes," she said, surging up with the figurine grasped tightly in one hand. "She's beautiful. Thank you so much."

Impulsively, Annie threw her free arm over Ted's shoulder and leaned over to kiss him on the cheek. At the same moment Ted turned toward her. Her pursed lips missed the side of his face and landed squarely on his mouth. Surprise held her immobile long enough for his arms to come around her as he deepened the kiss, the empty box tumbling to the stairs, forgotten. As their breaths mingled, the fingers of Annie's free hand tangled in the hair at the back of his neck. It was silky smooth, even where it met the crisp edge of his formal shirt collar.

She sighed as Ted moved his mouth on hers. His lips were soft, yet insistent, so that Annie found herself responding to his silent command and opened her mouth wider as his lips nibbled at hers. An unfamiliar tightening in her chest constricted her breathing. Dizzily, she wondered why she had never experienced this euphoria before with any of her dates.

A crash came from the direction of the kitchen, followed by the sound of splintering glass. Annie's fingers tightened reflexively on the figurine in one hand.

The feel of the cool ceramic snapped her out of her daze, and she drew back in Ted's arms. His lips were moist from their kiss, and she felt drawn back to them before muted exclamations behind her made her blink in awareness of where she was and what she was doing. Her free hand slid to Ted's shoulder to push him away, but he tightened his hold.

The noise level from the kitchen increased, and Annie felt constrained to say something, anything, to break the tension between them. "Thank you," she whispered.

"No, it's I who should thank you," he said cryptically in a low guttural tone. He leaned down, and as his face loomed nearer, Annie's heavy eyelids slid shut. His lips met her partially opened ones in a gentle caress before disappearing. Her lids fluttered open when his lips didn't return. Finally releasing her, Ted stooped over and retrieved the box from the floor. Taking the figurine from her nerveless fingers, Ted replaced it in the box, covered it, and handed it back to her.

"I was going to say that this was from both Jim and me, but now, selfishly, I don't want to share it." A wry smile twisted his lips, and Annie fought the urge to lean into them again. "I wish you success."

Annie didn't know how long she would have stood there, staring at him, if Ted hadn't pulled her around with one hand on her shoulder and opened the back door to the restaurant. She walked through the doorway and turned to stare at him again. He looked the same as he had looked before their interlude in the hallway, except that his expression was gentle now and contained a hint of puzzlement rather than his earlier uncertainty.

"Good night," he said softly and closed the door.

Annie stirred the huge pot of simmering stew, then stepped back and wiped at her damp forehead.

Lord, she was tired. Despite that, a satisfied sigh escaped as she looked around the bustling kitchen. If the last few days were any indication, Apple Annie's was a success. Business had picked up so much each day since their opening on St. Patrick's Day that more and more of the faces Annie saw in the restaurant were strangers rather than relatives and friends. Last night she had even spied a couple of the city's prominent politicians among the mixed crowd. By lunch on Thursday they were packed to the rafters.

And her varied though limited menus seemed popular. She offered and sold everything from Asian cuisine to good old pot roast, a testimony to the eclectic taste of a multiracial city sprinkled with restaurants from around the world. And the food was healthful, but not conspicuously so.

Annie again leaned over the huge black stove and gently stirred crab in a light curry sauce in preparation for the luncheon crowd. Next she sprinkled almonds over the lamb pilaf before sliding it back into the oven.

Deciding to whip up an extra batch of curry sauce, Annie worked at the counter adjacent to the stairwell wall and heard footsteps clumping down the back stairs. After a few moments she felt someone watching her and glanced over to the open back door. Ted and his partner stood there. With great exaggeration, Ted sniffed the air and smiled with what she thought might be a tinge of arrogance.

Jim's cherubic face was free of guile. The two of them reminded her of the Mutt and Jeff cartoons, one tall and slender, the other short and rather chubby. Jim's personality was the opposite of Ted's, too. She didn't know who was older, but she had immediately felt at ease with Jim Linden upon meeting him. Getting to know him was like putting on an old shoe, effortless and comfortable.

"My nose led us to the best restaurant in the city," Jim said. "Should we go out and come in the front, or can we enter through the kitchen?"

"Certainly you can come this way . . . on one condition." Annie walked toward them, wiping her hands on a towel, determined to clear the air on one matter at least. Both men seemed surprised, but waited politely for her to continue. "You have to tell me why you were sniffing by the door. Is the smell of curry that heavy?"

Jim immediately shook his head, but it was Ted whom Annie watched. He smiled slightly as he said, "It wasn't that noticeable until we reached the bottom of the stairs. Your exhaust fan would probably be more effective if you kept the rear door closed."

"Yes, but you try telling that to everyone who comes through that door. The delivery people are worse than children. I guess they figure as long as the outside door is closed, everything is okay. Maybe I should get a sign for the inner one," Annie mused.

"If the odors are no worse than this, I wouldn't worry about it too much," Ted said. "Maybe just keep an eye on the door on the days you have a particularly . . . fragrant dish. Besides curry, what's on the menu today?"

Resisting an impulse to tell him humble pie, Annie led Ted and Jim through the kitchen, introducing them to the myriad relatives working there, and placed them in the back hallway at a table usually reserved for family. Since the ceiling sloped to accommodate the second story stairs, she only used it for customers when the main area overflowed.

A little while later, she wandered out of the kitchen to the adjacent coffee and soda area to get a drink and overheard Ted telling Jim that he should probably eat two servings of the delicious curried crab since all he was going to get for dinner at Veronica's was some kind of vegetable salad. Annie knew she should move, either around the corner to make herself known or return to the kitchen, but she couldn't help herself. She had barely seen Ted since he had kissed her Monday night, and after those fleeting moments he'd acted like nothing had changed. For her, everything was different.

"It's getting so I can't stand to look at anything green," Ted's voice continued. "You can laugh, old friend, but the only thing that's saved me so far is the fantastic lunches I have here or the samples of new dishes Aunt Nola smuggles up to me. How does she do it, do you think? Annie, I mean. Did you see that menu? You could have a choice of about three fantastic vegetables à la carte for about the price of a dinner and any two of them would suffice for a normal meal." At the renewed crack of laughter from Jim, Ted chuckled, too. "Well, it would fill up an ordinary person. Where do you find room for it all, anyway? By the way, that lamb looks and smells delicious."

Jim continued to laugh. "You could be having this, too, if you weren't so determined to be a vegetarian. You really started something when you became a health freak. Of course, it *is* the chic thing to do, so maybe I shouldn't be surprised Veronica took to the idea so readily. Maybe you should introduce Veronica's chef to Annie, spice things up a bit. Speaking of Veronica, have you two set a date?"

"No. That is, I haven't asked her yet."

"I thought you had pretty much decided to pop the question."

"I had. I mean, I am. I think. Look, was I a little heavy-handed about the curry and the exhaust fan? You know, when we were talking to Annie earlier?"

"What's your concern, her feelings or your comfort?"

"Don't start sounding like a lawyer on me, Jim. I'm serious."

"Well," he drawled, and Annie could hear the clink of a spoon against a cup as one of them, presumably Jim, vigorously stirred his coffee, "the only reason I ask is that I happened to catch your act on Monday."

"What? What act?"

"You know. Your Lassie act by the back door before noon." He chuckled and said, "It took me a few minutes to realize what you were doing, but I wasn't quite sure *why* you were sniffing there."

A few beats of silence passed, and Annie became aware of the murmurs of other diners and sounds in the restaurant. Lord, she hoped none of her cousins spotted her and called to her about something now.

Ted's "Oh," was so soft she almost missed it, "you saw me, huh?" Another beat of silence, then, "Well, it's just that I was expecting corned beef and boiled cabbage. After all, they *are* Irish and it was St. Patrick's Day! How was I supposed to know she'd serve lamb stew?"

"And what would you have done if our halls had been permeated by the scent of corned beef and cabbage? Tried to void the lease?"

"Don't be silly. Of course not."

"Well, what then?"

"I don't know. It's just that for some reason the argument about odors seems to have become a point of honor." Ted cleared his throat. "Anyway, I made it up to Annie later."

"What do you mean?"

"Uh, well . . . I bought her a sort of grand opening present at lunchtime on Monday. You know, for opening day."

"Did she know it was an act of contrition?"

"No." Ted cleared his throat again. "And you might say that I received my comeuppance anyway."

"You coming down with something? You keep clearing your throat. No? Okay, what did Annie do?"

"Do? Oh! Well, she . . . thanked me rather warmly. Made me think, I can tell you."

"Good. Any day someone can jar you out of your rut, it's good news as far as I'm concerned."

"Some friend you are," Ted said, sounding good-natured despite his words. "This is turning out to be a week of revelations. Why are you insulting me?"

"Because that's what I am—your friend. You've become so predictable lately that I'm really worried about you." A chair scraped across the wooden floor. "Though now at least there's a glimmer of hope."

"What do you mean, hope?" Ted demanded, but Annie fled the area back to the safety of the kitchen and didn't hear Jim's reply.

The conversation had become too personal for her to eavesdrop on, and she flushed with guilt at having listened to as much as she had. But after Jim's comment about Ted popping the question to Veronica, a fire in the kitchen couldn't have dragged her away from hearing more. Her heart had stalled at the thought of Ted and Veronica together, especially after the kiss she had shared with him. At least he sounded reluctant to become engaged to Veronica. Maybe that moment had made a difference to him, too. Maybe—

"Annie." Aunt Nola nudged her. "Phone."

Taking the receiver, Annie heard her cousin Shelia's voice.

"Since all the family sitters are working at the restaurant, I'm going to have to bring the boys with me. The baby can stay with a neighbor. That's the only way I can do the early dishwashing shift.''

''All right. Maybe I can get one of the younger girls to keep an eye on them here.''

Hanging up, Annie made arrangements for one of her younger cousins to help with the boys at dinnertime. She hoped she would have some response soon to her ads for kitchen help. Oh, well, how much trouble could two little boys get into in a couple of hours?

As the thunking noise coming from the back stairwell continued, Ted sighed. He had planned to get caught up on some paperwork since it was after five and the phones had stopped ringing for the day, but the unusual sounds from below kept him from concentrating. God only knew what Annie was doing now. In fact, thoughts of her had been disturbing him for several hours, since lunch with Jim and facing his reluctance to propose to Veronica. Every time he tried to rationalize his decision to marry, visions of Annie in his arms returned and nature kicked in with a swift physical response. Ted swore softly under his breath. Just as he decided he was acting like a teenager with a terminal case of raging hormones, a particularly loud thud from the stairwell diverted him. Giving up work or thought as a lost cause, he gathered the folders on his desk and threw them into his briefcase. Maybe he could get something done at home.

Ted opened his pocket calendar and studied it. He'd better make sure he hadn't forgotten any files he might need for later in the day tomorrow since he wouldn't be coming directly to the office. As his gaze went down the list of appointments, a notation at the bottom of today's calendar caught his eye.

Damn. He'd forgotten about promising to escort Veronica to a fund-raiser at the Terra Museum of American Art.

By the time he changed and freshened up, drove through rush-hour traffic to pick her up, and reached the museum, they'd be cutting it close. And Veronica hated to be late for these blasted things. Swearing under his breath, Ted ripped off his tie and unbuttoned his shirt on the way to the washroom and the shaving supplies he kept there for just such an emergency. Thank God, he'd stashed an extra tux and dress shirt at the office.

Freshly shaved and changed ten minutes later, Ted picked up his briefcase and made his way grimly to the back stairs. The unusual thunking noise had been joined by a murmur of high-pitched voices which increased in volume as he jerked open the stairway door.

"I've got a secret," a childish voice chanted.

At the sight of two little boys jumping from one step to another, Ted felt his heart stutter as memories drowned out sight and sound. A moment later, he again heard the childish voice singing. After his fright had passed, temper took over at the scare the boys had given him.

"You two," he said, his voice unnecessarily loud in the confines of the stairwell. In a slightly lower, but no calmer voice, he said, "Just what do you think you're doing?"

The two little boys stopped in mid-hop, one grabbing the stair rail to keep from toppling over in surprise to the landing a few steps below. Ted's breath stopped in his throat. Almost as one, the two turned and, breathing again, Ted thought at first they were twins. Then he realized one boy looked slightly larger than the other. He thought they might be five or six, but what did he know about children? Just that the stairwell was not a playground. At least, not his stairs. He glowered at the boys. They both had dark, rioting curls so there was no question in his mind where they had come from.

"Does Annie know you boys are playing here on the stairs?"

Two pairs of little shoulders shrugged as the boys stared up at him open-mouthed.

"All right, I'll handle this." Starting down the stairs, he said, "Don't move! Either of you." The two boys shook their heads from side to side in unison. Ted clamped his lips together in a grim line to stop from saying anything that five- or six-year-old ears should not hear. He wouldn't be so cautious with their dear, scatterbrained cousin though. What the hell was Annie thinking about letting the boys play on the stairs?

Stepping cautiously around the children, he pulled open the rear door to the restaurant, closed for once. Wouldn't you know it? he thought, his ire building. The one time she should have the door open to listen in case one of the boys fell— Ted glanced quickly around the kitchen looking for the target of his present anger and frowned at the disorder.

Tubs of lettuce were stacked at the end of one of the stainless steel tables while Annie and one of her cousins— Moira, Morgana?—chopped something on the wood-block table. Today under her apron Annie wore what looked like a pair of khaki fatigues with bright orange suspenders. It should have looked ridiculous, but on her it looked right somehow. Pushing the thought away, he refused to acknowledge the softening of his anger at the sight of her.

Ted's gaze continued around the kitchen, disorder meeting his eye wherever he looked. Gray plastic tubs were stacked along the floor leading to the door. Some contained food, but others contained platters, pans, a huge coffee pot, and plastic bags filled with who knew what.

Finished with chopping, Annie flew from one task to another, answering questions, pointing out where something was to be found, all the time her hands busy doing something. She was energy in motion, and he marveled that she didn't seem rushed or confused by the constant interruptions. In fact, the whole tone of the kitchen was a happy one with everyone smiling and laughing.

Great, just great! Not one of them concerned about the two boys who might have broken their little necks on his stairs and sued him up the wazoo for untold thousands, perhaps millions—

"Ted." At the pleased exclamation, Ted switched his gaze back to Annie. She smiled at him, wiping her hands on a towel before coming over to where he stood by the door. "What can I do for you?"

Hardening his heart, Ted stifled any tender feelings and unburdened himself of several hours, worth of bottled up frustration. "What can you do for me?" he inquired in a deceptively mild tone. "I'll tell you in just so many words," he said, his voice rising several notches.

"First, you can remove those two imps who are playing on the back stairs like Gene Krupa on the drums. Next you can refrain in the future from letting them *near* the stairs! Of all the idiotic ideas. Didn't you stop to think about the possibility of their falling and breaking an arm or a leg? Or their precious necks? And just what is this mess?" he demanded, flinging a hand toward the row of containers lined up on the floor.

"And just what is *that* supposed to mean, Mr. Carlyle?" Annie's expression had changed from shocked surprise and fear for the boys to outrage, but she spoke so calmly that it penetrated Ted's anger.

"What?"

"I said, just what is—"

"No, no." Ted rubbed at his face in distraction. "Wait a minute." When he removed his hands, he saw a side of Annie he'd never seen before. She stared back at him, her eyes slitted with cold fury, her mobile features frozen in a mask of hard planes. This at least was an anger he recognized and was used to dealing with. But did he want to? Suddenly, he realized it was very important to him to erase that particular stamp of emotion from Annie's face.

His shoulders slumped and he held out one hand pacifically as he said, "Look, I'm sorry. I don't even remember what I said." He didn't notice any lessening of the tension in Annie's expression, so he tried to explain why he'd been so upset. "The boys on the stairs . . . When I was about nine, a friend and I were horsing around as we came down a flight of stairs at his house. He pushed me and . . . as I scrambled to grab hold of the railing to keep from falling, my friend tripped over my outstretched leg. He fell instead. He was paralyzed by the fall."

From far away, Ted heard Annie's sigh as the tension drained from her body and she made an involuntary movement toward him. "I'm sorry," she said softly. "I had no idea the boys were playing on the stairs," she continued in a firmer voice. "One of the younger girls is supposed to be watching them. Let me see what's going on."

Annie pushed past him into the hallway. "Bryce, where's Lucy?"

The two little boys had remained exactly where they were when Ted ordered them to stay put, and he tried to smile to let them know that he wasn't angry with them. Unfortunately, his very presence seemed to render them mute, but one boy finally raised his arm and pointed at the outside door.

"In the cold?" Annie asked, opening the door. "Lucy! Why are you out here when you're supposed to be keeping an eye on the boys?"

Ted peered around the door and Annie's shoulder to see a girl only a few years older than the boys themselves. Or at least he thought she was that young until she sprang up from the back step, her clinging sweater revealing otherwise. With a figure like that, she had to be a teenager. Another movement drew his gaze to the boy also rising beside her. He hid a smile as Annie sent the boy on his way and scolded the girl for neglecting her charges.

He shifted out of the doorway to face the boys again. "Why don't you two come down here and do something safe like play with the kittens?"

At the same moment that Annie hustled Lucy inside, asking her to take the boys inside for a Coke, Aunt Nola stepped into the now crowded hall.

She stopped beside Ted, tilting her head back to look him in the eye as the youngsters trooped by her. "Don't you have somewhere to go, all dressed up like that? I don't mean to be rude, but we're busy. Go away. We'll see you tomorrow."

"Aunt Nola!" Annie protested at her dismissal.

But apparently Ted had decided to take Aunt Nola's bluntness with amusement because he simply grinned at her before leaning down and giving her a peck on the cheek. "Good night, dear lady. Parting is such sweet sorrow."

"Oh, go on with you," Aunt Nola said, swatting at him with her hand. But Annie noticed her aunt had stopped scowling before she turned away. Poor Aunt Nola. She was feeling the strain more than most of them. They were all tired, but she most of all. Annie trailed after her to the doorway.

Without thinking, she said aloud, "I hope I get some response soon."

"Response to what?"

"Hmm? Oh." Annie glanced over her shoulder at Ted and lowered her voice. "To an ad I placed in the paper for kitchen help. Aunt Nola is not in favor of introducing strangers into our midst, but we've been successful more quickly than I'd thought we'd be. We've got to have some more help."

"What? With all your relatives, I wouldn't think that would be a problem."

"It's okay to depend upon the family and our friends to get me over the rough spots, but I can't impose upon them forever. Once school's out for the summer I'll have plenty of help from all the younger cousins. Some of my aunts and older cousins work here full-time, but most of them are stealing a few hours from their already busy schedules to help me out."

"Annie," Aunt Nola bellowed from the other side of the kitchen, "where's my favorite knife?"

Annie thought for a second, then pointed to the wood-block table. "Under the cloth."

As Aunt Nola retrieved her knife, Ted leaned close and said, "If you have any problems convincing Aunt Nola you need help, send her up to me. Lawyers are good at persuasion."

Annie smiled at the thought that she might need help in handling Aunt Nola. She'd been doing it for fifteen years. Still, it was nice of Ted to offer.

His face changed. Reaching for her hand, he said, "I've got to go." Her palm was lost between his two bigger ones, but he held it gently with just the slightest pressure. She searched his expression for some clue to what he was thinking. "I'm sorry about earlier, the boys and all." He removed one hand and absently rubbed his neck while a rueful smile tugged at the corners of his mouth. "It's been one hell of a week." He leaned forward and placed a kiss on Annie's forehead. "Take care."

His black tuxedo and crisp white shirt set off his tan beautifully, not to mention those incredible blue eyes. And apparently he had freshly shaved for the evening because she could still detect the faint scent of his after-shave, something fresh like herbs. As he turned at the door, she smiled and thought it was a shame all that elegance was to be wasted on someone else—probably Veronica. It took Annie a moment to realize that the pang she felt must be jealousy. With a start she realized she was still standing there, staring after Ted Carlyle.

Turning to help Moira go over the catering order, Annie saw that Aunt Nola was watching her with an air of smug satisfaction.

FOUR

Annie and Aunt Nola held their usual postmortem around the kitchen table late Thursday evening, filling Celia and Lynn in on the day's events, including Ted's tirade over the boys playing on the stairs. Despite Annie's best efforts, her voice became a little testy as she recalled the scene.

"That poor boy," Aunt Nola said, apparently electing herself Ted's champion. "And none of it would have happened if Lucy had been attending to her job. I'm going to give that girl's mother an earful."

"I've already spoken to her," Annie said.

"And just why are you so down in the dumps, miss? From where I stood, it looked like you and Ted parted on pretty good terms."

"This time, yes. But what about the next time? And even allowing for the distressing history behind his tantrum, Ted was less than kind about the state of the kitchen—which had absolutely *no* bearing on what had happened and was certainly none of his business." Leaning her elbows on the table, Annie rubbed her temples. "I feel like a yo-yo around him. One minute he's kind, the next ranting."

"*Now* look who's exaggerating." Aunt Nola glared at Annie. "Maybe you'll be able to see things clearer in the morning. I'm off to bed. And if the rest of you had any sense, you would be, too."

It was quiet for a few moments after Aunt Nola tottered off, then Celia asked about the size of the dinner crowd.

"Oh, good. We served the last dinners about nine o'clock, so I guess we'd better plan on Friday and Saturday running at least until ten before full meals are cut off."

Annie told them she had a couple of interviews set up for the next day to find more kitchen help, then the conversation drifted back and forth over the four days the restaurant had been open. Especially opening night.

Celia and Annie were laughing about how Uncle Tully had had to be helped as he left the restaurant singing "My Wild Irish Rose" in a deep baritone. Although Lynn chuckled, too, Annie noticed her youngest sister was watching her.

"What is it, Linette?" she asked, slipping into the familiar family name. Among their huge family, the duplication of Irish and Celtic names became confusing and everyone had adopted a nickname for everyday use. "Is something wrong?"

"Oh, no. It's . . . I was just wondering if you're happy, that's all."

Celia gave an unladylike snort. "Why wouldn't she be happy, you silly goose? This has been the realization of a dream."

Annie studied her two sisters: one so sure of herself, the other like a fawn ready to bolt at the first sign of trouble. She reminded herself that Celia probably didn't realize her impatience was intimidating to Lynn. For all that Annie was the eldest by two years, Celia was the one who made pronouncements with the assumed wisdom of Methuselah. It was just during spring break when she was around the girls constantly that Annie had noticed how Lynn would withdraw from a confrontation with Celia, always deferring to her judgment. Since that moment early on in the vacation the girls had taken to coincide with Kit's, Annie made a point of not spontaneously replying to Lynn's faintly put questions or comments, but instead looking for a hidden meaning. Her sister's insight was surprising when given a chance to explain what she meant.

Annie was so tired she almost groaned aloud, but realized now was the perfect opportunity to let Celia know that Lynn had a mind of her own.

"No," she told Celia. "She means more than that. What is it?" Annie probed gently, reaching over to squeeze Lynn's hand.

Glancing between them uncertainly, Lynn took an audible breath. "It's just that I wondered after our conversation Monday in the kitchen—you know, about dating and everything. Well, I got to thinking about you never dating anyone seriously and Celia's comment about why. It's the first time I ever really thought about it. I didn't realize—"

She broke off at a movement from Celia, and Annie sent her impatient sister a warning look before turning back to Lynn. "Go on, love. You didn't realize what?"

"Oh, it's not so important," Lynn said in a rush. "It's what happened later that really made me wonder." She paused, studying the series of rings she made on the table with the bottom of her wet glass.

When it didn't look as if Lynn was going to be any more forthcoming, Annie, thoroughly confused, asked, "What happened later?"

"When Mr. Carlyle stopped by to talk to you. When you came back into the kitchen, you looked . . . different somehow. Dazed, almost. Then I remembered how worked up you were earlier when everyone was questioning you about him. And again this evening." Wetting her lips, Lynn said, "I don't remember you ever reacting to anyone like that before. You simply didn't seem to care enough one way or the other. Now I think you do."

She had invited this, Annie realized, swallowing her immediate denial. Talk about being hoisted on your own petard. How did she explain what she herself didn't fully understand? Ever honest, she tried to put her feelings into words so Lynn could comprehend her confusion.

Patting her sister's hand, Annie said, "You're right in that I seem to be reacting to Ted. And I don't know why. He's so infuriating sometimes that I want to shake him, and yet other times I enjoy sparring with him." She shook her head. "Sometimes I think he's nothing but a conceited fusspot, then I catch a glimpse of something . . . maybe the inner man, or," she said suddenly, remembering Ted's expression as he handed her the gift, "or what he could be if he'd just let go."

"You've got that dreamy look again," Lynn said softly.

Taking a deep breath, Annie released it as a sigh. "Dreamy or not, I meant every word I said tonight. Experiencing"—she caught herself before blurting out the fact that Ted had kissed her—"the emotions he causes are confusing enough. Besides the fact we seem to rub each other the wrong way, who has time to decipher all the complications? I've got other fish to fry, and right now Apple Annie's is it. That's my number-one priority," Annie said, putting finality in her tone. "And I certainly don't need some know-it-all to tell me how to run my business."

Celia groaned, a long-suffering sound in the silence of the kitchen. "Lord, you're naive. You've practically given a textbook description of someone falling in love and don't even know it. You wouldn't recognize love if it fell into a pot of your own soup. No, I take that back. If it happened in the kitchen, you might be paying attention. Go on, laugh," Celia said when Annie smiled at her, "but whether you realize it or not, you don't have any choice about when you fall in love. Take my word for it, that's what it is.''

"Well, always being at loggerheads with someone is not my idea of love, so I don't feel there's any choice to be made." Annie stretched as she yawned. "And thank goodness. I don't think I can deal with anything more right now. The restaurant business is draining enough. Speaking of which, I've got to get to bed. Come on, you two.''

It was a long time before Annie fell asleep, though. Celia's statement filtered through her every thought. Finally she faced it. Was her sister right? Was she falling in love with Ted Carlyle? On the surface, the idea certainly seemed ridiculous, yet Lynn had been right too about her reaction to Ted. But was that love or simply that she found him different from anyone else she had known? Irritatingly so.

The thought was comforting. Celia might speak from experience, but that didn't mean she knew everything. Her brush with a serious relationship had ended in disaster her fourth year in college and had left Celia with a brittle edge. Annie worried about her becoming so cynical and knew she would have to talk to Celia about it soon. And about being more patient with Lynn.

Problems, problems, problems. And she considered Ted Carlyle just one more of them. There. Put in the right perspective, she could handle the confusing emotions he raised in her. With a determined sigh, she turned over and snuggled into her pillow.

A moment later, Lynn whispered from the next bed in the large room all three sisters shared. "Annie?"

"Yes, love," she mumbled, now barely awake.

"I hope you don't mind my asking, but . . . he kissed you Monday night, didn't he?"

The thought flashed through Annie's mind that maybe

Lynn was fey. She released the breath she hadn't realized she was holding and whispered in turn, "Yes, he did."

"Was it nice?"

"Yes, love. *Very* nice."

"I thought so. Sleep well, Annie."

Fat chance, now that the specter of those particular emotions had been raised. Just thinking about it made Annie warm all over again. Her skin tingled, and sleep was the last thing on her mind.

The next morning Annie felt sluggish as she began the day's preparations. She ruined a batch of croissant dough she was preparing and had to start over again. The incident reminded her of her own principle. She had to concentrate on what she was doing and let the rest go hang. She'd spend time thinking about Ted Carlyle when she had to. *If* she had to. And since she was determined to keep him mentally in a slot designated strictly as "landlord," she shouldn't have to spend too much thought on him.

As the day progressed, Annie regained her equilibrium and zest for her work. By early afternoon she was positively sparkling because after interviewing several applicants, she'd found one relief cook and a dishwasher. She had a couple of interviews lined up for tomorrow as well and, with any luck, would be able to add more to her staff.

The only cloud on her horizon was that Shelia had called and said she had to bring the boys with her again. She arranged for Lucy to watch the boys with strong admonitions to leave her boyfriend at home. Now, if they could just keep the boys occupied, everything would be fine.

Several hours later, the squabbling voices of her two young cousins brought Annie back from her preoccupation with dinner. She'd had to find a succession of jobs for the scamps during the past hour to keep them from getting under everyone's feet.

"Come on, you two. I have some giant carrots and two peelers just your size. Will you help me?"

"I've got a secret," a child crooned in a high-pitched, singsong voice.

"No, you don't," another childish voice refuted. "You just say that."

"Do, too."

"Do not. You always say that."

Ted halted on the back landing, intrigued by the childish voices raised in argument. Already late leaving the office, he nevertheless stuck his head around Annie's door and recognized the two little boys sitting on newspaper surrounded by scattered peelings and a small mound of carrots. It looked to him as if there were more peels off the newspaper than on. Stepping in for a closer look, he noticed crayons and colored drawings littering the floor of Annie's office and their cousin Lucy on the telephone.

"Hello, boys. I see they're keeping you busy today." Ted heard the ring of false heartiness in his voice, and he smiled to show there were no hard feelings from yesterday. The boys stared at him, their eyes round with surprise, then peeled carrots more furiously than ever.

Ted set his briefcase down by the door and turned back to the kitchen, disorder once more meeting his discerning eye. Gray tubs filled with food and odds and ends again lined the walls leading to the back door, only this time there were more of them. In fact, there seemed to be filled boxes and gray plastic tubs wherever he looked. Searching the milling people in the kitchen for Annie, he found her with five young women dressed in identical uniforms of white blouses, black skirts, and tiny, ineffectual black aprons. They finished going over a list, and Annie handed a file folder to one of the women.

"That's it then. The invoice is inside, with the gratuity already added. Just give the original to the sales manager when he gives you the check. Bring out the tray of cheesecakes and you can start loading the cars." Three of the women turned to do her bidding, and Annie looked at the two remaining waitresses. "And this is your file. All of your things are lined up beside the proofing ovens, except the dessert which is in the cooler. Make sure you don't grab the wrong one. The cake box is marked chocolate decadence. Okay?" The two young women nodded and walked over to examine the boxes against one side of the kitchen.

Annie looked up and caught Ted's eye as he stood over the boys, who were still shaving carrots. Wiping her hands, she moved toward them. "Hi. I don't believe you were formally introduced to our budding chefs yesterday. This is Bryce and the one peeling the carrot over your shoe is Casey, Jr." Ted winced at the orange blob on the European leather and gravely shook their small, stained hands while Annie absently bent to wipe the peel off his shoe. "Come along, you two. By the time we get this and you cleaned up, it will be time for Mommy to take you home. Lucy, time to go," she called to the girl still on the phone.

The smallest boy, Casey, nudged his brother. "I *do* have a secret," he whispered loudly, glancing up through thick lashes at Ted.

"Okay, Casey," Annie said indulgently. "What's your secret?"

The youngster snuck another glance at Ted and seemed to turn bashful.

"He doesn't have any old secret," Bryce proclaimed in patent disgust. "He's always saying things like that."

"Yes, I do," the little boy blurted. "I saw Annie kissing him." Casey's chin rose in Ted's direction before ducking again.

Annie flushed at the memory of Ted's first kiss before realizing Casey could only mean last night after Ted had caught the boys on the stairs, and his innocent peck as he left for the evening. Since that had happened in the kitchen in front of anyone who happened to be looking, it was no secret. But Annie thought she knew what Casey was getting at.

Bending down to his level, she hugged him. "I think what Casey means is that he knew something that Bryce didn't, isn't that it?"

The little boy nodded, and Annie ruffled his hair. Honor restored, he turned and smiled triumphantly at his brother.

Ted watched, mesmerized, as Annie whisked the towel over the two boys, sent them over to the sink with Lucy for a wash up, briskly threw peeled carrots into her apron and, within the space of moments, cleared the peels and papers from the floor. As she stood up, some spicy sweet scent that seemed familiar floated to him. Ted smiled, amazed at her efficiency. "That was quick."

"With a family the size of ours, you learn to be quick or be quickly inundated."

Ted's gaze involuntarily swept over the kitchen again. "Is it always so . . . busy?" "Disorganized" was the word he wanted but was too polite to use.

"Oh, this isn't busy," Annie said, watching the young women parading past as they carried out the catering materials. "We're just in a bit of a muddle right now filling a last-minute catering order."

"Which I said you were foolish to take on so late in the day," Aunt Nola muttered in passing on the way to the refrigerator. She expertly shifted the tub of greens she carried in one hand and opened the door before Ted could do it for her. "But does she ever listen to anything I say? Of course not, and one of these days, mark my words, she'll—" The closing door shut off her words.

Ted started to ask something, but Annie held her finger

to her lips saying, *"Sh-h-h,"* with amusement dancing in her eyes.

"—ere will she be, I ask you?" Aunt Nola continued as the refrigerator door swung open a minute later. She stopped beside Ted, hands on her hips, and cocked her head to look up at him as the waitresses filed past with their catering orders. "Every time I see you lately, you're stopping up the works. Why don't you either come in or stay out of the way?"

Ted grinned at her cheekily. "My timing does seem to be a little off, doesn't it?"

"In more ways than you know," Aunt Nola muttered half under her breath as she turned away. Abruptly, she turned back. "By the way, you're looking a little peaked to me. I'll bring lunch up to you tomorrow if you're working."

"I don't usually work on Saturdays, but having been gone so long I'm afraid there's no other way so, yes, I'll be here. And thanks for the offer; it's very kind of you. By the way, I hope you've been keeping a tab for me." Ted rocked back on his heels, deliberately baiting the older woman. He had immediately taken to her and her whiplash tongue. Aunt Nola was so different from his mother. "If not"—he pulled his pocket calendar from an inside coat pocket—"I'm sure I can reconstruct it."

"Phoo! Can't let a perfectly good specimen of a man waste away to nothing. And you're my taste tester, remember?" Aunt Nola continued to mutter as she walked away, but Ted distinctly heard the word "vegetarian" in a disparaging tone.

He cocked an eyebrow as he turned to see Annie's reaction to her aunt's edicts. She was shaking her head, but a grin tugged at her lips, and he caught a glimpse of her dimple as she pulled him into her office out of the way of the waitresses. "Rather autocractic, isn't she?"

"Yes," Annie agreed, "but she means well. You seem to handle her all right, though."

"Why are you so surprised? Besides my gift of persuasion," Ted added, tongue in cheek, "I might add those of a diplomat. Very conciliating, I am. I learned as a very young attorney before the benches of some of Chicago's toughest judges. If you didn't learn how to handle the old buzzards, your goose was cooked . . . so to speak." Annie's dimple deepened, and Ted looked at her warily. "Why, all of a sudden, do I have the feeling you don't believe me?"

Annie tried to hide her smile. "You might be conciliatory to little old ladies and venerable judges, but you'll never convince me you have the makings of a diplomat. I'm the lady with the smelly restaurant, remember?"

Ruefully, Ted rubbed the back of his neck. "I was rather obnoxious about that, wasn't I? I tried to make amends, but perhaps an apology would have served better." He straightened, tugging at the tail of his suit coat and clearing his throat. "Miss Rafferty." He reached for her hand and bowed over it. "Your servant, Theodore Camden Carlyle, humbly begs your pardon for any offense given in the past and swears that in the future he will act only in a gentlemanly fashion." He glanced from under lowered lids to see her face lit with childish delight. "Friends?"

"Friends," Annie agreed and laughed out loud just as Aunt Nola passed by.

She poked her head back around the door and asked, "Aren't you gone yet?" Then she apparently caught sight of their linked hands and added, "Forget you saw me," as she whisked herself out of the doorway.

Ted's grin grew as color swept up Annie's cheeks, then he took pity on her. "You heard the lady. She wasn't here. And as much as I'd like to stay and enjoy exchanging sweet insults with you, I've got to go. I'd better retrieve my briefcase before it disappears with all your catering paraphernalia." He squeezed Annie's hand, which had remained in his. "Good-bye, friend. See you tomorrow."

Feeling energized the next morning by the hours he had put in at the Y, Ted looked forward to cleaning up a backlog of work. He parked his car in the alloted alley space and thought that spending a Saturday afternoon doing paperwork wasn't everyone's ideal, but it suited his sense of order.

He locked his car door and smiled, remembering the beautiful twisting hook shot he had pulled off at the end of basketball practice. Maybe he'd have time to get in a couple of workouts before next weekend when the nine and ten-year-olds would expect him to duplicate the feat. Pure luck, but the boys weren't to know that. Awed, they had begged him to prolong the practice so they could match the coach's skill. Ted was willing to put in as much time as the boys needed, but their opponents had already begun assembling for the game. It had been a close one, with his boys pulling ahead by two points at the last minute.

As Ted entered the rear hall, he noticed that the back door to Apple Annie's was closed. He was tempted to visit Annie and her relatives for a few minutes before tackling his paperwork. There always seemed to be something interesting going on. Yet even as his hand reached for the doorknob, his smile of anticipation faded. Drawing his hand back, Ted frowned. His desire to be around Annie was becoming something of a habit. He needed to give this some thought. Absently, he bent down and scratched Charlie behind the ears.

As he slowly made his way up the back stairs, a burst of laughter from the restaurant came through the wall. He heard Uncle Tully's booming voice and smiled in response. Annie's family certainly had a zest for living.

Reviewing the traits of Annie's numerous relatives he had met so far carried Ted into his office. He removed his lambskin jacket and hung it over the back of one of the chairs in front of his desk deciding that, on the whole, he rather liked the boisterous Irish clan. But was it all of them or one of them in particular that caused his interest?

He sat at his black lacquered desk and stared blankly at the files awaiting his attention lined up in perfect precision across the shining top. He'd tried not to think too much about that accidental kiss he'd shared with Annie. Or his response to it. After all, it was not planned on either of their parts and as such, there was no reason not to enjoy the moment for what it was. Or at least, so he had thought.

But the little incident in the hallway downstairs just now made him realize how much he looked forward to seeing Annie every day. Yes, her family was wacky and wonderful, but he had to admit it was Annie that drew him like a magnet.

And what about Veronica? He knew her through and through, and in some respects she paled in comparison to Annie. But Annie was an unknown quantity for the most part. He had almost made up his mind to get married after long, careful thought. He knew what he wanted, and his mother was right: Veronica fit the bill perfectly. They both came from socially prominent backgrounds; his mother liked her, in fact had introduced them; Veronica had the right contacts, so socially and professionally she would be the perfect mate. Why then did he still hesitate about popping the question? What in the world was he doing throwing odd variables like Annie into the equation?

He smiled, visualizing her reaction to being called a variable. Maybe "distraction" was a better word. She was certainly that; a damned attractive one. And that's all she was, all he'd allow her to be. Once decided on a course of action, he rarely changed his mind. But that was part of the problem, too: he hadn't actually made the decision to marry Veronica . . . yet. Something was holding him back.

Sighing, Ted pulled the stack of files toward him, and the sound was loud in the silence of his office. With his office door shut, it was quiet as a postgame gymnasium in here. He shook his head; he really was getting fanciful lately. Opening the first file, he settled with determination to get through the backlog of paperwork.

"Are you going to keep a body standing on the doorstep all day?"

At the sound of Aunt Nola's voice coming through the rear door, Ted looked at his wristwatch. One o'clock. He was surprised to find he'd been working for almost three hours. With his stomach already rumbling in anticipation, he hastened to let Aunt Nola in.

When he opened the door, she awaited him with a laden tray. Behind her on the stairs stood Annie and two of her cousins, their arms weighed down with flowers. Surprise held him mute.

Aunt Nola greeted him and bustled past with the tray. "Come on, girls. Let's get these things settled."

Annie took in Ted's stunned expression and said, "I made the mistake of wondering out loud if you'd want a plant or two for your office. We've been inundated all week with opening gifts and our house is already overflowing." Stepping into the hallway, the other girls followed her. "Whatever you don't want I'll send over to Children's Hospital."

"Now, we have oodles more where these came from," Aunt Nola said, coming back into the hallway and immediately taking charge. "Annie, take those into Ted's office. You two come with me. There's Mrs. Marshall's desk, the reception area, and I'm sure Jim would appreciate having his office brightened up, too."

Annie looked helplessly at Ted and was relieved to see his bemused smile. "Seems we've been given our orders," he said, waving her into his office.

She preceded him and immediately became lost in viewing his inner sanctum. It was like him in some ways but mostly not, she decided. The lines of the furnishings were crisp, the massive pieces bold, everything sparkling clean, but the colors were so . . . bland. Suddenly she knew that Veronica or someone like her had decorated Ted's office. This insipid scheme was not representative of the real man. Not when he could stand toe-to-toe with her and argue up a storm. Nor did it portray the inner man, she realized, thinking of his face when presenting her with the figurine. Glancing at the bookcase and tables, she didn't see one whimsical item, unless you counted the crystal paperweights, and even they fit into a tightly structured pattern on the shelves. That might be one face Ted presented to the world, but it certainly wasn't the only one.

And to be fair, she had probably jumped the gun in accusing Veronica of decorating his office. After all, if he was contemplating marrying her, surely she knew him better than what this montage of gray and black barrenness represented.

"What do you think?"

Ted's question startled Annie, and she whirled to face him, almost dropping the plants in her arms. She wracked her brain for something complimentary to say and blurted, "Well, it—it has a certain . . . purity."

"That's certainly saying a lot of nothing," Aunt Nola put in from the doorway.

Annie's gaze swung from Ted's frown to her aunt's mulish expression.

Aunt Nola turned to shoo the younger girls back downstairs and faced the two of them again. Seeing Ted's tray on the desk, she took his arm and led him over to the desk. "Better eat before this gets cold." She removed the napkin, shook it open, and looked up at him until he settled himself at the desk. "Now," she said, turning to Annie, "let's get to work."

She took two small mum plants from Annie, leaving her with the cherry-colored azalea and a vase containing tulips with pussy willows that looked almost Oriental. Annie wondered at Aunt Nola's plan to put all four in Ted's office. For a man who lived with virtually no color, it was bound to be a little overwhelming.

Since Aunt Nola headed for the bookcase at the far end of the room, Annie turned and surveyed the rest of the office. Ted's desk sat at an alcove of windows, giving him a sliver of a view of the Chicago River between one skyscraper and the next, while a tall ficus tree filled in the corner behind him. A rectangular conference table and chairs occupied the rest of the space adjacent to a whole wall of books.

"My law library," Ted said when she stood before the floor-to-ceiling shelves.

Annie looked from the dark, discreet book bindings stamped in gold to the table's ebony surface. The silvery velvet of the catkins and the gray vase fit the color scheme perfectly, she decided, and the pale lemon of the tulips added a spot of warmth to its austere setting.

"There, I think that's got it," Aunt Nola announced from the far end of the room.

Annie looked to where she stood surveying her handiwork. Yellow mums sat on a shelf of the bookcase along with crystal paperweights that Aunt Nola had rearranged, and a bronze mum sat on a small table between two charcoal leather-upholstered chairs that her aunt had pulled forward into the room by the east wall of windows. Still holding the azalea, Annie weighed the balance of color. The only decent place left was the glass and brushed steel table before the sofa. Deciding that the cherry colored blossoms would fight the room's only declaration of color, a painting of Chicago's skyline at sunset, Annie switched the azalea with the bronze mums and placed those on the long cocktail table.

It still needed something, and she looked longingly at the paperweights. Several of those scattered on the table would help soften the feeling of rigidity, and the crystal facets would reflect the coppery flowers. She elected not to suggest it though when she looked up and saw Ted's reaction to their impromptu decorating.

He seemed to be eating mechanically because the fork rose and fell with regularity as he glanced with a slight frown from one end of the room to the other, then from side to side.

Finally, wiping his mouth, he said, "I have to admit that the flowers look very nice." He came around his desk and gazed at the new arrangements appreciatively.

"Nice?" Aunt Nola looked indignant. "I'd say that they add some blooming life to the place." She chuckled, adding, "No pun intended. I told you, Annie, when you suggested sharing the plants that it was the very thing this office needed."

Turning to Ted, she said, "Now, if you were to turn Annie loose in here, she'd really do a bang-up job for you. The girl's gifted when it comes to color. Maybe that's why her food always looks so appetizing."

"You won't get any argument from me there." Ted smiled in Annie's direction, but she thought he also looked a little wary. "And thank you for the decorating offer, but the offices were recently redone."

When it looked as if Aunt Nola were going to take issue with him on that point, he continued, "I can't tell you how much I appreciate you sharing your bounty with me. And for the lunch. It was delicious, as usual."

Aunt Nola perked up again. "You liked it, huh? Annie makes the best lasagna I've ever tasted."

Annie turned to her, her brow wrinkled. "But I didn't think there was any of the vegetable lasagna left."

"Oh, there wasn't." She beamed at Ted who was looking at the empty plate in astonishment. She said to him, "If you had complained about it not being vegetarian, I was going to get you more manicotti. That was the other dish. But you lapped it up. I can't tell you how relieved I am you gave up that nonsense."

Looking thoroughly confused, Ted said, "You mean I ate meat and never knew it?" He shook his head as his hand came up to rub his neck. "Come to think of it, I really don't remember eating. All my stomach knew was that it was being fed and that it tasted great. I guess I was watching you two and not thinking much about anything. Certainly not about what went into my mouth."

"Aunt Nola," Annie said in a warning tone, "shame on you. It wasn't fair to pull a fast one like that."

"Fair?" Looking up at Ted towering over her, the older woman said, "He's a big boy. He can take care of himself. Why in the world a big, strapping man like him would want to be a vegetarian anyway is beyond me."

"Yes, but you can't just go around reorganizing everyone's life to suit yourself," Annie protested. "How would you like it if—" She broke off at the tap on Ted's office door.

"Ted, darling," Veronica said, opening the door. Her smile slipped when she saw others present. "I beg your pardon. I naturally assumed you would be alone."

"Veronica." Ted stepped to her side and slid one arm around her shoulder rather heartily. "You remember Miss Rafferty and her aunt?"

"Yes, of course. You have something to do with a restaurant, don't you?"

Annie nodded, her breath constricted at the sight of

Ted's arm around Veronica's silver fox–draped shoulder. With hair the color of champagne, the silvery fur, and an oatmeal-colored wool dress accented with a buttery brown belt, shoes, and gloves, Veronica looked ready for a fashion show. Eyeing her, Annie changed her mind again and decided that Veronica probably *did* have something to do with the way Ted's office was decorated. She seemed partial to bland colors herself.

After a short, uncomfortable silence, Veronica turned to Ted. "Darling, I came to see if I could drag you away for lunch. Surely you don't want to spend *all* afternoon cooped up in here? I heard about the most delightful place . . ."

Her voice trailed off as Aunt Nola marched over to Ted's desk and made a show of tidying up the tray of dishes. The metal covers rattled as she replaced them.

Clearly displeased, Veronica said, "I see I'm too late once again. How . . . convenient for you to have a restaurant on the premises. You must take me there sometime."

"Veronica, I'm sorry—"

"No, darling." Veronica's smile was too bright and obviously forced as she interrupted him. "It was just a passing whim. I know how busy you've been since you returned from vacation. *I'll* leave and let you get back to work." She patted his cheek. "Now don't forget, we have to be at the Jeffersons' by eight-thirty. I'll expect you at eight."

She reached the door before she paused and turning said, "Good-bye, ladies. So nice to have seen you again." The door closed gently behind her.

Ted stuffed his hands in his pockets and whistled silently through pursed lips. Annie and Aunt Nola stared first at Ted, then at each other.

Just when Veronica's steps had grown fainter, they heard a loud yeowl from Charlie, followed by Veronica's scream.

FIVE

Their blank stares became ones of concern, and all three started forward. Annie darted around the door as Ted opened it. He glanced back at Aunt Nola, but when he saw she was encumbered by the tray he rushed after Annie.

If it hadn't been for the frightened look on Veronica's face, Annie would have laughed. A grown woman cowering in a corner of the hall held at bay by a cat, even a growling one, was pretty ludicrous. Annie scooped Charlie up in her arms to quiet her. She could feel all ten claws at once as Charlie made her displeasure known.

Ted halted at the bottom of the stairs and frowned as he looked from Veronica, now edging toward the rear door, to Charlie. "Veronica! What is it?"

"Oh, darling." She threw herself into his arms, turning her face from Charlie. "It was horrible! That beast attacked me. My leg—I'm afraid to look. You know I don't like the sight of blood."

"Blood!" Annie and Aunt Nola, who had stopped behind Ted, spoke in unison.

Ted held Veronica away from his chest and leaned over, turning her from one side to the other to see where she was injured. Annie was close enough to hear his sigh of relief at no sign of attack on one leg, but she caught her breath at the evidence of a torn stocking and tiny pinpoints of red where Charlie's sharp claws had gone home.

"I'm sorry," Annie said quietly. "I don't know why Charlie would do something like that." And she *was* sorry, but from the screech Veronica had let loose you'd have thought a wild animal had attacked her. "I've got a first aid kit in the kitchen. I'll get it."

"No!" Veronica's unequivocal tone halted Annie. "I won't stay here a moment longer." She turned to the door and drew her dignity around her like the fur cape she straightened. "Ted, take me home."

He stared helplessly at Annie for a moment. With Veronica already walking through the doorway, he took a moment to squeeze Annie's shoulder.

Early Sunday afternoon Ted stood outside the rear entrance to his building wondering what he could possibly say to Annie and Aunt Nola as an excuse for Veronica's behavior. He had had enough trouble dealing with it himself. He'd explained that Charlie was only protecting her family, but Veronica was unforgiving of the cat's attack. In the face of her dramatization of the incident and her demands, Ted said he thought they needed a respite for the evening and canceled their plans. When Veronica asked in an icy tone if his new plans included a certain restaurant, he turned and left. He had gone to a movie, but watching the romantic comedy hadn't stilled his thoughts. He didn't particularly like this newly revealed side of Veronica.

Ted poked his head around the kitchen door and stared at the strange occupants. A huge black woman loomed over the stove, energetically stirring something in a pot not much bigger than her hand. His glance took in another unfamiliar woman rinsing dishes. The sound of laughter erupted from somewhere in the restaurant, then Annie's cousin Moira walked into the kitchen and saw him standing uncertainly by the door.

"Hi. If you're looking for Annie, she's sitting down in the back room with some of the family. Come on through."

Before they rounded the corner by the coffee and soda machines, another burst of laughter rolled toward Ted. Moira led him past the smattering of diners that remained to the smiling group in the back hall where he had eaten lunch with Jim. Annie looked ridiculously young with her hair pulled up into a ponytail and tied with a light green ribbon that matched her blouse under the ever-present apron.

Uncle Tully hitched over another chair, saying, "Take a load off and join us."

"Yes," chimed in Aunt Nola who sat on the far side of the table. "Looking up at you gives me a crick in the neck."

Amid the laughter and general shifting to make room for Ted between Uncle Tully and Annie, she asked quietly, "Is Veronica okay?"

"She's fine."

He didn't have time to say more as Uncle Tully wanted to introduce Ted to the man seated next to him. "Marmaduke Sullivan, another of Annie's uncles. Duke for short," Uncle Tully informed him with a wink. Ted didn't think anyone had ever called the massive, graying Irishman by anything other than his nickname to his face. "Next to him is his son, Trevor. He's got a twin sister around here somewhere. Moira," he said, putting an arm around the girl who had led him to the table, "you already know. Now those three young ones over there," he pointed toward a group between Annie and Aunt Nola, "are more directly related to Annie. Next to her is her sister Celia, short for Cecilia; then Lynn, short for Linette; and the man of the family, Kit, short for Christopher.

Now, Annie isn't short for anything. She's just short, period.''

Groans greeted his words, giving Ted time to study Annie's brother and sisters.

Celia, clearly the next in age, had lighter hair than Annie with an auburn tint and two dimples to Annie's one; Lynn had the lovely reddish gold hair of Shelia and several others that obviously ran through the family. She was also shy if her bent head was anything to go by. Kit, whom Aunt Nola had said was in his last year of college, was a masculine version of Annie.

Shaking Ted's hand, he said, "Now, I know why the name sounded familiar when Annie mentioned it. You coach at the Y, don't you?''

Ted agreed, scrutinizing him. He didn't recognize the young man and said so with an apology.

"No reason why you should. Since I'm still in school, I'm only there on holidays and during the summer, usually during the week. I admired the moves some of the boys were making, and they were only too happy to tell me about their awesome coach.'' His wide grin was as infectious as Annie's.

"You forget how impressionable nine and ten-year-olds are,'' Ted replied, returning his smile.

The talk became general about basketball and the Chicago Bulls' chances for the play-offs. As unobtrusively as possible, Ted pulled out his notebook and scribbled down their names. Eventually Moira said she had to help Maureen out front.

Aunt Nola leaned over and tapped Annie on the arm. "If you don't get a move on, you're going to miss going to that exhibit you wanted to see.''

Annie, with her feet propped on Cecilia's chair, looked slightly rebellious. "I'm too comfortable.''

"Well.''—Aunt Nola gave an indignant sniff—"now that you've got that help you wanted, you should take advantage of having some time to yourself. Go on. Take your apron off and scoot.''

As Annie headed for the kitchen, Aunt Nola eyed Ted speculatively. ''I take it you saw the mountain in the kitchen called Dora? And Consuela, the dishwasher?'' At his nod, she said, ''We're becoming a regular United Nations around here.''

''Aunt Nola,'' Celia protested, ''you're being unfair to Annie. You know she's not pushing you out. She just wants you to supervise the catering jobs and take things a little easier.''

Ted remembered Annie's comment about needing help and her covert glance at the time toward Aunt Nola. He saw that the tiny lines around the older woman's eyes were etched a little deeper and realized her tongue had been a touch more astringent the last couple of days. Well, he *had* promised to help handle Aunt Nola.

''I imagine,'' Ted said with a glance at Annie's siblings to see how they took his interference, ''that the extra help will be a relief to everyone. Annie's been looking a little worn lately.'' Aunt Nola looked surprised, then thoughtful. Good. He had pegged her as a benevolent tyrant who hadn't considered things beyond their impact on herself. To be fair, she had been in charge of the family for a long time, and it must be hard for her to realize that her chicks were growing up and able to make decisions on their own. ''And remember,'' he told her, ''that if anything happens to you, then Annie would have the responsibility of looking after you *and* the restaurant.''

''You may be right about Annie.'' Aunt Nola nodded her head after a moment. ''She has been looking a little peaked. Maybe I've been a bit crotchety about the whole thing.'' She glanced around the table and saw Celia and Kit staring at her, and Lynn's eyes round with surprise. ''A body has a right to change her mind,'' she huffed.

''You, Kit. What are you still doing here? You have

studying to do. Celia, where's that fellow of yours? Is it now considered good manners to keep people waiting? And you, Linette, you can take me home as soon as Celia leaves. No niece of mine is going out with someone until I've met him.'' Aunt Nola gazed at the circle of smiling faces defiantly.

Kit rose and kissed her on the cheek. "It's good to see you back to normal. Had me worried there for a minute.''

"Well, it's about time,'' Aunt Nola said as Annie appeared with Shelia in tow. "What kept you?''

"The boys wanted to introduce me to Sugar, their parakeet. I promised Shelia I'd take him to the vet tomorrow to have his wings clipped, so he's staying here overnight.''

Looking at Shelia, Aunt Nola said, "And why can't Shelia take the bird in herself, I'd like to know? Never mind,'' she added, as Annie opened her mouth, "I'm sure you've got a reason. You usually do every time the family talks you into something. First a pregnant cat, then parakeets. Before you know it, we'll have a menagerie in here to match the United Nations. Well, what are you waiting for? Be on your way.''

Before Annie could reply, Bryce erupted from the kitchen shouting, "Mommy, Annie. Come quick! Sugar's loose!''

"What'd I tell you?'' Aunt Nola said, but everyone ignored her in their dash to the back of the restaurant.

As people crowded into the kitchen, Ted thought it was the funniest thing he'd seen in a long time. Consuela, obviously the new dishwasher, let loose a torrent of Spanish and stood poised with the spray hose, while Dora flapped a dish towel in the air to keep the bird from flying anywhere near the food. Casey hopped up and down on one foot, holding an extended finger in the air for his parakeet to land on. Everyone babbled at once.

Dora kept flapping her towel, saying, "Shoo, bird,'' as she advanced on the fluttering parakeet.

"Come on, Sugar," Casey and Bryce begged.

"*Madre de Dios!*"

"Will everyone be quiet?" Annie pleaded. "You're scaring the bird."

She was practically drowned out by advice offered from the onlookers on how to catch the parakeet. He fluttered from side to side, apparently afraid to land anywhere. Kit and Trevor were poised on opposite ends of the floor-to-ceiling shelves, leaning over and trying to snatch the blue and white bird as he flew by. Dora's advancing dish towel snapped close to Sugar, and he made an abrupt U-turn and flew out the back door into the hall.

Casey began to wail before Byrce assured him that now they would catch Sugar. Annie dashed to the door and halted the flow after the parakeet.

"No, the noise is only frightening the bird more. Give him a chance to settle down, and I'll get him. The doors are closed so he can't go anywhere."

Ted made his way through the throng to Annie's side. Sotto voce he said, "Guess what? I think we left all the doors to my office open yesterday. I never even went back for my jacket, so I'm assuming the doors are like we left them." Louder he said, "Annie's right. There're too many of us making noise. Since he's likely in my offices, I'll help her. Do you have something to put him in?" he asked the boys.

Byrce produced the cage which Ted took and followed Annie up the stairs. When he could tear his gaze away from her swinging hips and shapely bottom ahead of him, he noticed there was no sign of the bird in the stairwell.

Annie proceeded up the stairs, constantly aware of Ted's presence behind her. She wished suddenly that she was wearing her usual uniform of a loose-fitting jumpsuit or baggy pants instead of tight jeans. She could almost feel his gaze upon her as she reached the landing.

She halted, listening for the fluttering parakeet. Nothing. The door to Ted's office, almost across from the landing, was standing wide open so chances were Sugar was in there. At least it wouldn't be difficult to find him. He should stand out in that nondescript room like pimento in olives.

With Ted on her heels, she walked slowly into his office, and he quietly shut the door behind them. Annie spotted Sugar atop the gray and charcoal plaid drapes. He was perched near the end of the rod just opposite the bookcase, the top shelf of which sparkled with reflected prisms of light from the crystal paperweights. She approached slowly and began talking to the parakeet.

"Poor Sugar. Bet you're one frightened bird, aren't you? You just stay put. I'm coming to get you." Glancing over her shoulder, Annie noted that Ted had moved quietly behind her. She turned back and judged the distance between the bookcase and the curtains. "I'm just going to pull over this chair to climb on and, before you know it, we'll have you safe and sound in your cage."

Ted waved her away and moved the chair for her. In a low voice, he said, "Are you sure you can reach the curtains from the bookcase?" Frowning, he judged the distance. "It doesn't seem close enough to me."

"Since I don't see how else we can get him down, I'm going to try it. You can brace my leg when I lean over." Removing her boots, she climbed from the chair onto the thin ledge of the bookcase and edged her way toward the window. When Sugar began squawking, she crooned, "Pretty bird. Just be patient a few moments longer. Then you can make as much racket as you want."

Teetering on the edge of the bookcase, Annie put one hand on the ceiling and, with Ted's hands bracing her right leg and hip, leaned as far over as she could while murmuring reassuring noises to Sugar. "Tsk, tsk, tsk, tsk, tsk," she trilled as she had seen the boys do. Extending her right hand, she said, "Yes, you're a pretty bird, and you're so scared you're trembling. Come on, get on my finger.''

She swung her left leg out to balance herself as she leaned further to the right. Just as Sugar hopped onto her finger, Annie felt herself overbalance and Ted's supporting hands falter as he tried to compensate for her angle.

She moaned as she tilted further to the right, and the parakeet flew off. Annie closed her eyes as she lost her balance. The sinking feeling in her stomach ended as she was caught in mid flight and held with rock-hard arms. She automatically wrapped her arms around Ted's shoulders and sighed in relief. It was short-lived. The herbal scent of his after-shave and the bunched shoulder muscles beneath the crispness of his shirt made her blazingly aware of him.

With her head on Ted's chest, Annie could hear the thud of his heartbeat over her own jumping one. Tilting back her head, she opened her eyes and stared at him. Her breath caught in her throat as a jolt shot along already tingling nerves, and heat sluiced through her body. She didn't understand any of the emotions flooding her. All she was aware of were Ted's blazing blue eyes and his lips tantalizingly close.

Her eyes slid closed as he touched her lips with his, their breaths mingling. The pressure from Ted's arms increased, and she felt one palm just beneath her breasts. She felt them tightening and moaned from the exquisite shock. As the muffled sound escaped, Ted's light duel with her tongue increased, and he let her legs slide down until she stood firmly against him. Annie felt drugged with the surge of sensations rocketing along every fiber of her being.

"I must say"—Aunt Nola's voice came from far away—"that's the funniest way I've ever seen to catch a bird.''

Annie blinked, trying to focus on her through the rays

of the sun that slanted though one edge of Ted's office window. Ted. She sneaked a peek at him from under lowered lashes. He didn't seem the least disturbed by the sight of Aunt Nola finding them plastered together as close as mackerel in a barrel. As his body shifted bringing her to his side under one arm, she searched for any sign that he had been as lost to reason as she had by their embrace. All that showed was an indulgent smile as Aunt Nola plucked the parakeet from the back of the sofa where he had apparently landed after Annie's abortive rescue attempt.

Confused as to why her legs still trembled, Annie rushed to explain what she was doing in Ted's arms. "I— I fell trying to capture that darned bird, and Ted was quick enough to catch me."

"And a good thing, too," Aunt Nola replied, carrying Sugar to his cage. "We may have some more help, but that doesn't mean we could do without you while a broken arm or leg mended." Closing the cage door after the bird, she picked up the cage and walked to the door. Before closing it behind her, she turned back with a roguish smile. "Why don't you two just continue where you left off?"

Annie stared at the door as it snapped shut and felt a vibration radiating from Ted's side. Her gaze switched to his face as the rumbling deep in his chest exploded in laughter. Her indignation at Aunt Nola's high-handedness dissolved in a chuckle at the irony. Her straitlaced aunt who wouldn't let the girls out of her sight without arranging for a bodyguard had left her literally in the clutches of a man who was almost a stranger.

No. That wasn't quite true. They might not have known Ted for long, but Annie realized she felt as comfortable with him as she did with any of her many male relatives. Or, she amended, she had until that kiss. With a start, she realized that Ted was returning her examination with interest. Her eyes slid closed again as he leaned toward her, and her pulse quickened in expectation.

He hugged her to him a moment as his lips met her forehead, then let her go, chuckling. "Your aunt is indeed one of a kind, but I think I can manage without her encouragement."

Disappointment shot through her, but Annie shut it down remembering Ted's entanglement with Veronica. She took a deep breath, gained a measure of control, and said lightly with a smile, "I think she just tries to see how outrageous she can be." She glanced around, pretending to look for her boots, and spied them under the chair by the bookcase. "Ah," she uttered in relief at having a reason to step away from Ted's disturbing closeness.

After pulling on her fashionable boots, she tugged at the chair, but Ted brushed her hands aside. He swung the chair up, muscles bunching across his shoulders, and replaced it in its proper position. He remained looming over it, his hands braced on its charcoal arms, looking at her with an expression hard to define. At a loss for something to say, Annie finally remembered her manners. "I never said thank you. For catching me, I mean. It could have been a nasty fall."

Ted smiled. "And have Aunt Nola haunting me for letting something happen to you? I have a way with little old ladies. You said so yourself, remember?"

And young ladies, too, but damned if she was going to tell him so. "Well, I'd better be on my way if I want to get to the Art Institute before they close. Thanks again." Swallowing her reluctance to leave, Annie turned toward the door. She reached it just as Ted appeared at her side.

"Are you going to see the French Impressionists?" he asked, referring to the traveling exhibit currently in Chicago. Annie nodded. "Good. I mean, I've been wanting to see it, too. Would you mind if I went with you?"

Sternly reminding herself about Veronica, Annie tried

to subdue the quickening of her heart and its leap of excitement at his request. Besides, Aunt Nola was bound to send her usual bodyguard along and that would take care of any further complications.

Less than fifteen minutes later, Annie and Ted exited a cab at the Michigan Avenue entrance of the Art Institute. She had been exasperated by Aunt Nola's attempt at matchmaking by sending them off alone, but was determined to enjoy the couple of hours left to see the exhibit.

Annie's artistic ability came out in her cooking and her blending brilliant colors together in decorating. She could not reproduce the lovely pictures she saw in her mind, but that did not stop her from enjoying the work of others. She loved to wander the halls of the Art Institute and look at the paintings. Particularly the work of French Impressionists and Postimpressionists. The institute's fine collection had been enhanced a month earlier by the Courtauld Collection of nineteenth and early twentieth century French paintings touring the United States.

As they climbed the long flight of steps between the famous stone lions, Annie noticed Ted glancing at her speculatively. She bore his discreet glimpses while Ted paid the entrance fees over Annie's protest. Finally, walking toward the designated gallery, she asked, "Do I have bird feathers or worse on me somewhere?"

Chuckling, he reassured her. "No, it's just that you seemed to be checking over your shoulder in the cab. Almost as if you thought we were being followed."

"In truth, I thought we might be." Her shoulder and hip brushed Ted as she turned slightly to look up at him with a rueful smile. "This isn't exactly a date, but you see, Aunt Nola has never let us girls out of her sight on a first date without a bodyguard." At his confounded look, Annie explained, "Oh, it took us a few years to catch on. We used to wonder at always bumping into one or another of our cousins wherever we went. In fact, Celia was the one who made the big discovery at the end of one of her dates.'' Annie grinned at the memory. "He tried to kiss her, only Celia wasn't having any of it. As she explained later, she'd only gone to the movies with him so she could see the latest picture. Anyway, when she pushed him away, our cousin Guy started snickering from behind the bushes. Celia jumped on him and gave him a black eye. That was the last time her date ever asked her out. He was scared to death of her right hook.''

Ted's uninhibited laughter rang out in the hushed gallery. He covered his mouth at the realization of where they were, but laughter erupted again when Annie giggled like a little girl. He had enjoyed watching the amusement ripple through her various expressions as she talked. She had an exquisitely expressive face. And he loved her husky voice. In relating the tale, it had dropped even lower, and though the words were not intimate, her tone was.

What a paradox. Annie had responded like an experienced woman to his kiss, yet her face was pure innocence while brushing against him a moment ago. What would have happened if Aunt Nola had not chosen to interrupt when she had? He'd been lost to the emotion of the moment and all sense of propriety. Hell, he'd been about to make love to Annie on the carpet then and there, and here she was telling him that she still had a duenna on first dates.

He looked back over his shoulder involuntarily before another thought struck him. He was inordinately pleased at the thought that Annie was untouched. If she was truly the innocent she seemed, what would she be like once initiated into the ways of lovemaking? Her body had been soft and sweet, fitting next to his naturally. He didn't remember being so lost in passion since a callow youth in the backseat of his Trans Am. Ted bumped into Annie and, jarred back to the present, realized she was mesmerized by the painting in front of them.

Leaning forward, he read the plaque below the enormous canvas: Seurat's *A Sunday Afternoon on the Island of La Grande Jatte*. Ted stared at the dots of color up close, then drew back as far as the crowd around them would allow.

Annie looked around and saw him shaking his head. "What's wrong?"

He gave her a rueful grin and, shrugging, ran his hand over the back of his neck before stuffing his hands into his pockets. "Guess I just don't understand Impressionism. I mean, what's the point? Give me something where what you see in front of you is exactly what it's supposed to be."

Annie cocked her head like an inquisitive bird. "Like what, for instance?"

"Oh, like the great masters. Michelangelo, Raphael, da Vinci. Or even more modern painters like Turner and Constable. They dotted their *i*'s and crossed their *t*'s, so to speak."

Annie's puckered brow smoothed into serenity once more. "Ah, I see." Taking his hand, she pulled him after her past several paintings before coming to a stop. "Look," she said, pointing to a small garden landscape by Monet. "What's the first thing that strikes you about the painting?"

Looking at the side of a house and paved court in shadow and a garden in sunshine, the lushness of summer was portrayed in greenery everywhere. "I guess the light," Ted finally said, pointing to where brilliant sunshine spilled over the garden to the courtyard and edged out the shadows. Then he frowned and stepped back, his eyes searching the canvas. "It's—it's sort of suffused with light, even in the shadows."

"Yes!" Annie grabbed his arm, almost dancing in

her excitement. "Come on, I want to show you some more."

She pulled him to paintings by Pissarro, Manet, Cassatt, Degas, Morisot, and more Monets, talking about fleeting images, animated brush strokes, visual impressions. She came to rest before a grouping filled with jewel tones and soft pastels alike. "I think Renoir's my favorite. His paintings are so lush and express so much—" Annie spread her arms, as if to encompass the brilliant colors "—joy." Moving on to *Impression, Sunrise*, she added, "But then I see one of Monet's brimming with vitality, and I'm torn between the two.

"But do you see what they all have in common?" Not waiting for him to answer, she rushed on. "They're all fragments of life caught as they happen, but the common thread is the quality of color and light." Annie's face turned up to his was shining. "When you mentioned Turner and Constable, I immediately thought of color and light. And because of that, I thought you might appreciate the spontaneity of the Impressionists' informal compositions and vigorous brushstrokes."

Ted nodded. "Despite the fact I like things a little more organized and realistic, I have to admit that they're beautiful."

But no more beautiful than Annie. At his words, her delicately tinted cheeks flushed with color and her dimple flashed as she grinned at him. He put an arm around her shoulders and hugged her to him.

Turning, he kept her under his arm as they continued through the labyrinth of corridors viewing Cézanne, Gauguin, Toulouse-Lautrec, van Gogh, and yet more Monets and Renoirs. As Annie, with her hands fluttering like birds' wings, talked about their animation and spontaneity, Ted began to liken her and her actions to those of the Impressionist painters she loved. He realized those very qualities were probably what attracted him to Annie, who was impetuous, energetic, and vivacious as well.

Suddenly, he wanted to know more about her. No, everything about her. He remembered what she'd told him as they entered the museum about her and her sisters' bodyguards. "Do you mean to say," Ted took Annie's elbow and steered her around a group stalled in front of a grouping of Sisley's landscapes, "that you girls put up with being followed once you knew of it?"

Annie looked up at him in surprise. "Oh, we ditched our cousins Brian and Guy a couple of times after Celia's incident. Then Aunt Nola started double-teaming: one cousin would follow us and one would be in place already. She knew where we were going and always had someone there ahead of us. Once in a while we'd succeed in losing our guards on the way home, but not often. Most of our dates, once they learned what was going on, thought it the better part of valor to respect the situation." A sudden grin deepened the dimple in her cheek. "Celia comes by her right hook honestly. All the boys were notorious fighters."

"And Aunt Nola actually continues the practice now that you're . . . what? Twenty-four, twenty-five?"

"No, twenty-seven. Celia's twenty-five and Lynn's twenty-two. And the reason we permit Aunt Nola to continue with the whole thing is that times have changed. In Celia's first year at college, a friend of hers was raped on campus. We came to realize that what we had considered interference in our lives was actually protection. We stopped giving the boys the slip and started making sure we could always keep them in sight. Besides, it's usually just until Aunt Nola is assured there's no reason for worry."

They both turned and scanned the thick crowd around them. Either whoever was following them was being damned discreet or Aunt Nola was slipping.

They moved on to the next painting, Renoir's *The Rowers' Lunch*, and Annie's gaze roamed the canvas, her lips curved with delight, before moving on to follow the flow of the crowd. "So how did you wind up in practice with Jim Linden?"

"A fraternity brother. And," Ted admitted, "my youthful idealism. I thought I would prefer serving the common man rather than a faceless corporate giant. As things have turned out, it's proven as lucrative as the family firm, even if Jim and I have to work a little harder by serving more clients. But then that's what we set out to do."

They spent the next hour gazing at paintings and drawings and talking. By closing time, Annie had related more of her family history than had Ted, who'd kept most of his comments confined to describing youthful follies with Jim in college and how they started up their practice.

As the cab left them at the rear of his building, Annie drew her thin spring coat more tightly against her throat while Ted fished for his car keys. With the sun had gone most of the day's warmth, and she regretted exchanging her usual sweater for a blouse this morning in a burst of spring fever.

Ted opened the door of his Mercedes and then leaned over it, propping his arms along the top of the window. The wind on Michigan Avenue had ruffled the usual perfection of his hair, and by the glow of the streetlight almost above them, Annie finally saw it mussed as strands of blond masked his forehead.

"I'd like to see you again where we can talk comfortably without being interrupted," he said into the Sunday quiet of the quarter. "If it isn't committing heresy, would you consider having dinner with me at another restaurant?"

Annie hesitated a moment, thinking about all the unanswered questions she had despite her resolve to look upon Ted as only a landlord, before her smile lightened her expression. Her yes corresponded with the opening of the back door.

Aunt Nola stuck her head out. " 'Bout time you brought her back, young man. Go away now and don't keep her standing out in the cold.''

Ted grinned at her and saluted smartly. Before he ducked into his car though, he leaned around the open door and kissed Annie lightly on her chilled lips.

SIX

Pacing the hallway waiting for Annie to arrive the next morning, Ted realized he hadn't been this nervous since his first junior high dance. As much as he wanted to see Annie, to hold her in his arms, and taste her sweet warmth, he almost dreaded her arrival. What if the reality of Annie didn't mesh with his dreams of the previous night?

He frowned down at Charlie and her kittens. He wondered how a man who prided himself on calm, well-thought-out decisions had arrived at the conclusion that Annie was the answer to what he'd been searching for in a wife. He sighed. How had his life been turned upside down in such a short time by a pixie who talked to cats? All he knew was that as much as he liked Annie's boisterous, fun-loving family, it was Annie herself who mesmerized him.

Ted frowned again, thinking about the two messages from Veronica on his answering machine last night. He had ignored them both. He knew he would have to settle things with her sometime this week, but he wanted to do it in person. For Veronica, there would be ego involved, if not emotions. Why hadn't he ever seen beneath the surface to her true character before? Perhaps because he'd never met anyone like Annie before. Veronica saw life as something to tiptoe through on the way to the grave, while Annie was like a free spirit who ran through life laughing and loving. She saw life as a celebration, and he wanted to share in that joy.

With a start, Ted heard a key in the lock. He'd been so lost in thought he hadn't heard Annie drive up. He turned and faced the door, then smiled as Annie gazed at him in surprise. Everything was all right. She was everything he remembered, and more. And she was going to be his. He enveloped her in a hungry embrace, his lips finding hers in urgency.

Annie responded to the magic of Ted's touch, her drugged senses bounding along in tandem with his demands as his kiss deepened. She was reeling as he unzipped her winter jacket and pushed its folds aside to run his hands under the edge of her sweater. Grasping her by the waist, he pulled her to him as his lips covered hers once more. His hands slid up her rib cage to the sides of her breasts. Annie leaned into his embrace as a thrill of joy shot through her: there was no denying this time that he was as affected as she, though she wasn't sure how far she wanted to test these uncharted waters.

As suddenly as Ted had fiercely gathered her to him, his touch changed and became gentle. Dazed, Annie drew back and studied his expression in the pale wash of spring light filtering into the tiny hall. He looked . . . pleased, proud, and possessive.

"Well, good morning to you, too," she said, striving for a light note.

"It is now that you're here." He lowered his head and kissed the side of her neck. "What time shall I make the reservations for tonight?"

"Reservations? Oh, dinner." It was hard to think with

him nuzzling her neck. "But, Ted," Annie protested, pushing at his chest. He didn't budge, except to use the opportunity to circle beneath her chin to the other side of her neck. If she didn't stop him, she was never going to be able to think. Putting some muscle into it, Annie shoved at Ted and immediately had his attention. "I can't have dinner with you tonight."

The satisfied gleam faded in a blaze of blue. "Why not?"

"Because for starters," Annie said, drawing a deep breath to steady herself, "I'm not sure how much dinner would be eaten."

Ted grinned. "Is this the lady Aunt Nola says is not afraid to try anything?"

Ignoring his taunt and the challenging glint of mischief that sprang into his expression, Annie smiled wryly. "I'm not going to touch that one. The real reason is that I have no one to leave in charge." At his frown, she explained, "I don't like to ask Aunt Nola just now because I think it would be too much for her and frankly, no one else is capable yet."

"So where does that leave us?"

Somehow Annie was back in Ted's embrace, her head tucked under his chin. "At the mercy of the applicants I've got lined up for interviews." Sighing, she wrapped her arms around him. She'd never realized that giving in could be such fun.

As the week wore on, Ted found the stolen moments alone with Annie in the early morning hours frustratingly short. They were both so busy during the rest of the day there was little time for more than a quick hello while surrounded by a multitude of others. In the evenings, he could see Annie was so tired that the kindest thing he could do for her was to let her go home to bed . . . when what he wanted was to take her home to his bed.

The week seemed endless as Annie interviewed first one candidate, then another, and yet each day overflowed with work. And different members of Annie's family had taken to coming upstairs to ask advice about one thing or another.

Uncle Tully owned the six flat apartment building he lived in, and he had a fractious tenant. How could he legally evict him? On Wednesday afternoon, Annie's cousin Kevin sheepishly appeared at his door asking for help with his calculus assignment. And every day, Aunt Nola appeared at his door with a lunch tray and conversation while he ate. He was kept fully apprised of Dora's and Consuela's activities in the kitchen, as well as those of other family members he had met over the last two weeks.

Ted's patience was rewarded when Casey appeared in his office later Wednesday afternoon with a note from Annie: *If your offer of dinner is still open, how about six tonight?*

He looked down at the little boy's dark head, which was cocked sideways trying to decipher the message. This was the little guy who liked secrets. "I'll tell you what, Casey. I'll let you in on a little secret." Bright blue eyes glowed up at him.

"I'm going to take Annie out to dinner. But it's a secret just between you, me, and Annie." The little boy's head nodded solemnly while Ted slashed a "yes" on Annie's note and gave it back to him. "You take this down to Annie and tell her you know a secret."

When Ted went downstairs to collect Annie, he found her in her office. His greeting froze in his throat as he took in the picture of Annie standing on tiptoe on one foot, the other leg bent enticingly as she stretched, trying to replace a thick binder on the top shelf above her desk. Gone were the baggy pants and concealing apron. In their place a dress, heels, and stockings. She actually had legs. And what legs! Ted swallowed and cleared his throat.

Annie glanced over her shoulder and saw him. "Oh, hi."

She shoved the binder in place and turned around. One hand swept down over the swirling blue-green skirt that hugged her hips before flaring into ripples around her legs, while her other hand crept up to smooth her dark hair. It was longer than he had thought. For the first time she wore it loose, and it fell in beautiful waves below her shoulders.

Before he could stop himself, Ted said, "You look good enough to eat." Her throaty chuckle escaped, breaking the spell. He grinned in response to the smile that lit her whole face with its warmth. "I mean it. You look lovely."

Twenty minutes later they were seated in Tratoria's because Annie said she wanted to try their northern Italian cuisine. Sampling the wine and nodding to the man hovering over them, Ted congratulated himself again on his choice of bride. Beauty, brains, *and* personality.

As Annie set down her wineglass he picked up her delicately boned hand and held it between his two larger ones, running a thumb over her palm. "We're going to have beautiful children."

Annie's smile slipped as she looked at him in astonishment. "This is what one glass of wine does to you? You'd better send back the rest of the bottle in self-defense."

She tried to tug her hand away, but Ted tightened his hold, gently but firmly. There was that particular smile again, the one she had noticed after his exuberant greeting earlier in the week. It was reminiscent of the ones Shelia's boys wore when staking out some particular territory or toy.

When he didn't say anything, but just looked at her

with that complacent smile, she bristled. "Children with or without benefit of clergy?"

Ted chuckled. "I don't know how brave I am, but foolhardy I'm not. I remember your story about the right hook, and I *do* know how to count. The odds are in favor of your family. I'm outnumbered, so I guess we'll have to make it legal."

"You can't be serious!"

"Why not?"

"Because you—I—" Annie sputtered to a halt, then tried again. "You've known me for less than a month."

"But I think I know you very well. All I had to do was watch you around your family. You're kind, resourceful, intelligent, personable, *beautiful*—"

Annie decided to tackle the issue head-on. "What about Veronica?"

"Ah, yes. Veronica." Ted squeezed her hand and kept it in his as he leaned toward her, looking at her directly. "There was never anything official between us. Just a lot of hope on my mother's side." He frowned. "Although I'm not quite sure how Veronica felt about it because the subject never came up."

Annie was pretty sure she knew how serious Veronica was, but there was a more complex issue at stake. "I know hardly anything about you—or your family. Do you have brothers and sisters? What about your parents? How are they going to feel about this?"

"We'll get to my family in a minute. I have a question for you first. How do *you* feel about it? Will you marry me?"

Annie gulped. There it was; in black and white, so to speak. Ever honest, she replied, "I'm . . . not quite sure."

"What *are* you sure about?"

"Well . . . I like you." Blushing, she added, "I—I'm attracted to you."

Ted flashed a variation of what Annie was coming to think of as his "Me Tarzan. You Jane" smile. "That's enough to go on for now." He broke off as the waiter put their salads in front of them. "Permit me to overcome your major objection—that you don't know anything about me. Go on, eat," he said, relinquishing her hand.

"First, my family. My father has been dead for about two years. He would have loved you," Ted said with a quick smile. "My mother—well, my mother is somewhat difficult, I guess. She's used to having her own way, even when my father was alive. To be honest, Veronica was her choice. She felt Veronica met certain . . . criteria."

"What do you mean?"

"It's going to sound pretty crass, but you have to understand where she's coming from." Poking at his salad, Ted continued. "My father died a very wealthy man, but when they married he was practically a pauper by the standards of my mother's family. Anyway, she's of the persuasion that marriage is almost a business arrangement. She felt Veronica could do a lot for my career."

Annie felt the bottom drop out of her stomach, and her fingers tightened on her salad fork. She no longer had an appetite. Putting down her fork, she asked carefully, "And how do you feel about this . . . arrangement?"

Ted leaned over and cupped the side of her face. "I don't think business has a damned thing to do with how I feel about you." His lips covered hers in a quick kiss. Picking up her fork, he placed it back in her unresisting fingers.

Annie felt warm all over, whether because of his words or his touch, she wasn't sure.

"Next," Ted said, "I have no sisters, but I do have a younger brother. Geoffrey Thornton Carlyle, Thornton being my mother's maiden name." He chuckled. "I have my father to thank that I wasn't named Theodore Thornton. He thought Camden, another family name, was bad enough.

"My brother did go into the family law firm. He's married to Priscilla and they have one point three children." With a grin, he explained, "Pris is three months pregnant with the next heir."

"Heir?" Annie asked faintly.

"As in big bucks. Pris is an heiress in her own right. Come to think of it, I guess Mother had something to do with introducing Geoff to her.

"What else?" Ted thought for a moment while Annie digested the thought of his busy mother working on her sons' behalf to snare each of them an heiress, because she was sure that Veronica had money also. Her clothing alone said money, though quietly and discreetly, of course.

"If you're interested, I attended prep school, Harvard Law School, summer camps before joining the family at the cottage on the shore." Ted rubbed the back of his neck. "I can't think what else to tell you."

Annie sighed inwardly. He'd already told her enough for her to realize they came from different worlds. Gamely, she pressed on. "What do you do for fun? You know, hobbies."

"Oh, sailing, racquetball, tennis, skiing. Some golf. I've tried hang gliding, mountaineering, white-water canoeing. In the fall, I play touch football with some fraternity brothers. During spring I coach basketball at the Y."

Warning bells were going off in Annie's head as she compared their lives. While he'd attended camps and climbed mountains or negotiated white-water rapids, she'd earned money by teaching inner-city kids how to mix colors in summer camp. He'd attended prep schools, and she'd catered to make money for the girls' and Kit's college fund. He had a flourishing law practice, and she was struggling to start a restaurant. He wore suits that had to cost several hundred dollars, and she wore jeans, jumpsuits, and overalls several years old in order to save money. He had wealth and a privileged background, while her sisters and brother had exactly what she could give them until they could provide for themselves. He even liked different artwork than she did.

Finally, she said so out loud, then watched closely for Ted's reaction.

He looked blank for a moment, then he frowned and said, "So what? Things aren't important; people are."

At least he had his priorities straight, Annie mused. But the gulf between their worlds seemed gigantic to her. "Don't you see how different we are? We have absolutely nothing in common."

It cost her to say that, but she felt in fairness she must. With a pang, she realized it didn't matter what she wanted; it wouldn't work anyway.

"I disagree. We may not have a lot in common, but there are some pretty basic things we share that are a lot more important than similar experiences."

"Name one."

"The attraction we feel for each other, whether you call it sexual or otherwise. Hell, look at Geoff and Priscilla. They're like two peas in a pod as far as common experience is concerned, yet I wouldn't say they have the happiest marriage. Geoff's already had one affair that I know of, and I'm not too sure about Pris."

Ted broke off at Annie's shocked expression. His poor, naive little love. As her look turned wary, he could just bet what she was thinking.

"Now, don't go getting the idea that that's what our life would be like. I'd probably break the neck of anyone who looked at you twice. As for me, I didn't wait this long to make a decision about marriage without careful thought.

"Your dinner is getting cold," Ted said, and Annie wondered in surprise when the waiter had cleared away their salad plates and brought their meal. She didn't remember his being there at all. The scent of garlic from the linguini and white clam sauce was overwhelming now that she noticed.

Rubbing the back of his head, Ted continued, "Look, I don't mean to sound conceited, but although I'm not sure of Veronica's feelings, I'm fairly certain that if I'd raised the question of marriage she would have been willing. But I was looking for something more," he said, reaching over to take her hand once more, "and I've found that—whatever it is—in you. Now that I have, I don't intend to let you get away."

Stalling for time, Annie picked at her dinner and said, "Do you realize I don't even know where you live?"

"That's easy enough. My family home is in Lake Forest. I'll take you to meet my mother this weekend."

"And your brother?"

"Oh, he and Pris live in a mausoleum in Winnetka, along with a nanny, a maid, and a chauffeur."

Annie groaned. "See, that's what I mean. You were probably raised the same way. What do I know about that kind of life?"

"But you're not marrying my family. You're marrying me."

She tried to snatch her hand away, but Ted held on to it firmly. She wondered if he were deliberately being obtuse. "You know what I mean. You've been raised to expect certain things, to live a certain way. For example, what do your mother and Priscilla do all day?"

"Well, Pris has her little girl, of course. Then there're the various clubs she belongs to, plus committee work for some charities. Pretty much like my mother."

"There," Annie said, stabbing a finger in the air almost under Ted's nose. "That's what I mean. When would I have time for things like that? I have a restaurant to run."

A sudden thought occurred to her that brought her upright in her chair. "Or would you expect me to give that up?"

He squeezed her hand. "Certainly not. Though I expect eventually the restaurant would not be so time-consuming for you."

A lot he knew, Annie pondered morosely before another thought that had been niggling at the back of her mind surfaced. "Ted," she said, leaning forward, "you said before that I'd be marrying you, not your family. But that's not quite true in my case. You've seen my family. They're as much a part of my life as breathing. They'd be a part of *our* life together."

"I wouldn't have it any other way. I *like* your family. And the proximity of the restaurant would insure that they'd remain a part of our lives."

"But you don't understand. You make it sound . . . compartmentalized. It wouldn't be that way. Family life, *my* family life, seems to spill over into everything else." Annie looked at him doubtfully. "Somehow I can't see that as your particular style."

"My style, your style. Look," Ted said, giving Annie's hands in his a little shake, "together we'd make our own style. We'd build a life together that suited *us*. All those differences you mentioned don't have to be a problem. The variety will just add spice to our lives, keep things interesting."

When she still looked doubtful, he sighed. Instead of playing devil's advocate, she was beginning to sound like a prosecuting attorney: one objection after another. That gave him an idea. He'd convince her the same way he won in court, by building a logical case.

Leaning over, he kissed her on the tip of her nose. "All right, Miss Rafferty. I guess I'll have to do what I do best. Prove my point."

An hour later Annie let herself into the hallway of her

home, her thoughts still in a muddle. Hanging up her coat, she wandered into the living room lit only by the glow of a streetlight outside. She could hear the others in the kitchen, but she wasn't ready to join them yet.

As Annie sat on the window seat in the bay window she saw Lincoln Park looming from the mist at the end of the street a half block away. She never grew tired of watching the changing panorama there of nature—human or otherwise. They had been lucky to find this place with a view of the park. Securing a home for them all had been a major accomplishment, and Annie loved the old near north brownstone they had lovingly renovated.

The long, narrow building's three floors had been parceled out to best advantage by making the ground floor a combined living space, with the middle floor for the women and the top floor for Kit. Over the years though, Annie and her sisters all eventually used the study at the front of the building on the third floor.

With a brick patio at the rear and the surrounding fence with its built-in stained glass portals, the brownstone was a tiny jewel. Annie ran her fingers along the glossy window frame she had helped strip and varnish herself. The windows ran from the seat almost to the ceiling, with a separate inset of stained glass at the top. The pattern was repeated on each of the three floors. She smiled, remembering how stubborn she'd been about keeping the stained glass and her search to find someone to repair several of the broken windows.

She sighed. It had been worth it. She had the perfect setting and a perfect life. Looking out at the fog creeping up the street and obscuring the lamplights, she wondered if she was ready to give up any part of it for an unknown life with Ted.

"There you are," Aunt Nola said, jarring her out of her reverie. Her aunt came to stand beside her saying, "I thought I heard you come in." She glanced out the window beside which Annie was seated. "Looks like it's warming up. Be pea soup by morning. What are you doing here in the dark?"

"Just thinking."

" 'Bout what?"

"How much I love this house . . . and my life here."

Annie felt Aunt Nola shift to peer at her. "What brought all this on?" When Annie didn't answer, her aunt lowered herself to the window seat beside her. After a moment, she said, "That boy must be a fast worker to have you tied up in knots so soon. What'd he say?"

"Just that . . . he wants to marry me."

Aunt Nola hooted with laughter. "He really is a fast one. But I don't blame him. It's the only way, as I see it."

"What do you mean?"

"Well, Annie, my girl, if he's fast enough you may not have time to squirm out of it."

"Squirm . . ." Completely mystified, Annie looked at her aunt blankly. "I don't have the faintest idea what you're talking about."

"Yes, you do. You just don't want to admit it. Sure as the sun's going to rise tomorrow morning you know that if given enough time and enough rope, this young man will hang himself in your eyes. You'll latch on to some excuse as a reason for not hooking up with him. Oh, I'm not saying that you haven't had some perfectly good reasons in the past for not marrying any of the clods sniffing around. But there were one or two who would have done if they'd stayed the distance."

"But that's unfair. It wasn't me. They were the ones who seemed to lose interest," Annie fired back, remembering the various men who had reconsidered after a good look at the barrage of cousins, aunts, and uncles looking over their shoulders.

"Honey, I got news for you. There can't be a fire without a spark. All I'm saying is that in the past you've made darned sure there was no kindling lying around. Think about it, Annie, me girl. You don't want to lose this one."

The next day, Ted found Annie elusive with protestations of being busy. And she refused to commit to meeting his family during the weekend on the grounds that she simply couldn't add to Aunt Nola's workload by leaving for several hours. Annie even bristled at Kevin when he asked for help again with another calculus assignment. She told everyone within hearing to try solving their own problems for a change without bothering Ted. He tracked the boy down, sitting morosely in a corner of the restaurant, and helped him anyway.

Thursday evening he even volunteered to *baby-sit*— him, who knew next to nothing about kids—for Shelia's children, obstensibly so she could work her last shift as the early evening dishwasher. In reality, he wanted to show Annie that he could pitch in and help, too.

Annie simply stared at him, while Aunt Nola exclaimed, "I think that's a great idea." She shooed Annie back to her catering order, and Consuela and Shelia toward the sink where the latest addition to the staff, a young man— Vietnamese or Thai—awaited instructions in the mysteries of the dishwashing system.

Having entered from the front of the restaurant for once after seeing the last client of the day off the premises, Ted looked around the huge kitchen for Casey and Bryce. Aunt Nola chuckled as she took him by the arm. "Have I got a surprise for you. Come on, they're in the back hallway."

Ted looked through the open door to the two dark heads of Casey and Bryce bent over the box of kittens. Next to them was a tiny little girl with reddish gold curls.

Startled, he turned and looked at Aunt Nola for an explanation. "Shelia's youngest, Cassandra. She's almost eighteen months old. Now don't look so worried. She's a sweetie, won't give you a bit of trouble. Not like these two limbs of Satan you've already met. Boys," she called out, "mind your p's and q's. If not, you'll answer to me." With a warning frown, she marched away, leaving Ted in the hallway with the children.

The boys nodded a hello and after peeping up at him through her lashes and tumbling curls, the little girl reached out slowly to the box.

"No, Cassie. I told you," Bryce admonished. "You can't pick them up."

A couple of caught breaths preceded an escaping sob as the little girl collapsed in a heap of tears.

"What seems to be the problem?" Ted asked, hunkering down by the children.

Bryce as the oldest apparently elected himself spokesman. "Cassie starts to pet the kittens, then she tries to pick them up. Annie said they're too little. You're just supposed to pet them, but Cassie won't listen."

"Well, Cassie," Ted said as the little girl turned her face up to his. Huge blue-green eyes wet with tears looked at him, and he promptly lost his heart. She was the most beautiful child he'd ever seen: tiny and delicate with rioting curls tumbling around her flushed face. He looked from the entreaty in her eyes to the box. After a second, he glanced back to Cassie and measured her position. "Would you like to see the kittens closer?" She gravely nodded, and Ted said, "I thought so.

"I tell you what, boys. Cassie is so little she can barely see into the box. I'm going to lift the kittens out onto the towel, and you can all pet them easier. How will that be?"

The brothers enthusiastically agreed, but Ted denied any need of help as he arranged the kittens on the soft towel in the center of three eager pairs of hands. Once Charlie reassured herself that all was well with her family, she jumped back into her box.

The minutes flew by as the children oohed and ahhed over the newborns. Eventually he looked up and found Annie studying him with a bemused expression. On this mild spring day, she had on a cherry red, long-sleeved T-shirt and a sleeveless, denim jumpsuit that looked outstanding with her coloring. The contrast between her vividness and the washed-out beige of Veronica's expensive silks came to mind. Congratulating himself once again, he grinned at her.

She said, "I see Cassie has won another beau. I think it's in the genes. Her mother is a beauty, too."

Ted silently agreed, but to him Cassie resembled Annie. Looking at the child, he thought he knew what Annie must have looked like as a little girl. He said, "I think good looks run in the family," and was rewarded with a blush.

"Would you mind," Ted surprised himself by asking, "if they came upstairs with me? I've got some things that might keep them occupied for a while."

"No, I don't mind. Just surprised. Somehow, you didn't seem the type to be at ease with young children."

He was surprising himself, too, but he wasn't going to let Annie know that. "How about it, Cassie? Would you like to see my office with your brothers?"

The little girl looked to Annie for approval. Receiving a smiling nod, she pushed herself up and took Ted by the hand.

More than an hour later, Ted looked up from the scattered papers on his desk and smiled. Cassie was asleep on the sofa, his jacket thrown across her for warmth. He had enjoyed watching the little girl's expression as he showed her his collection of crystal paperwieghts, most of them imbedded with swirls of striking colors. He had gone so far as to tape two half spheres together to make a ball for Cassie which they rolled back and forth across the pale gray carpeting.

He gave the boys each a pad of paper and colored markers and turned them loose while he played with Cassie. When she began rubbing her eyes, he tucked her up on the sofa with her favorite, and one of the most expensive, paperweights. Next he showed Casey and Bryce how to outline the crystal bottoms to make perfect wheels for cars, then geometric designs.

Where had this predilection for children come from? First the YMCA teams three years ago and now Annie's little cousins. Obviously, at thirty-three his nesting instincts were getting stronger. Lost in thought, he didn't hear the clatter on the stairs until just before his door opened. Annie burst into his office. "Ted, come quick! You have to do something! They're going to arrest Consuela. They say she's an illegal alien."

SEVEN

Annie went into Ted's arms as naturally as coming home, muffling her tears against his chest. She took the handkerchief he pressed into her hand and a deep breath to calm herself.

"Have they taken her away?"

"No, I told them my attorney was upstairs, that they had to wait." Annie blew her nose and said, "I'm sorry. After telling the family to keep their problems to themselves, I dump on you. But I didn't know what else to do." Fresh tears spurted at the memory of Consuela's terror when she realized the two men were from Immigration.

"You did the right thing."

Ted continued to hold her with one hand while the other absently swept caressingly over her hair, the same way, she realized, that she soothed Cassie when she was upset about something. Only who would soothe away Consuela's anguish? Getting a grip on herself after a moment, Annie moved back. "What are we going to do?"

"The first thing I have to do is make a telephone call. Then I'll go downstairs and see what this is all about." He squeezed her shoulders and stepped behind his desk.

116

Annie blew her nose again and wandered into the hall at the top of the stairs, listening to the sounds below. She didn't want the agents or whatever they were to get tired of waiting and take Consuela away. Concentrating on listening for raised voices in the kitchen, she was only faintly conscious of Ted's phone conversation.

"—without me. I'll try to join you later. Yes, I said it was an emergency. I'll explain when I see you, Mother. Good-bye."

Annie only had a moment to feel a twinge of regret for messing up Ted's plans for the evening before he gave her a peck on the cheek and went below. She sat down on the floor by the boys and tried to show interest in the drawings they shoved at her.

The minutes ticked by with agonizing slowness for Annie, but at last she heard a step on the stairs. However, the figure that appeared at the door was only Shelia come to collect the children.

"What's happening?" Annie asked, taking Cassie's jacket and blanket from her to bundle up the still-sleeping child.

"I don't know." Shelia handed the boys their jackets and began to pick up papers from the floor. "Ted took Consuela and the two Immigration people to the back table and has been there with them ever since. The tension level seemed to have dropped though, the last time I looked."

Finally, Annie helped Shelia load her family into their car and sped back to the restaurant. She rounded the corner by the soda fountains in time to see Ted shaking hands with the two men. She hung back as they left, then went to put an arm around Consuela.

Ted couldn't decide who looked more frightened, Annie's employee or Annie herself. Still holding Consuela protectively, she said, "Well?"

He motioned them to sit down. "They weren't here to arrest Consuela. This is a civil proceeding, not criminal.

What they had was an order to show cause, the beginning of a deportation proceeding."

"Deportation!" The word, barely breathed, sounded incredulous in Annie's husky voice. She reached over and took Consuela's hand. "We must be able to do something to help her."

"It's not as bad as it sounds. We have some options." Ted glanced admiringly at Consuela.

That was one of the things he liked about his work. People were full of surprises. Even though he had become better acquainted with Consuela over the past week, what he'd learned tonight had made him realize once again not to take things at face value.

Taking out his notebook, Ted asked Consuela for her full married name.

"But, Mr. Carlyle," she replied in a lilting accent, "I don't have the money to pay a lawyer."

Before Ted could tell her not to worry about it, Annie jumped in with, "I'll take care of whatever expense is involved, Consuela." At the woman's protest, Annie insisted they would work it out. "You concentrate on your studies and taking care of Maria."

Heartened by her attitude, Ted looked at Annie. If she knew about the child, she probably also knew about the medical complications. "Your daughter, Maria, is our ace in the hole."

When both women looked at him in confusion, Ted explained to Annie. "Consuela was a student here on a visa. She met her husband at school and after they married filed for conditional residency."

"I know all that," Annie interrupted. "She married an American. Surely that means she's safe."

"No. What's crucial is what stage of the immigration process they were in vis-à-vis her application for conditional residency before her husband's death. Since he died, the Immigration Service probably wouldn't grant her conditional residency because the reason for the grant is gone.''

Annie looked at him, her brow contracted in a frown. ''Then where does that leave us?''

''With Maria. Because of her medical condition, humanitarian reasons may prevail in preventing Consuela from being deported. Besides the fact Maria's mother is her only relative here, her rare blood disorder is only treatable at a few centers in this country. It's probable there are no such facilities in Mexico. Since Maria's a U.S. citizen, I don't believe Immigration would push it.''

''Thank goodness,'' Annie breathed.

Ted hated to burst her bubble, but . . . ''There's also the little problem of you perhaps being in trouble with the Immigration Service because of not doing what was required under the law.''

''But I checked her papers,'' Annie protested. ''Here, you can see for yourself. She has permission to work. What else was I supposed to do? And what do you mean, I might be in trouble. What trouble?''

''Possibly fines, penalties.''

''How extensive?''

Ted shrugged. ''Several thousand.'' At Annie's shocked expression, he leaned over and put an arm around her shoulders. ''Don't worry. I doubt it will come to that. As you say, her papers seem in order. The only fly in the ointment is the untimely death of Consuela's husband. That changed everything. Unfortunately, Consuela didn't understand she needed to file new papers.''

Ted picked up his pen again and, poised over his notebook, said, ''Let's get all the information down, then I can get busy on your behalf tomorrow morning.''

Annie automatically stuffed pita bread with chopped chicken as she kept one eye on the back door. Surely Ted would be returning any minute. At the thought of him,

Annie's hands grew still. He had been so wonderful, turning his work over to Jim so he could take care of Consuela's problems this morning. And Ted had been reassuring about her own position. A smile tugged at Annie's lips as she remembered his parting words, "As if I'd let anything happen to you," as well as his embrace and farewell kiss last night. That could become addictive.

Sighing, Annie forced herself to continue working. Things of late seemed to be turning out differently than she intended. Despite Aunt Nola's comments and her own feelings to the contrary, she had decided after a mostly sleepless night Wednesday that there was no future in a relationship with Ted. Disappointed that they didn't have more in common and determined not to make the same mistake her sister Celia had in the past, Annie believed focusing on her business and not a questionable relationship was a wise choice. Not for her the long road back from a broken heart if anything went wrong.

She had put Ted off yesterday with protestations of being too busy and not wanting to impose on Aunt Nola. What she didn't tell him was that her aunt was more than willing to fill in for her. Annie felt pressure now on two fronts to move the relationship along to a new plane. Resisting, she had informed everyone within hearing that they should leave her *landlord*, as she referred to Ted, alone and take care of their own business as they had in the past. Annie snorted. And what had she done at the first sign of trouble? Run straight into Ted's arms. And wonderfully comforting it had been, too.

Of course, having taken a proprietary interest in her employees, she would have danced with the devil if it would have helped Consuela. But the fact remained that she hadn't hesitated a second. And Ted had come through. Her instincts had been correct, if not her mind. Sighing, Annie wondered what she was going to do about the situation. Then a grin surfaced. Hah! Who was she trying to kid? No matter how much she denied her attraction—no, her feelings for Ted—they were still there. Maybe Celia knew what she was talking about after all. You just didn't have any choice when it came to the moment Cupid loosed his arrow. Mere mortals were left with the messy details of trying to deal with it.

An image of Ted in the back hallway with the children yesterday surfaced in Annie's memory. And his efforts at helping Kevin with his homework, plus Uncle Tully over that worrisome lease, and goodness knew what else. Honesty made Annie admit that despite the layers of structure Ted had imposed on his life with his schedules and that notebook of his, he really was a caring, loving person underneath.

A movement at her elbow drew her attention to Consuela, also anxiously watching the back door. Poor Consuela. As if she didn't have enough to worry about with her daughter seriously ill, now she had to contend with the Immigration people. Keeping her busy helped . . . and not only Consuela. As soon as Annie realized the young woman was creative in the kitchen, she had promoted Consuela to the cooking staff. She had proved invaluable in providing some new and interesting recipes the customers seemed to relish.

In the pre-noon hush, Annie and Consuela heard a car in the back alley and waited for the sound of a car door closing. By the time Ted entered the hallway, they were both waiting for him. Somehow it seemed the most natural thing in the world to go to him when he reached for her. Looking up from the shelter of Ted's arm into his smiling face, Annie wondered at the crazy calypso beat of her heart. When had he started to have this effect on her? She could understand it after a kiss, but just a look?

Her knees turning to mush, Annie threw caution to the wind. The timing might not be to her liking, but she'd always been one to seize the moment. "Hello, counselor. Were you very diplomatic today?"

Ted had been nodding reassurance to Consuela, but at the husky intimacy of Annie's question, he looked down into her eyes. And was lost in what he found there. Her gaze was always bright, but now it seemed suffused with a radiance that was positively hypnotizing. Annie melted against his side as his hand found her hip.

His grip on his briefcase slipped and Ted was about to abandon it, the better to properly kiss Annie's tantalizingly close lips, when a sound made him glance up.

Aunt Nola grinned at him from the back door of the restaurant. "Oh, good. You remembered the rest of us."

Undaunted, Ted chuckled and leaned over to plant a quick kiss on the exposed side of Annie's neck as she turned toward her aunt. "As if I could forget you," he said, looking up.

But even his insouciance was tested when he faced the barrage of expressions watching with interest over Aunt Nola's shoulder. Was there anyone left to take care of the customers?

Allaying their concern, if not their interest in the immediate situation, Ted said, "All is well. Or at least I believe it will be." Turning to Consuela, he added, "I've filed the necessary motions. Now we just have to await our court date. The one encouraging note is that the judge we drew is a woman . . . with a family."

Consuela smiled back at him through a mist of tears and, retaining his hold on Annie, Ted reached over and squeezed her shoulder in encouragement. There was a collective sigh from the others gathered at the door.

"Well," Aunt Nola groused, "what are you all waiting for? You heard the man: everything's going to be okay. Now, back to work with you."

Kendra, Dora, Maureen, and a few others that Ted had only glimpsed drifted off. Aunt Nola stepped into the hallway and reached up to pat his cheek, then his shoulder wordlessly. Turning away, she put an arm around Consuela. "Come on, honey. Let's go check on Sompong to make sure he knows what he's doing with those dishes." Leading the unresisting Consuela through the back door, Aunt Nola closed it behind her muttering something about the United Nations.

"She never changes," Ted said, smiling down at Annie once more.

Snuggled at his side, Annie shook her head. "You wouldn't think so, but it's just for appearances. Actually, she's had to adapt to many changes over the years."

Putting down his briefcase, Ted gathered Annie into his embrace. "A fascinating tale, I'm sure, and one that I want to hear sometime. Right now," he murmured against the silken texture of Annie's throat, "there's something else that needs tending to."

"And what would that be, counselor?"

"If you keep calling me that in *that* particular tone of voice," Ted murmured, nuzzling the side of Annie's neck, "the only conversation we're going to have is the one referred to in legal depositions."

"Should I be worried about my virtue?"

"Not as far as I'm concerned. My intentions are honorable, remember?"

Annie only burrowed closer to him. And while it provided easy access to the back of her neck, it played hell with his pulse rate. What he wanted to do was forget about the double load of work Jim was carrying upstairs, forget about Immigration officials and worrisome tenants, and take Annie back to his apartment on the Gold Coast. Only he knew Annie wasn't ready for that. In fact, her reception after yesterday surprised him.

Ted held Annie away just far enough to see her expression. "Am I mistaken or is there a definite warming in the climate around here?"

"Transparent as that, huh?" Her voice was teasing, but he noticed a slight tensing of the figure in his arms.

"Let's just say I'm attuned to every nuance of your behavior and, although I'm delighted with your response, somehow I think right now you're . . . uncomfortable for some reason. Want to tell me about it?"

Sighing, Annie wrapped her arms about Ted's neck. "I'm not uncomfortable with you," she promised. Far from it, in fact. Nestled against his chest with his lips playing at her temples, there was no other place she wanted to be. "It's just that everything seems to be happening so quickly."

Annie could feel Ted's face next to hers change and his smile was reflected in his voice as he said, "Now, that does surprise me. Everything you do is lightning quick. Why should meeting someone and falling in love with him be any different?"

At that, Annie pulled back and grinned up at him. "You *do* know me pretty well, don't you?"

"Yes, I think so. That's why I'm wondering what else is bothering you."

"Ah, counselor, you give no quarter, do you?"

Annie peered at Ted through the blinding shafts of sunlight coming through the hall window. His smile had slipped into a look of concentration, as though he were listening with his whole body, feeling vibrations to define her response. With his back to the window, the sun's rays danced over his blond head, creating a golden aura. Wise as well as beautiful, Annie decided, wondering at her good fortune. As suddenly as it had come, her tension drained away leaving her with a feeling of lightness. She wasn't her sister, and Celia's problems didn't have to become hers. The past was history, and she and Ted had a future to write together. She stood on tiptoe to reach his finely etched lips, lips she now felt free to explore and enjoy to her heart's content.

Heedless of time and place, Annie gave herself up to the delicious heat stealing through her. With the sunlight playing on her closed eyelids and the herbal scent of Ted's after-shave filling her senses, Annie thought of wine . . . warm red wine racing through her veins, faster and faster in time to the beat of her heart. Her fingers met at the back of Ted's neck and tangled in the softness of his hair against the rigid rim of his collar.

An image entered her mind and refused to be dislodged. As it intensified, Annie's hands slipped to Ted's shoulders and felt the ripple of powerful muscles there as he changed position slightly, bringing her even closer to his body. The image persisted and behind sun-warmed lids, Annie wondered what it would be like to taste wine on skin warmed by the sun. In her imagination, they stood in a golden field surrounded by blazing white light, she tasted the tart dryness of a ruby red wine as her lips played over the taut muscles of Ted's chest, and she wondered at the heat. The warmth of the sun beat at her, making her more thirsty for the wine she tasted on the back of her tongue, and her lips raced back to his for more of the precious liquid. The heat continued to build, and Annie thought she would burn up as the fire raced through her.

Ted broke away from the kiss, drawing in a harsh breath of air. Annie blinked, awareness of her surroundings returning once more. She could have sworn her temperature dropped ten degrees in those split seconds before Ted's hands came up to frame her face.

"Lady, I think I'm going to like it when you make up your mind. You do it so well."

Annie chuckled, but she could feel the warmth of embarrassment creeping up her neck to her face. She'd never known she had such a vivid imagination.

"Which is not to say you didn't successfully distract me for a few minutes there," Ted murmured, almost against her lips. "However, the fact remains you still have

some explaining to do, and right now"—he grinned down
at her—"it's a hell of a lot safer to concentrate on that
than resume where we left off."

"You can say that again." Annie turned and, taking
Ted by the hand, led him to the back stairs. As he sank
down beside her, putting an arm around her shoulders,
Annie said, "If I can gather my few scattered wits, I'll
try to explain."

Wrapped in Ted's warmth, it was hard to think. Visions
of the sun-drenched field started to creep back, and Annie
struggled to focus on her sister's first serious love affair
so he would understand her own apprehensions.

"It's because of what happened before," she blurted.

Annie felt the jerk in Ted's body. She looked up at his
startled expression before it changed to confusion. "Wait
a moment. I thought you said—"

"No, not me. I mean Cecilia." Taking a deep breath,
Annie tried to think logically. "In her last year at college,
in fact during her first months there, Celia fell in love with
a young art instructor." Frowning, she said thoughtfully,
"Afterwards, I blamed Aunt Nola and myself for keeping
her so sheltered that she'd never had a chance to build
defenses. You know, experience puppy love and gain and
lose a few serious boyfriends before being exposed to the
heady wine"—there was that word again—"of more, um,
more mature relationships."

Annie decided the only safe way to get through her
tale was not to look at Ted and the blazing blue of his
understanding gaze. Her own had a tendency to drift south
to that tempting mouth of his and the sorcery he could
perform. Clearing her throat, she stared with determination
at the pattern of sunlight on the slate floor of the entryway.

"Anyway, she fell hard. And I have to admit he was
a charmer, as well as devastatingly handsome. By the time
Christmas holidays rolled around, there was talk of an
engagement. At least, Celia fully expected to receive a

ring for Christmas. And"—Annie's throat tightened with remembered pain—"she might have, too, if things had been as Ramon visualized them."

"Ramon?"

Glancing back at Ted, Annie smiled at his quizzical expression. "Yes, Ramon, as in Ramon Luis Carlos Neval." Concentrating with a frown on the floor once more, she continued. "Ramon was supposedly of an aristocratic Spanish family making his own way in the world, you know, second or third son and all that. He was an artist and an expert on some technique or other who had been convinced by the Art Institute to lecture during the fall season at the University of Chicago to students in the design program.

"What he discovered when Celia brought him home, however, didn't mesh with the elaborate scenario he had apparently built in his mind of a wealthy, business-owning family." Annie sighed. "The business, my catering business, was real enough but it seems Señor Neval had visions of something on the scale that catered not to the masses, but to the select—more specifically, exalted public figures, royalty, etc."

"How on earth—"

Annie smiled wryly through remembered pain. "Once, Celia had shown him a clipping with a photograph featuring me smack dab in the middle of the mayor of the city and the Princess of Wales, surrounded by ambassadors and Chicago blue bloods. She had only wanted to show him what I looked like, but he latched on to the notion that we were some elite service.

"I'll never forget the look of shock on his face when Celia brought Ramon into the cellar kitchens of the Clark Street brownstone where we prepared our catered meals."

Ted looked at Annie, her sadness reflected in her face as well as her husky voice, and tenderness engulfed him. He shifted closer to her, pressing her head to his shoulder

and stroking her hair softly. But he waited patiently for
Annie to tell her tale without further interruption.

After running his hands through her mass of rioting
curls for a few moments, Annie said as if far away, "Celia
looked so beautiful that night. She was wearing a full-
length, black velvet evening gown and a fur coat one of
our aunt's had pressed on her for the occasion. She was
also wearing diamond earrings from another aunt, and a
diamond pendant from Aunt Nola. So I suppose"—Annie
sighed heavily—"I shouldn't have been surprised that
Ramon had the wrong idea about us."

She shook her head under his hand, creating small
waves of scent Ted had come to associate with Annie.
"There was Ramon dressed in a tuxedo and top coat,
looking every inch the Spanish grandee, as he looked
down his nose at me working in the kitchen with everyone
else.

" 'But what is this,' he said." Annie's mimicry
sounded amazingly real. " 'You are shorthanded this evening because of the holidays? That is too bad. You will
not be able to enjoy a party yourself?'

"When I explained that, no, I always worked like this,
the poor man looked thoroughly confused. I didn't have
too much time to waste just then because I was trying to
get three parties out the door, so I turned to the waitresses
I had lined up and gave them their orders. Also, one of
the bartenders I was supplying for the evening hadn't
shown up, and I was on the phone bullying one of my
male cousins into doing it for me.

"When I finally turned back to Celia and Ramon, I
heard him saying something to her about where were the
butlers, where was all the silver featured in the photograph
she had shown him."

Annie shifted next to Ted, snuggling closer to him.
"When I finally got everyone out the door, Celia and I
disillusioned Ramon about any ideas of grandeur. Every-

thing for that special party in the photograph had been supplied by other services. I was only there dressed as I was because I was supplying the hors d'oeuvres and was overseeing their preparation and distribution. I could see his olive complexion turning ruddier by the minute so I took them both into my office away from the kitchen staff who remained to clean up. Unfortunately, they could hear everything anyway when Ramon lost his temper as he realized his mistake.''

Ted could hear the catch in Annie's breath, and he reached inside his jacket pocket and handed her the silk handkerchief tucked there.

Dabbing at her face, Annie sniffed, but was unable to control the tears streaming down her face. "Poor Celia. Not only was her big evening ruined, but everything else, too. It turned out that Ramon was a down-at-the-heels artist looking for a wealthy American wife to provide the cachet he thought he deserved. When Celia couldn't provide it, he dumped her and went looking for another, more plump-in-the-pocket pigeon.''

"The heel," Ted muttered.

"Yes, but—the worst part was what it did to Celia.'' Annie sniffed and dried her tears once more. "She's become so . . . cynical about life in general. And about men in particular.''

"And you're afraid something of the same sort will happen to us, aren't you? I mean, that I'll turn out to be different or that things won't work for some reason.''

Annie pushed away from his side. "I was, but not anymore.'' Raising her head, she looked at him. All Ted could see were tear-drenched eyes luminous with warmth. "I realized that even if things didn't go as planned, I still had to try.''

"Thank God for that.'' Ted gathered her to him once more, unable to resist the allure of her soft lips.

After a few minutes, he asked, "When did you begin to think I might be husband material?"

Annie chuckled against his throat where she was busy planting fleeting kisses. "After seeing you with the children yesterday afternoon. I know you coach young boys at the Y, but you never struck me as someone who would know what to do with really young ones."

"I'll let you in on a little secret," Ted admitted.

Annie laughed out loud. "What?"

"I'm sorry. It's that for a moment, you sounded just like Casey with your *secret*."

Ted grinned back at her. "Yeah, well, maybe it's catching. About the kids, though. Somehow it seemed natural. I didn't have to think about what to do." He hugged Annie to him again. "A lot of strange things have started happening to me since I met you and your wonderful family."

"Me, too," Annie said cryptically.

He looked down at her in question, but the sound of the back door to the restaurant opening drew their attention. They both leaned over, looking in that direction.

Aunt Nola stood framed in the doorway. "Oh, there you are. Phone, Annie. It's a television producer who wants to talk to you about doing some sort of cooking show."

"Thanks. Tell him I'll be there in just a moment, please."

Aunt Nola withdrew, and Annie looked at Ted with a question in her eyes. Interestingly, a flush began to creep up her neck.

At last she said, "I know you like wine because we had white wine at dinner together, but . . . by any chance do you also like red wine?"

EIGHT

"Quit fidgeting. You look great."

Annie flashed Ted a grateful look, then returned her attention to the ribbon of highway as it wound through the North Shore's wooded hills and manicured lawns. Propping her elbow on the armrest, she rested her chin on one fist and peered out the window. Signs of spring were everywhere, from daffodils and tulips waving in the gentle breeze to the chartreuse of willow trees bursting into leaf. But after a few minutes, even studying the stately old homes in their new finery began to pall, and she sighed.

Ted reached over and covered her balled fist lying in her lap. Her fingers relaxed under his reassuring warmth. "What is it that's worrying you so much? Surely you can't be that concerned about meeting my mother?"

After a moment, Annie turned to him and tried to match his smile. "No," she admitted. "It's not that so much as feeling like I'm intruding." When Ted had called his mother and asked to bring Annie to meet her, she'd told him about having a brunch on Sunday and suggested he bring her then. "Tell me again who's likely to be there."

"You're no more intruding than I am," he said, squeezing her hand under his. "Other than Geoff and Priscilla, I imagine one or two of my father's partners will be there and a few of my mother's closest friends."

Ted had already given her the names of those Mrs. Carlyle considered her bosom buddies and Annie shuddered, remembering that the list read like a who's who of Chicago blue bloods. Her despair deepened, and she looked doubtfully at the flower arrangement by her feet. The pink and white rosebuds had seemed like such a good idea yesterday. Now the gift struck Annie as ludicrous.

She envisioned handing the petite arrangement to Ted's mother and saying, "Hi, Mrs. Carlyle. Here's a posie for you in exchange for your son." Because she was sure Mrs. Carlyle was no dummy and had already assumed from Ted's request that Annie must be of some importance to him. And that wouldn't sit well if indeed she had hand-picked Veronica for his bride. Mrs. Carlyle was going to be prejudiced against her, which didn't allow for a comfortable time as far as Annie was concerned. She sighed again.

Ted turned her hand over and laced their fingers together. "I'm going to be by your side every minute. I wish you wouldn't worry about it so much."

Annie, contrite at the frown marring his handsome profile, tried to think of something reassuring to say. Failing that, she fell back on a tidbit of news that might divert both of them.

"I almost forgot to tell you. You're looking at the newest potential star in WGN's television schedule."

Ted's glance whipped to her. He must have been reassured by what he saw there, for a grin spread across his face and his grip tightened before he released her hand to attend to his driving. "You mean I'm going to have to share you with an adoring public?"

"If I'm lucky." Annie smiled at his nonsense. "That phone call Friday morning from the producer led to a brief meeting yesterday. They seem to think I could be the next Galloping Gourmet.''

"What do they want you to do? I mean, how would it work?''

"Demonstrate some of the recipes I've developed over the years. According to their demographics, there's been a rise in the popularity of ethnic restaurants and because I seem to cross a number of culinary boundaries, I was their logical choice.''

"And the fact that you're lovely and articulate would be definite pluses.''

Annie shook her head. "There was also a mention of a cookbook tie-in. Originally, they suggested it as a possibility if the show took off, but Aunt Nola seems to think I should do it on my own now to capitalize on the free publicity.''

"And she's right. Remember, though, don't sign any contracts until after I've looked at them.'' Ted again reclaimed possession of one of her hands now lying calmly in her lap. "Good thing you've got a lawyer in the family.''

Chuckling, Annie said, "What would we do without you?''

"Thankfully, you won't have to find out.''

"Aunt Nola badgered me last night until I brought out all my old recipe cards. The whole family sat around the table mulling over favorites and trying to decide upon an approach.''

"You know, I just figured out that the public's gain is going to be my loss.'' Annie looked at Ted in confusion, then caught the teasing gleam in his eyes. "I'm already sharing you with dozens of people. Just how much is a man supposed to do for his country?'' He shook his head, then turned rueful. "Are you sure you're not biting off too much? The restaurant and catering seem to keep you on the hop constantly.''

"Fortunately, I already had ads in the papers for an assistant manager. I've one interview tomorrow and, of course, today's ad may produce more results." She knew Ted had been teasing, but she caught at the edge of his concern and turned toward him in her seat. "Things are beginning to calm down at the restaurant, you know. It's really been just a matter of getting things organized. Once that's completed, I'd be sitting around wondering what to do with myself."

Ted laughed out loud and squeezed her hand. "I doubt if you're ever still long enough to be bored. Besides, *I* have some ideas that might keep you busy." Annie smiled back at him and he said, "Just so long as you leave room in your schedule for a honeymoon. Speaking of which, do you have a preference? You know, hot-cold, sand or snow?"

Annie shook her head and, for a moment, the rapidity of events threatened to overwhelm her. Everything was happening so quickly lately. She swallowed and fought down the hollow feeling in her stomach rising to choke her. It was just nerves at meeting Ted's mother. Gamely she said, "Surprise me."

Snapping on the turn signal, Ted said, "Okay. How about if we start with the fact that we've arrived."

Startled, Annie shifted in her seat to stare straight ahead as he completed the turn. They had left the asphalt highway behind and were on a tree-lined, brick driveway. Bricks, for goodness sake, that stretched practically to the next county. Since the trees were still bare, she could see an imposing edifice in the distance. Eventually the car swept into a circular drive and past the house to park, and "edifice" was still the only word Annie could think of to describe the imposing pile of rosy brick.

She leaned over to pick up her floral offering, being careful not to tip it or crush the paper wrapping, while Ted came around to help her out of the car. All she needed to do to get off to a really good start, she thought ruefully, would be to hand a dripping arrangement to his mother. With Ted's hand at her elbow, Annie faced the house and squared her shoulders.

The chateau-styled mansion would look equally well in the French countryside, she decided, flicking a glance along its facade. The flanking wings were two stories high, but the center portion obviously had another floor above the rows of windows divided into two pairs of four on either side of the entrance. Annie craned her neck, but she could only see dormer windows in two sets along the roofline. Maybe that floor only contained attics.

Ted noticed her actions and followed her glance. "I guess it looks rather intimidating, but in summer the effect is softened by overhanging trees. I forget how old it is, but it was really rather a warren until my mother had it renovated. All I remember is that Geoff and I preferred all the tiny rooms. They provided a lot more scope for the imagination than all this."

He waved a deprecating hand toward the house, and Annie wondered again at her decision to link her life with this man. How could he dismiss *all this* with a wave of his hand?

As they stopped before the doors, Ted brought Annie to a standstill by grasping her upper arms. Out of the sun, the air was cool and she was grateful for his warmth. She might look fashionable in her "best bib and tucker" as Aunt Nola called her outfit, but the rose-colored spring coat and matching wool jersey turtleneck dress did little to warm her today of all days. Ted leaned down and planted a quick kiss.

From a distance, Annie heard a deep, melodious chime, but only seconds passed before one of the massive doors before them opened. The young man before them was of foreign parentage, although Annie couldn't decide which nationality as he bowed them into the hall. She missed his name as Ted murmured a greeting and introduced her. In the flurry of removing their coats, she absorbed only an impression of marble floors, Oriental carpet, wainscoting and wallpaper and, out of the corner of her eye, a beautiful carved stairway with more Oriental carpet that took flight to some upper reaches in the two-story entrance.

In heavily accented English, the man said, "Mrs. Carlyle is in the morning room, sir."

With Ted's hand at her waist guiding her, Annie trod on the jewel-toned Oriental runner past silk-covered walls artfully touched here and there with oil paintings. They passed several closed doors and came at last to the end of the hall surrounded by more closed doors. Moving his hand to her shoulder, Ted opened the door on the left and stood aside so Annie could enter.

All she was aware of at first was the blinding light from the floor-to-ceiling windows and the warmth of the closed room with the sun pouring in through uncurtained glass. Then Annie heard the crackling sound of paper and noticed the woman who looked up at them from the folds of the Sunday news. Even seated at a banquette and table in an alcove, Ted's mother looked of impressive height. Annie couldn't see her features since her back was to the light, but it seemed a long time before the woman spoke.

"Ah, Ted. I see you're early." Annie wondered briefly if there was an accusatory tone to her gruffness or if that was her normal voice. Rising at last, Mrs. Carlyle came around the end of the table. "And you must be his little friend Annabelle."

"Annie, Mother. Her name is Annie Rafferty."

"Actually," Annie broke in, "my name is Anne Marie. But my friends call me Annie. Hello, Mrs. Carlyle. I'm pleased to meet you."

"Yes. . . ." Mrs. Carlyle's voice trailed off as she took Annie's outstretched hand briefly. Her eyes lacked the depth of color and warmth of her son's, but went with her barely blonde hair. She turned her perfectly coiffed head almost at once toward Ted. "Well, darling, did you misunderstand the time? I thought I said eleven."

"Yes, I know, Mother." He leaned down to kiss her proffered cheek. "But I thought I'd arrive a little early so you could chat with Annie before the horde descends upon us. Here," he said, taking the flower arrangement from Annie and presenting it to his mother. "These are from Annie. I told her how much you love roses."

Mrs. Carlyle set the bowl on the linen-draped table and peeled away the layers of paper. Lifting the miniature bouquet, she sniffed the roses. "How sweet. But pink . . . let me see, where shall I put them." Walking around the table to a bombé chest set beneath a baroque mirror, she rang a hand bell made of crystal.

While Ted's mother continued to study the arrangement, Annie glanced around. With the walls and ceiling painted a pale yet warm shade of yellow, almost every surface in the room reflected sunlight. The only dark elements were the mirror and marquetry chairs drawn up to the breakfast table and a few ornaments scattered around the lovely octagonal-shaped breakfast room. The door across the room opened and more light spilled across the golden parquet floor.

A black maid, dressed in the traditional uniform with a small, starched apron and a matching white headpiece on her graying hair, stood poised in the doorway. "Yes, Mrs. Carlyle?"

"Oh, there you are, Mary. Would you place these roses in my sitting room. And is everything ready in the dining room?"

"Yes, Mrs. Carlyle." Mary moved to her side and took the flowers.

As she returned to the open door, Ted greeted her and Annie blinked in astonishment as the maid winked at him. He stopped her, clearly surprising the maid. "Mary, I'd like you to meet Miss Rafferty. She's done me the honor of saying she'll marry me so don't tell her too many tales about my youthful misdemeanors."

"Why, Mr. Ted. Congratulations. When—" Mary broke off at a movement by the table, and her face and posture underwent a lightning change. "I wish you happy, Miss Rafferty." With a regal nod, Mary left, closing the door behind her.

The door had barely snapped shut when Mrs. Carlyle set her cup down with enough force to make Annie cringe for the fragile bone china. "Honestly, Ted. How many times must I ask you not to be so familiar with the servants in front of others? It's bad enough that you do it at all." She fussed with the stems of narcissus in a crystal vase on the table, fire flashing from the heavy rings on both her hands.

"As much as I dislike having to correct you, Mother, I hardly consider Annie as *others*. She's practically family."

Mrs. Carlyle's mouth tightened and her hands became still, halting the dancing light from her rings. Almost immediately, she beamed at Annie with a hostess smile. "Well, since we have time, why don't we take Annabelle on a tour of the house so she can have a clearer picture of you, hmmm?" Without waiting for an answer, she crossed to the door through which Annie and Ted had entered earlier.

Annie carefully avoided looking directly at Ted to see his reaction to his mother's insistence on renaming her. Raising her chin, she straightened to her full height. It was going to be an interesting morning.

Mrs. Carlyle waited only long enough for Ted to open the door for her, then crossed the hall and threw open the door opposite. "This is what we call the terrace room. As you can see . . ."

Ted's mother droned on about the terrace, but Annie

was lost in the beauty of warm woods and colors. Here, too, floor-to-ceiling windows flooded the richly but simply decorated room with light. Only here, the windows were a series of French doors opening onto the terrace on the long side of the room at the back of the house which faced Lake Michigan. At the opposite side of the room from where she stood, half the wall was an arch-shaped window with brass struts that fanned into a crisscross pattern at the top, reminding Annie of a Gothic church. The cream-colored walls reflected the rosy glow of shrimp-pink silk on several Regency armchairs, and touches of that color and aqua were repeated in needlepoint on several others. Islands of conversational areas had been created by placing the chairs and tables on beautiful Oriental carpets scattered throughout the room. On the wall opposite the French doors was a fireplace with an ornately carved wood mantel.

Mrs. Carlyle walked beyond it and opened another door. Ted urged Annie on, and she followed his mother reluctantly. She wanted to stay there and feast on that simple but elegant beauty. The room she entered was striking, but somber in contrast.

Annie heard Mrs. Carlyle murmur, "The library," but could have figured that out for herself by the series of shelves built into the burled mahogany panels. The huge window now at their backs was partially covered by silk balloon shades, again creating a rosy glow as the light gleamed on highly polished wood. Overstuffed chairs and a sofa in shades of taupe, beige, and terra cotta were surrounded by shelves filled with books and artifacts that alternated with niches filled with artwork and groupings of collections—here a forest of candlesticks, there a series of carved statues. The parquet floor was stained darker, and at its center lay an oversized zebra skin area rug. On the shared wall with the terrace room was another fireplace.

Again Mrs. Carlyle only paused a minute before opening a door cleverly concealed in the mahogany paneling. Annie trailed after her into the light again as they entered the formal living room at the front of the house. The overall effect there was dazzling whiteness, from the delicate lace sheers hanging at the sides of the mammoth windows to the overstuffed baroque feel of the furniture to the lush white carpeting and grand piano which filled the end of the room where they entered. The only touches of color were the floral-printed blue valances framing the windows, the hues repeated in myriad cushions and ornaments throughout the huge room.

On decorative overload, Annie could only murmur, "Lovely," but Mrs. Carlyle didn't seem to need her accolades. She simply looked around as if ascertaining that everything was in its place and walked through the room to the main hall, clearly expecting Annie and Ted to follow.

His mother tapped her way across the marble entry to the double doors opposite and opened them to reveal more opulence. As Annie came to a standstill beside her, she realized that Mrs. Carlyle was only about an inch taller than she, but the woman appeared taller because she carried herself ramrod straight.

She said, "As you can see, I'm using the dining table as a buffet, but we'll be eating in the greenhouse."

Annie eyed the long table with misgiving. There looked to be enough silver chafing dishes to feed a small army, and she began to wonder just how many people Mrs. Carlyle considered an *intimate* group to be. The setting was beautiful though: silver and crystal gleamed on the linen and lace tablecloth. High-backed chairs had been set back along the walls for easy access to the table and revealed a beautiful pattern of yellow and gold silk repeated from the pale yellow silk walls.

The click of Annie's heels on the dark intricate pattern of the parquet was squelched by a thick cream, gold, and blue Oriental carpet which covered a major portion of the room as she again followed Ted's mother. She pulled herself up just short of bumping into Mrs. Carlyle though when the woman stopped abruptly halfway down the room.

Ted brushed by Annie. "Here, Mother, let me help you." Together they moved a folding silk screen which had effectively covered another set of French doors.

Mrs. Carlyle's mention of greenhouse echoed in Annie's mind as she stepped down into a room bordered completely on two sides by glass, alternating with pristine white frames, while overhead glass panels arched into a Gothic vault. Looking at the canopy of bare branches overhead, Annie thought the room would be lovely and cool in the summertime.

It might not yet be green outside, but Mrs. Carlyle had made it seem so with a profusion of palms and hanging plants. White cloths draped over periwinkle blue ones covered the round tables that littered the room; the chairs themselves were dressed in covers of bluish green whose edging matched that on the white tablecloths. Enhancing the table settings of white china and clear crystal water goblets were dark blue champagne flutes and arrangements of salmon-colored orchids and lillies in silver baskets.

The tinkle of water led Annie to discover a verdigris fountain in the shape of a boy across the room, then the deep tones of the door chimes distracted her.

Behind her, she heard Mrs. Carlyle say, "Ah, you're not the only early ones this morning. Why don't you finish showing Annabelle around?"

When Annie looked over her shoulder, the older woman had disappeared and Ted gazed down at her, his somber expression at odds with the air of festivity around them. "It seems my mother truly has the bit between her teeth today. I can only apologize for her outrageous behavior."

Annie shrugged. "It's understandable, though. She

obviously doesn't like being thwarted." She moved into Ted's embrace as he put an arm around her shoulders.

"It's funny," he said with his chin resting on the crown of her head. "I've watched her make the same maneuvers over the years and most of the time admired her singleness of purpose. But I don't like it aimed at you."

"I'm a big girl and can take care of myself. Besides, I have all those years of dealing with Aunt Nola under my belt."

Ted hugged her to him just as his mother called to them. "Sounds like Geoff has arrived. Let's go meet the rest of the family and see if they're as bloody-minded today as my mother."

Although she hadn't consciously thought about it, Annie had expected Ted's brother to be a replica of him. Instead, where Ted was blond, Geoff's hair was darker, a sandy color closer to brown, and he didn't match Ted's height. His wife, Priscilla, came closer to Annie's vision of what she'd be like: pencil thin with a haughty look. She tossed her mane of dark hair back over her shoulder, adjusting a beautiful blue silk maternity dress that almost totally disguised her condition.

"No, darling," she said to the toddler trying to hide behind her skirt, "don't pull on Mommy. Here, Monique, take Victoria away to the nursery."

A young girl, speaking with a coaxing French accent, removed the child's grasp on her mother's skirt. Gathering a bag by the door, she moved away up the stairs with the little girl in her arms. Annie gazed after them, picturing Cassie dressed in silk to match her mother like the lucky Victoria, then shook her head. It wouldn't be safe for more than ten minutes.

"Honestly," Priscilla said to her mother-in-law, "I look more like a pumpkin every day. And it doesn't help when Victoria pulls on my clothes and makes me look fatter than I am." She looked down ruefully and patted the swell of her abdomen.

"Nonsense, Pris." Ted leaned over and gave her a peck on the cheek. "You look beautiful."

Ted's sister-in-law looked at him skeptically and glowered at her husband. "This is absolutely the last one. I mean it, Geoff," she added when he only laughed.

Mrs. Carlyle hastened to make the introductions and called to a butler in the dining room to bring them a tray of mimosas.

Standing by the grand piano an hour later while someone played a tune, Annie gazed around the mammoth living room at the multitude of people. She didn't know if Geoff and Priscilla were being particularly difficult today. All she knew for sure was that not one of his family had a tenth of the warmth and charm of Ted.

She shifted a little closer to him for, true to his word, he had remained by her side introducing her to people and making her a part of the various conversational circles that ebbed and flowed around them.

"Here they are."

Annie turned at the sound of Mrs. Carlyle's voice behind her, her grip tightening on the champagne flute in her hand as she recognized the blonde beauty Ted's mother had in tow. At the same moment, Ted's hand slipped around her waist as though in protection or comfort.

"Annabelle," Mrs. Carlyle said, moving in front of Ted and pulling Annie a little forward, "I believe you already know Veronica. And this is her father, James Mellinger."

Annie nodded to Veronica, her eyes having been locked with the younger woman's icy stare from the first moment. She pulled her gaze away to that of Veronica's father and felt the power radiating from the rugged and formidable-looking man.

He inclined his sandy gray head and immediately looked

over her shoulder. "Ted, I've been trying to reach you about our contracts for the state-run project."

Mrs. Carlyle chuckled. "I know I can't keep you men from discussing business," she said, linking her arm with Annie's, "so you just go ahead. Don't worry about Annabelle, Ted, darling. I've promised Aunt Edith that I'd bring her along. She's holding court in the petite salon."

Annie smiled reassuringly at Ted and permitted herself to be separated from the group, almost grateful to escape Veronica's presence. She didn't see how she could stand there and carry on polite conversation as convention dictated in the face of someone who so obviously disliked her. Well, the feeling was mutual.

"Here's someone I must introduce you to, dear." Annie was almost startled by the sweetness in Mrs. Carlyle's voice as Ted's mother led her to a group of three men deep in conversation. Annie recognized one of them from recent newspaper photos of the Washington social scene. "Annabelle, I'd like you to meet Senator Langly. Senator, this is Annabelle Rafferty, a friend of Ted's." Mrs. Carlyle allowed them a moment to shake hands and continued, "And this, my dear, is Judge Reardon and Congressman Hallerton.

"Annabelle, gentlemen, owns a restaurant. Yes, in your district, Charles," she teased the congressman. "Just doing my part to increase your constituency." Everyone laughed. "Now, I mustn't let you monopolize her. Aunt Edith awaits us."

Mrs. Carlyle again took Annie's arm and continued across the room. When they were a few steps away, she leaned close to Annie and said sotto voce, "The senator is Veronica's grandfather on her mother's side and Judge Reardon is an uncle by marriage."

They made slow progress through the shifting throng of people, stopping every few paces so that Ted's mother could introduce Annie to someone or other. After the third set and the whispered confidence establishing who was who, Annie began to get the picture. Veronica's name figured large in each connection.

As they neared the side of the room where Annie had entered earlier from the library, she could see that lace sheers had been pulled back exposing double French doors now flung open to expose another room. Mrs. Carlyle introduced her to a wizened lady tucked into a wing chair with cushions and a shawl, but did not allow Annie to remain with Ted's great aunt for long. Saying there were others to meet, Ted's mother led her toward the back of the room and Annie was surprised when Mrs. Carlyle motioned her through a beautifully carved door.

This room too was a delight, furnished like a feminine library, except that Annie noticed a computer tucked into the shelves by a lovely Queen Anne desk. Her gaze roamed over the delicate antiques, her artistic eye appreciating the subtle blend of old and new and the color scheme of cream and apricot. The whole house was a lovely foil for Mrs. Carlyle's coloring: soft, warm, and inviting. Too bad it didn't match her personality.

Annie turned at the sound of the closing door and found Ted's mother studying her. The woman's thoughts didn't appear to be happy ones, for her face was set in hard lines, her mouth pinched in distaste.

She walked by Annie, saying, "Let's sit over here and get to the bottom of this." With butterflies beating a tattoo in her stomach, Annie followed and sat upon a quilted love seat as Mrs. Carlyle leaned over to open a cigarette box. "Now," she said, after lighting a cigarette, "what is this nonsense all about?"

Annie searched her expression through the haze of smoke, but saw only petulance marring an otherwise remarkably well-preserved face. Not pretending to misunderstand her, she said, "I know you're unhappy about the . . . collapse of your plans for Ted to marry Veronica."

"Unhappy is too mild a word for how I feel. Well, what is it going to cost me to make you see reason?"

Blood pounded in Annie's temples, and she fought the impulse to slap the country and cream perfection of the face taunting her. She took a breath to steady her voice. "Money can't buy some things, Mrs. Carlyle."

"Oh, spare me your naiveté." Ted's mother sprang up and began to pace around the perimeter of the Oriental carpet before the sofa. "You obviously saw that Ted is a wealthy man and made a beeline for him. I never thought he could be bewitched by anything in skirts, but obviously I was wrong." She took a quick drag from her cigarette and looked back at Annie. "I can see the attraction, of course. Your looks are . . . exotic enough to blind him for a time. But when your physical appeal has abated, what's left?"

In a quiet, controlled voice, Annie said, "I love your son, Mrs. Carlyle."

She was answered by a bark of derisive laughter. "Love!" The older woman continued pacing and drawing distractedly at her cigarette. Finally, she stopped in front of Annie and looked at her shrewdly. "All right then, miss. If you love him so much, you must see that you're completely wrong for him."

Annie raised startled eyes to Ted's mother. "Yes, I see the thought is not completely new to you. What can you offer him, after all, except your body? That might suffice in your world, but I assure you it won't in ours."

Lowering her lids so that the woman couldn't see how her shafts had gone home, Annie maintained a rigid control. Not by so much as a twitching muscle would she let Mrs. Carlyle know how her words hurt.

"You see how we live." Still standing before her, Ted's mother threw out one hand. "I introduced you around today so you could see with whom Ted is used to dealing. Senators, presidents of large companies, ambassadors even. These people can help him in his career. He won't remain a small-time lawyer for long, you know. I have plans for him and so does Veronica."

At that, Annie's head came up. "And what if Ted doesn't want to fall in with your plans? What if he wants something different?"

Mrs. Carlyle laughed derisively. "Men never know what they want, my dear girl, until they have it. Most of the time they only reach a level of excellence because of the hard work and dedication of the women behind them. Then they think they did it all by themselves!

"Ted has the personality to become a great politician. Veronica saw his potential and became a willing ally to further those aspirations. Tell me, just whom do you know that could influence his career? Would you even *know* what to say to accomplish what you want without being blatant about it?" After a small silence, Mrs. Carlyle grinned maliciously and ground out her cigarette. "Your social status would be a definite liability to any political career. And really, the two of you have so little in common, how could you possibly think a marriage would work?"

Annie stared at Ted's mother, unable to say anything.

"You've seen today that we have an inside track on the national political scene, and if there's someone we don't know personally we know someone who does. That's the way of our world and we know it well. You don't.

"If Ted carries through with his plan to marry you, he will remain a storefront attorney, squandering his talent. If you really love him, you'll let him go."

Mrs. Carlyle stared down at Annie, her words echoing in the air like the repeated stabs of a stiletto in Annie's heart. "You may think I'm cruel, but I love my son. I orchestrated today so he could see you in his milieu. Because I believe once he sees you here rather than in *your* world, he will know you are not the woman for him despite your love. If, as I hope, he comes to that decision, you won't have to worry about a scene." Serenely, she shrugged. "He will act like a typical Carlyle and simply back off.

"As a matter of fact," Mrs. Carlyle said, arching an elegant brow, "I'm arranging a little weekend tête-à-tête for Ted and Veronica. He has some fence-mending to do in that quarter."

Annie looked away, ostensibly out the window, and willed back threatening tears. She wouldn't give this woman the satisfaction of seeing her pain, her doubts, and confusion. The click of the door brought Annie's head around, but Mrs. Carlyle had gone, leaving her to suffer in silence.

NINE

Ted threw down his pen in disgust. He shoved his hands into his pants pockets and walked away from his desk over to the windows. Leaning a shoulder against the cool panes of glass, he stared blindly at the gray-green water of the Chicago River below.

He couldn't concentrate on his work, and he frowned at the general sense of unease twisting through him. There didn't seem to be any particular point he could put his finger on, but somehow things were a little out of kilter.

Yesterday had gone about as he expected, with the exception that perhaps his mother's tongue had been a little more acerbic than usual. All in all, though, he thought she had taken his announced intentions of marrying Annie remarkably well. And while her reception of Annie had definitely been on the cool side, she would probably come around when she realized there wasn't a damned thing she could do besides accept the situation gracefully.

No, his apprehension sprang from Annie. She had been somewhat subdued on the ride home yesterday, but she had claimed it was simply exhaustion. It *was* tiring meet-

149

ing a bunch of people you didn't know, let alone being on an emotional highwire about meeting his family. If he'd had any idea his mother intended to invite so many friends and acquaintances, he wouldn't have subjected Annie to that particular ordeal. Hadn't she said the brunch was only for a few close friends?

His musing was interrupted by a tap at his door. He looked around to see Annie's brother framed in the doorway. His mood lightening, he said, "Come on in."

"Just dropped by for a few minutes to ask your advice about something." Settling in the chair before Ted's desk, Kit picked up a crystal paperweight and fiddled with it.

When the young man didn't say anything after a few moments, Ted prodded with, "Advice on anything in particular?"

"A job offer I've had. For after graduation."

Again Kit seemed reluctant to explain any further. As he examined the facets of the paperweight, Ted studied the youngest of Annie's siblings. He probably was the closest to her in personality, and his air of subdued distraction reminded him of Annie's behavior yesterday on the way home. His gut tightening for no reason he could think of, Ted leaned forward. "What's the problem?"

Kit's keen gaze pierced his, and after a moment the boy nodded as if making up his mind about something. Placing the crystal paperweight back on the desk, Kit's face smoothed into its normal expression of pleasant anticipation. "It's like this. The engineering job is a really good offer, but it's in Peru. The only reason I even considered it is because . . . well, according to Aunt Nola you and Annie plan to get married."

"Yes, we do."

"Yeah, that's what she said. And I thought, great, I wouldn't have to worry about the women in the family. You could watch over all of them for me while I'm gone." Kit grinned at him, man to man. Then his brow puckered, and he looked confused. "But this morning when I was sounding out Annie on the subject, she just said I wasn't to worry. That she had looked after the family for fifteen years and thought she could manage to carry on for the few years I'd be gone. And when I mentioned you and that at least she wouldn't have the entire burden, she just looked at me. Or through me. Anyway," Kit said, bracing his elbows on his knees and rubbing his forehead, "her eyes sort of glazed over, and all of a sudden Annie seemed completely unapproachable. I've never seen her like that.

"Her final words were, 'I'm quite capable of managing by myself, thank you.' And when I asked Aunt Nola what was wrong with Annie, she just looked worried." Kit raised his clear blue gaze to Ted's once more. "So I thought I'd try to find out if there was some problem—not that I want to interfere, mind you. It's just that I have to let Hartman International know about the job. Whether I want it or not."

Despite his increased concern, Ted grinned at the boy. "Well, at least I can put your mind to rest. I aim to marry your sister as soon as decently possible. I'm not sure what's on her mind, but I don't think it has anything to do with our plans. Therefore,"—Ted stood up and shook hands with Kit—"you should definitely take Hartman up on that job. It's a great company and a good start for you."

After seeing him off, Ted asked Mrs. Marshall to hold all calls until he finished going over the pending state contracts for Mellinger Industries. He flipped back open the contract pages on his desk and tried to concentrate, but his original unease of early morning had been increased by Kit's visit. He was getting to know Annie pretty well, and Kit's comments added fuel to his notion that something was up.

Ted had had to stop at a client's before coming to the office this morning, so he had missed out on the early morning routine established with Annie the week before. He arrived to find the kitchen full of people. He could understand her desire not to create a spectacle for the entire staff, but dammit, he'd only been going to kiss her on the cheek. At the last second, she turned her head and he wound up kissing her on the ear.

Even that he could excuse by way of distraction with what she was doing at the time, except that Annie definitely lacked her usual sparkle this morning. In fact, he recalled dark circles under her eyes. What was causing her to lose sleep?

A glance at his watch showed him he had only twenty minutes to finish this contract. He forced his thoughts into legal channels with the carrot dangling before him of time with Annie as a reward for his concentration. He could hardly wait to see her reaction to where he took her this morning. Miss Rafferty didn't know it, but she was about to acquire an engagement ring.

When Ted finally made his way down the back stairs a half hour later, the door into the kitchen was shut. Opening it, he noted the closed door to Annie's office before scanning the kitchen for her presence. He didn't see Annie, but Aunt Nola was there, scolding the hapless Thai dishwasher. His nose twitched, and Ted was drawn to the stove where Dora was browning something in a saucepan that made his mouth water.

She saw him sniffing appreciatively and grinned. "I know what you're having for lunch."

"Not today, unfortunately. I have something more important to do."

"More important than eating Miz Annie's food? Don't let Miz Nola hear you say that. Ever since she got you off that green stuff, she's been strutting 'round here like a peacock. She'll likely think you're sickening."

Ted chuckled. "No, she'll understand. I'm taking Annie out before lunch. Then I've got to dash for a court date."

Dora set the pan of bubbling sauce aside and placed a tiny frying pan the size of her hand in its place with a dollop of butter in its center. With a couple of flicks of a huge carving knife, she whisked off two thin slices of something rolled in dough and dropped it in the sizzling pan. "Now this here isn't going to be fixed exactly according to Hoyle, but it should stick to your ribs. Take just a minute."

"What is it?"

"Miz Annie calls it veal caprese, but just between you and me it's veal rolled in pastry that gets baked and covered with this fancy sauce here."

"Hm-m-m. Is that what smells so good?"

Ted felt a nudge in his ribs. Aunt Nola demanded, "What are you doing down here in the middle of the morning bothering Dora?"

Despite her glare, Ted leaned down and gave her a hug. "Getting a preview of lunch while I wait for Annie. By the way, where is she?"

Aunt Nola flicked a look at Dora who nodded. "She's still shut up in her office interviewing." Her face registered disapproval.

Glancing at his watch, Ted asked, "Do you think she's going to be much longer?"

"If I'd had my way, there wouldn't even *be* an interview!"

Ted looked down at the indignant figure still under his arm. It was obvious Aunt Nola was very unhappy about something. "What's wrong?"

Dora chuckled on the opposite side of the huge kitchen stove. "What's wrong is that the applicant for assistant manager is a man, and Miz Nola don't want no men in her kitchen."

Ted feigned shock and put one splayed hand to his chest. "Aunt Nola! Never say you're sexist."

"Watch your tongue, young man." Aunt Nola swatted

his hand where it grasped her shoulder, and Ted pulled away in a pretense of hurt. "The nuns would have paddled you good where the sun don't shine." She sniffed. "Sexist indeed. I just don't cotton to the idea of *any* man giving me orders, and I'm too old to change my ways at this late date." Her words might have sounded like a battle cry, but the expression on her face showed consternation.

Sobering at the hint of trouble for Annie if she were serious about the male candidate in her office, Ted tried to placate her aunt. "Didn't Annie or someone say that you were going to be running the catering? It sounds to me like managing the restaurant and managing the catering business are two completely different areas."

Aunt Nola cocked her head sideways as she looked up at him, obviously weighing what he had said. Acceptance came as she pulled away from Ted, straightening her dress with another sniff. "That's as may be. Just so long as he doesn't go poking his nose into my business.

"Speaking of business," she said, rounding on him, "why aren't you attending to yours instead of wasting my time and Dora's?"

Glad to see the fire back in her eyes once more, Ted restrained a laugh. "I'm waiting for Annie. We have a date."

At his words, Aunt Nola's expression changed once more, and she glanced doubtfully toward Annie's office. "You sure about that?"

"Well,"—Ted pulled out his appointment book—"since Annie couldn't get away Saturday as planned, we agreed on today. See," he said, pointing to the entry, "ten o'clock."

"Did you mention it to her this morning when I saw you in here?"

"No, I forgot to remind her, but I had Mrs. Marshall call her as soon as it occurred to me. Annie did say something to her about the interview." Feigning a calm air, Ted said, "It's okay. I'll wait."

He sat by Aunt Nola on an adjoining stool at the wooden chopping block. She was oblivious of his presence, though, as she sat watching the closed door of Annie's office, absently rubbing her hands together. His uneasiness grew as he watched her restless fingers tapping a tattoo on the wooden table.

Dora placed a dish before him, but the fragrant smell had lost its appeal. Aunt Nola was clearly worried about something, and it wasn't the possibility of Annie's hiring a man to work over her in the kitchen.

When the towering black woman moved to the other side of the kitchen, Ted used the opportunity to probe. "Aunt Nola," he said quietly, placing one hand on her arm, "what's up?" At her startled look, he added, "And don't tell me nothing, because I got the same impression this morning that something was wrong with Annie. Kit only confirmed it."

"Kit? What's he been saying?"

"It wasn't so much *what* he said as the *way* he said it. Annie's too good-natured for any aberration of her behavior to pass unnoticed." Ted picked at the veal Dora had fixed for him, giving Annie's aunt a chance to respond.

"I don't know what's wrong with the girl," she said querulously. "All I know is that she practically snapped my head off this morning when I mentioned it was time to make some hard plans for this wedding." She sighed. "Like you, apparently, it wasn't so much the words that bothered me, but her attitude. She just isn't acting like herself."

Feeling as if he'd choke if he tried to swallow another bite, Ted put down his fork. "What did she say?"

"I don't remember exactly. Something about there *was* no timetable for the wedding and she wished everyone would leave her alone to arrange her own life." Aunt

Nola sniffed. "Something about being capable of deciding things for herself."

Ted slumped a little on his stool. Not so much, all told, to get upset about. Still, this was Annie they were talking about, not someone like his mother or even Veronica who were peevish in the normal course of events. Tension bringing him upright once more, he said, "Do you think it might be just prewedding jitters?"

"I tell you honestly, I don't know what to—" Aunt Nola broke off as the door of Annie's office opened.

They watched her lead a tall graying gentleman to the rear entrance where she continued to talk to him in a low voice. Eventually, she shook his hand and after his departure, turned to face them.

Annie swallowed when she saw everyone waiting for her. Her gaze roamed over Ted, absorbing every detail of his appearance, until the pain constricting her heart threatened tears. She had decided to cool the relationship to give Ted some breathing space. But in order to do so, she had to be deceptive. How could she do that when she loved him so much? Then another thought occurred to her that straightened her shoulders with determination: loving him as she did, how could she not?

As she came to a stop by the wooden chopping block, Annie deliberately widened her eyes and gazed around the kitchen at the tableau. "What? No one has anything to do?"

Dora and Sompong immediately busied themselves, and her cousin Maureen who had halted at the doorway whisked herself back into the serving area. If only it was that easy with the two people remaining. She eyed Aunt Nola warily to see how she was taking the possibility of a man in their kitchen and was relieved to see that the storm warnings had abated somewhat.

Her aunt said, "Well, did he get the job?"

"I'm not sure. I have one more candidate to interview.

She called just as I started talking to Claude. In fact,''—Annie looked at her wristwatch—''she should be arriving any minute.''

Ted frowned. ''Does that mean you won't be able to come out with me this morning?''

''Oh, Ted.'' Contrite at her duplicity, Annie crossed her fingers behind her back. ''I'm sorry. The only time this woman could come was now. I didn't know how Claude was going to turn out, and I haven't exactly been overrun with applicants. I didn't dare *not* take the chance to interview her.''

His smile looked forced, but he said, ''Business is business. We'll go out together tomorrow morning.''

Annie bit her lip. ''I'm afraid I can't do it then either. I have an appointment with the TV production people.''

''I see.'' Ted studied her for a long moment then said, ''And what about Wednesday?''

''I—I promised an old professor that I'd stop by. She wants me to take over a nutrition class for a colleague who's ill.''

''Thursday?''

Out of the corner of her eye, Annie saw Aunt Nola's head going back and forth, like a ping-pong ball, and felt an urge to giggle. Realizing it was nerves, a spurt of adrenaline rushed through her. Darn it! Why should she be made to feel like the one in the wrong? It was hard enough being magnanimous.

With an edge to her voice, Annie said, ''I'm sorry, but this week is turning out to be impossible. It's difficult to keep all my commitments straight.''

She saw the instant hurt in Ted's gaze that she apparently didn't consider him or their plans a commitment. Annie couldn't stand it. As much as she wanted to remain in his company just to be near him, she couldn't stay and inflict more pain. ''If you'll excuse me, I want to jot down some notes about Claude Auberge so I don't forget them.''

Her office offered a momentary escape, but she couldn't shut her ears to the drone of Ted's deep baritone as he answered something Aunt Nola asked. Annie fought the prickling sensation of threatening tears and swallowed repeatedly to clear a suddenly clogged throat. She would *not* cry.

The sound of footsteps stopped at her open door, and Annie glanced up from the resume she had been blindly staring at. Ted practically filled the doorway.

"I just wanted to tell you not to be upset." His tender smile was almost her undoing. "Everything will fall into place." He moved into her tiny office and, leaning over to cup her chin, brushed her lips with his. "You'll learn that I'm a very patient man."

Annie still tingled from Ted's touch after his steps faded up the stairs. Feeling something wet on her hands, she looked down and was surprised to see drops of moisture falling.

She thought she had cried herself dry during the long night she had lain awake. Her mind would not let her body rest as it scurried around and around, trying to find a solution that would allow her to have Ted's love and yet not be a hindrance to a political career. Because his mother was right about that. He would make a wonderful politician; he was so fair and honest. With the gray light of a cold dawn, Annie finally accepted that there was no choice. Ted's mother was right about that, too. She loved him and, therefore, she couldn't stand in his way. It would be selfish of her to keep him from a career of public service.

The only difference was, she at least was willing to let Ted make up his own mind. He had now seen her in his world and had to decide for himself whether or not she would fit into his life. If Annie tried to push a decision either way, she'd never be sure she was what Ted really wanted. But giving him the space to work it out was the hardest thing she'd ever done. At the thought she might have to give him up entirely, pain lanced her heart and her head. Ted's mother had seemed so sure.

With the sky brightening outside, Annie acknowledged something else. She had thought she understood Celia's pain from Ramon's desertion for greener pastures, but she hadn't even come close. Somehow she would have to learn to accept her loss, if it came to that, without becoming bitter as her sister was in danger of doing. Sleep had finally come as she made a mental note to tackle Celia on her attitude.

The sound of someone rapping on their back door brought Annie out of her trance, and she looked up to see Aunt Nola standing in the doorway watching her, her expression a mixture of puzzlement and compassion.

"Your applicant is here," she said gruffly. "What's her name?"

"Gina Antonelli."

Aunt Nola rolled her eyes. "God, give me patience. First a Frenchman, now an Italian." Pulling the office door toward her, she said, "You fix yourself up and I'll keep this lady on ice for you." She shut the door, but even so Annie could hear her muttering, "The United Nations don't have a patch on us." A watery chuckle escaped as Annie reached for the tissue box.

She didn't feel like laughing the next night, though. Dinner was a strange and strained affair with Ted's flowers in the center of the table a silent rebuke. No one had taken her seriously about eating at home, but Annie was determined to escape the restaurant.

She had decided to hire Claude *and* Gina. She'd spent all afternoon training Claude to manage the restaurant at night, and tomorrow morning she'd do the same for Gina on the day shift, deciding that the less time she had to spend at the restaurant the better off she'd be. But her presence was necessary for the next week at least, and the prospect of continually running into Ted left her feeling drained.

She looked up as she took a bite of perch filet and met the unblinking stare of Aunt Nola. Glancing to both sides of her, Annie could see that no one else was even making a pretense of eating anymore. With a sigh, she dropped her fork. Apparently the family grapevine had been at work. While cooking dinner, she'd received a phone call from two aunts and one from Uncle Tully ostensibly about the restaurant. But every conversation had worked its way around to her forthcoming wedding or questions about her visit to Ted's mother. She was tired of having to think up evasive answers, and she wanted the pressure off Ted.

Taking a deep breath, she said, "Okay, here it is, folks. There won't be a wedding. I'm not marrying Ted."

A stunned silence followed her words before everyone broke into speech at once.

Aunt Nola drowned them out and when she had everyone's attention, she turned to Annie. "You want to explain that?"

"What's to explain?" Annie shrugged. "I've simply come to the conclusion that Ted and I basically don't have that much in common. It's hard enough to stay married these days without going into a marriage with two strikes against you."

"Two strikes?" Aunt Nola asked sharply.

"Yes. Besides the fact that our tastes are opposite on almost everything, we . . . come from different worlds. I saw Sunday that I would never fit into Ted's kind of life."

"But Annie," Lynn started, "you love him. I——"

"Women," Kit said in disgust and left the table.

Aunt Nola muttered under her breath, but several of her words were audible among the voices raised in protest. ". . . harebrained . . . obstinate . . . foolish girl . . ."

"You can't be serious!" Celia stared at her, shocked for once out of her self-absorbed air.

Annie stood up, pushing her chair back. She braced her hands on the table and looked at each one of them, including Kit who leaned against a kitchen counter, until their voices stilled. "I might be all of the things you called me, Aunt Nola, and yes," she said, looking at Lynn, "I do love Ted. But the fact remains that a marriage between us is unsuitable."

She raised a hand to stop Aunt Nola's words before they began again. "I've thought about this very carefully, and there's nothing you can say that I haven't already considered."

Ted grinned gleefully as his office door closed. Good, now he had another reason to talk to Annie. Only the visit this morning, like the others for the past two days, would be quick. Just long enough to give him an excuse to hold her briefly in his arms or drop a quick kiss on her tantalizing lips after he made whatever comments he'd planned in advance.

The idea had come to him on Monday after their visit to the jewelers was scuttled and he'd seen Annie's reaction to his words in her office. He'd stay out of her way, give her a chance to straighten out whatever was wrong, but let her know he was there waiting in the background whenever she was ready. His lightning sorties on her distancing tactics had made no difference so far, but he was a determined man. Flowers, candy, a book, or notes about Consuela's case had all found their way downstairs by one means or another.

He rubbed the cushiony velvet of the small box in his jacket pocket. He was still undecided about when to present the ring he'd picked out for Annie, but carried it with him in case an opportunity presented itself.

Ted checked his pocket calendar now to see what else

he had pending today, but decided he'd have time for a quick trip down to Annie's before his next client was due. The visit from her twin cousins, Trudy and Trevor, just now had provided the perfect excuse.

It seemed Trevor wanted to go on to law school after college and be a lawyer rather than the policeman Annie's Uncle Marmaduke wanted him to be, and Trudy wanted to follow in her father's footsteps as the next cop in the family.

A few minutes later in Annie's office, she stared up at him in shock. "Trudy wants to be a policeman?"

It was all he could do not to take her in his arms, wrapping her in his protection as well. Whatever the demon riding her, it was taking its toll: dark bruises under Annie's eyes proclaimed her lack of sleep, and she looked like she had lost weight as well.

"I don't have time to go into all the details now. I received an emergency call just as I started downstairs, and I'm literally buried in work." Ted explained briefly about Trudy and Trevor, adding, "Trudy seems to have a level head. She wants to be a cop, but only for the street experience. What she really wants is to wind up in youth services where she'll be dealing with kids. I think she'd be good at it. Trevor I'm not sure about." He frowned, trying to arrange his scattered thoughts. "He's young yet, of course, but I'm not sure if he realizes what a grind law school is. How about it? You know him better than I do."

"Ted,"—Annie put a hand to her forehead crinkled in a frown—"I'm sorry. I didn't realize the family was burdening you so much. I've tried to let everyone know they're not to bother you with family problems. In fact, maybe now's as good a time as any to—"

"Don't be silly," he interrupted. He was sure somehow that the look of determination on Annie's face did not spell good news for him. "It's not a burden. I've enjoyed helping them. In fact, knowing your family has enlivened my existence considerably. I didn't realize how dull I'd become."

Deciding that continuing the conversation later, preferably this evening, would give him another excuse to see Annie, Ted bent over. From his position sitting against the edge of her desk, it was easy to lift Annie from her chair to lean against him. She didn't have a chance to react. He lowered his lips to hers and after a momentary stiffness, she relaxed as her lips melded with his.

It was damned difficult to only sample lightly what he wanted to plunder, but Ted kept a tight rein on his physical response to Annie's soft curves. A whiff of her spicy scent as she leaned into his embrace almost made him lose control, and Ted pulled away with a groan.

"You have a potent effect on me. I'd better go before someone catches us flagrante delicto, so to speak." But he couldn't resist brushing her lips with his once more, leaving a silent Annie behind.

Two hours later, the tap on his door didn't make Ted look up from the contract he was studying. Instead he called out, "I told you, Mrs. Marshall, that I don't want to be disturbed."

"Well, it isn't Mrs. Marshall's fault," Aunt Nola said from the doorway as his secretary held the door open for her. "You can eat while you work if you want, but eat you must."

Realizing it was futile to argue with that tone of voice, Ted cleared his papers to one side to make room for the tray she carried. It was a few moments before he noticed Aunt Nola was pacing at the side of his desk. He sighed. More problems.

He removed the metal cover and inhaled the flavor of barbeque that rose to greet him. Knowing that Aunt Nola would unburden herself when she was ready, he took up his knife and fork, poking at the chicken and rice and something else he couldn't identify. "What is this?"

Aunt Nola made a face and said, "Barbeque chicken with lemon grass and rice. Sompong's contribution to the menu. Tomorrow there's something with fish in ginger sauce." She stopped pacing and faced him across his desk. "Ted, there's something I have to tell you, but I don't want you to take it at face value."

"What is it?"

"Last night Annie . . . Annie said she wasn't going to marry you." Dumbstruck, Ted's mind raced with a dozen questions before he formulated a coherent one, but as he opened his mouth Aunt Nola held up her hand. "There's something going on I don't understand, but I'll get to the bottom of it."

"What did she say exactly?"

Scowling, Aunt Nola started pacing again. "Some nonsense about it being unsuitable. I ask you!"

Ted's mind raced with all the normal reasons people usually gave for not marrying someone, but after Annie's reaction this morning to his kiss, he knew for certain it wasn't because she suddenly found him repugnant. *Unsuitable*. That stumped him.

Frowning, he absently tapped his fork and reached a decision. "Officially, I don't know that Annie said she wouldn't marry me, so I'm going to carry on with the quiet campaign I've been running all week." His expression clearing, he grinned at Aunt Nola. "I don't give up easily." He wiped his mouth and rose from his desk. "I'm sorry, but I've got to meet with my partner before I leave for court. Thanks for lunch and"—leaning over he hugged her—"don't worry. Annie will come around."

He escorted Aunt Nola to the door and wandered down the hall to Jim's office. Since his partner was on the phone, Ted sat in a chair with his pocket diary before him, trying to bring some order to the chaos of his schedule.

Jim's chair squeaked as he leaned over to hang up the phone. "You look harassed."

Ted looked up and smiled ruefully. "I *feel* harassed."

"You, too? I thought it was my imagination that we were driving ourselves into the ground."

"I didn't see it coming, but we're getting more business than we can handle without some help. And it doesn't help when my personal life starts edging over into business hours."

Jim grinned at him. "Thought you'd been running up and down those stairs a lot this week."

"It isn't that I begrudge the time spent with Annie's family. They provided an insight into family life I only saw when I stayed with you during some college vacations." Crossing his leg, Ted rested one elbow on his knee and rubbed the back of his neck. "But it plays hell with my carefully arranged schedules. This morning alone I took on helping one of Annie's cousins find out about scholarships for law school. And I'm supposed to help convince his father that becoming an attorney is smarter than being *just* a policeman. The whole family is littered with men in blue!"

Jim chuckled. "Looks like you've got your work cut out for you." The two friends smiled at one another. "About the business, though. I've got an idea it might be time to bring another partner on board. Maybe two."

"I knew there was a reason we get along so well." Ted smiled back at him. "I'll bet you're thinking the same thing I am. Junior partners, right?"

"Yep. Every campus is being innundated with recruiters. Now's the time for us to make a move. Besides, if you think you're busy now, wait until you're married." Jim grinned at Ted's look, but went unchallenged. "Thursday and Friday are some of the biggest days on the eastern campuses. Want me to tackle them?"

Ted groaned and yearned to tell Jim yes, because then

he'd be here for the weekend with Annie. But he knew he couldn't do it to his partner. Jim's wife, Alice, was expecting another baby and his place was here with her as much as possible.

"No, you handle Northwestern and Loyola and take over seeing Mellinger for me about those state contracts. The sooner I'm rid of any connection to Veronica, the more comfortable I'll be.

"I'll fly out tonight so I can be bright eyed and bushy tailed for all those eager young candidates tomorrow." Rising, Ted grimaced. "But I'd sure rather be here with Annie than spending a whole weekend digging into the backgrounds of earnest potential associates. And on top of that, I have to be in New York on Monday for the Stratford case."

After telling Mrs. Marshall to book him on an early evening flight to Boston, Ted went downstairs to find Annie. She wasn't to be found, though, among those caught up in the bustling activity of the kitchen. Catching Aunt Nola's eye, he asked her whereabouts.

"Out front with a customer."

Ted was going to ask if she thought Annie would be long, but she turned away to answer a question from Dora. Glancing at his watch, he decided he didn't have time to wait for Annie. Besides, he required more than five minutes with her. Annie's maneuvers had convinced him that she needed to know he was committed to their relationship. And he had just the thing in his pocket. Only it took more than a couple of minutes to win a woman over and, if he wasn't careful, he was going to be late for court. The best thing to do was to clear his calendar, then he could go after Annie full steam ahead next week.

Deciding to write her a note, he pushed open the door to Annie's office and discovered Bryce and Casey playing with their hot wheels on the floor. "Hi, boys. What are you doing here? I didn't see your mother."

As usual, Bryce elected himself spokesman, saying, "She's having lunch. Casey and I are supposed to play here quietly and stay out of the way."

Ted hid a smile. "And you're doing it very well, too. I'll leave you to it," he said when his searching gaze found nothing on Annie's desk that he could write on.

He had turned away when the angle of Casey's head triggered a memory. This was the little guy who loved secrets. Just then the boy's car shot out the door of Annie's office, and Ted took advantage of the brothers being separated to squat down beside Casey as he retrieved his car from under the metal racks.

"How would you like to know a secret?" The little boy's eyes lit up. "Just between you, me, and Annie, like before. But I need you to tell Annie about the secret because she's busy right now and I can't wait for her. Will you tell her for me?"

Casey's head bobbed up and down. "Good boy. Here's the secret: I have to go out of town, but I'll be back next week. Can you say it back to me so I'm sure it's the same secret?"

A minute later Ted started up the back stairs with Casey already chanting his favorite theme. The door at the top opened and his secretary peered down at him myopically. "Your mother is on the phone, Mr. Carlyle."

"Tell her I'll be right there, Mrs. Marshall, but I've only got a minute before I have to leave for court." Ted had a feeling he was doomed to have one of those days. Then he grinned as Casey's piping singsong voice followed him up the stairs.

"I've got a secret, I've got a secret."

TEN

Annie escaped the unnatural warmth of the early spring afternoon on Tuesday into the coolness of her home. Wearily, she hung up the light coat she had needed just that morning and, hoisting her heavy briefcase once more, made her way into the kitchen. What she needed was a cool drink.

After a long draught of iced tea, Annie held the glass to her temples. Her headache, which had begun in the television studio earlier, was now in full bloom.

"You look beat." Celia's voice startled Annie, and she jumped, nearly dropping her glass.

Spinning around, she tripped over the briefcase she had dropped at her feet and spotted her sister sitting at the kitchen table. Her gaze dipped to the floor where half the contents of her briefcase had slid out in disarray. "Great," she said, sinking to her knees and starting to gather the scattered papers. "The way my day is going . . ."

Annie left the thought unfinished. Things were bad enough without calling more bad luck down upon her head. In fact, things were about as black as they could get.

She didn't realize that her hands had stilled until Celia squatted down beside her. "Here, let me help you."

Annie didn't dare look at her sister. She knew what she would find there, and she didn't think she could stand any more sympathy. Everyone had been treading lightly around the subject of Ted and his whereabouts, but by now her whole extended family must be privy to the fact that he was nowhere to be found. He'd left. Decamped. Gone.

Annie sighed. After six days, it was time to accept the fact. She had been surprised but not too concerned when Ted didn't put in an appearance on Thursday or Friday. After all, she'd practically warned him away. But when Saturday rolled around without sight of him, Annie didn't need it spelled out for her where Ted was. She knew in her heart what had happened.

His mother had been right. Ted had simply walked out of her life and back into Veronica's, if Mrs. Carlyle was to be believed. Hadn't she said she was arranging a weekend reconciliation for them? And hadn't she said Ted wouldn't create a scene, but simply fade away? Annie's lips twisted wryly and she wondered if Ted's mother had expected *her* to make a scene.

No, that wasn't her style. And neither was it her style to be comfortable with constant cosseting and to have subjects talked around as if they were fragile glass. Her family had been wonderful . . . loving, supportive, kind, first as they tried to convince her of the sound judgment of marrying Ted, then later as they gradually came to accept that he no longer would be a part of their lives. Annie felt as if she'd been entombed in cotton wool. It was suffocating and she didn't like it. Sighing as she got to her feet, she realized she was also the only one who could do anything about it. She dumped her briefcase on the table and sprawled in a chair, thinking it was time to put her life back on track.

"What's the matter?" Celia asked. "Didn't the contract negotiations at the studio go smoothly this afternoon?"

Annie swallowed. Here was her opening, if she could pull it off. "Yes. Or at least," she amended, "as well as could be expected since I didn't have my attorney with me."

"Annie . . ." Celia began tentatively.

"It's okay." Annie smiled wanly at her sister. "It's best if we all face it. Ted's gone and he's not coming back. At least, not back into our lives."

"You don't know that."

"Oh, but I do." Annie straightened and gazed at Celia directly. It was easier than she had thought. All she had to do was pretend that Ted was some stranger, who meant no more to her than . . . No, what she had to do was *not* think of him at all. And the only way she could do that was to let her family work Ted out of their system so she wouldn't have to hear his name dropped in conversation a half dozen times a day. No matter how much it hurt, she had to begin sometime. "No question about it. He's gone."

Celia stared at her in disbelief. "How can you sit there so calmly? Don't you want to scream or cry or throw something?"

"All of the above." A ghost of a smile hovered on Annie's lips. "But what good would it do except make all of us uncomfortable?"

She took another sip of iced tea and set her glass down, deciding that maybe she could kill two birds with one stone if she stretched the truth a little. "You see," Annie said, reaching across the table for Celia's hand, "I finally realized that Ted's desertion was not a rejection of me personally, but of a lifestyle he couldn't embrace. Just like with Ramon." Celia's hand jerked in hers.

"Ramon?" Her sister stared at her as if she were mad. "What are you talking about?"

"Ramon wanted something you couldn't give him. Money. So he had to find it elsewhere. It had nothing to do with you personally." Annie tugged at her sister's hand for emphasis. "And that's what you have to hang on to. His rejection had nothing to do with your love, your talents, or even your body. It simply came down to a matter of money. Not you."

"Why are you telling me this now?"

Annie captured both of Celia's hands and spoke gently. "Because I've noticed a brittleness about you, a hardening veneer that is totally unlike the lovable sister I know." Celia started to pull her hands away, but Annie hung on. "You're a wonderful person with great talent and a lot of love locked up inside. I don't want to see all that wasted in futile anger on something you had no control over." Annie gazed at her earnestly. "You're better than that, Celia. You *deserve* better than that."

Celia sighed, her shoulders slumping, yet her forehead remained pleated in perplexity. "But it hurt so much."

"Yes," Annie agreed, "it does at first. But we have to get beyond that and take control of our lives again."

Her sister's gaze swiveled to Annie. "We . . . you mean, you . . ."

"Yep." Annie forced a smile. "And you've got to promise me that you'll give me a kick in the pants if you hear me getting too sassy."

"What are you going to do?"

"Do?" Annie glanced at her briefcase ruefully. "I have plenty to do. I just have to rediscover my will to do it. Know anything about contracts? No? How about teaching a nutrition class?"

Celia brightened. "I *do* know something about recipes. I could help sort them into the various chapters for your cookbook, then subdivide them by nationality."

Annie beamed at her with gratitude. "You angel. With Aunt Nola heckling me to work on that, too, I was wondering how I was going to find time to get everything done.''

Her sister laughed. ''Unfortunately, your system of keeping recipes for meals or occasions together is not conducive to cataloging.'' She rose, looking eager to start.

''Thanks, Celia. Everything is piled on our desk in the study. I started but didn't get very far. I didn't realize I'd collected so much in ten years.''

''You've accomplished a lot in those ten years, Annie.'' Her sister leaned over and hugged her. ''Sometimes I forget I have a lot to be grateful to you for.'' Annie shook her head, but Celia said, ''We all do. Thanks for being there.'' With a final hug, her sister left the kitchen.

What self-pity hadn't been able to accomplish, her sister's words did. Annie sniffled and fumbled in one side of her briefcase for the items she'd placed there from her purse. ''Oh, sugar!'' she said, unable to find any tissues in the jumbled mess.

''Here, use this,'' Aunt Nola said from behind her, passing a pristine handkerchief over Annie's shoulder.

Wiping her eyes, Annie said, ''This is not what you think.''

Aunt Nola walked around and sat in Celia's vacated chair, her eyebrows raised. After glancing at Annie though, she said, ''I was going to ask how you know *what* I think, but that's taking unfair advantage of your condition. It just so happens I heard the whole thing.''

Annie looked at her unrepentant aunt over the folds of her handkerchief. ''Just so happens, huh?''

Aunt Nola shrugged. ''Well, I didn't eavesdrop on purpose. But once I realized you were taking Celia in hand, I didn't want to interrupt. She's needed a talking to for a good while now.''

Her wide, innocent look didn't fool Annie. She was included in Aunt Nola's statement just as plainly as if her aunt had said so. Straightening, Annie said, "Since you heard what I said, you know that I'm okay."

"And just what is it Ted wanted that you couldn't give him and don't take personally?"

Annie sucked in her breath, wondering how long it'd be before just his name no longer had the power to hurt her. "A lifestyle," she prevaricated, "that he was used to."

Aunt Nola made a sound close to that of a snort. "Pish! What do you take me for, girl?" Her aunt glared at her, daring her almost to try another fabrication.

"In one sense, it's true," Annie said and with an effort relaxed in her chair. If she could convince Aunt Nola, then her aunt would calm the pack of relatives who had been nipping at her heels these last few days with questions. And if she stuck close enough to the truth, her comments would sound more convincing. "I think last Sunday Ted had a chance to see me, *really* see me for the first time."

"And found you lacking, huh? I'm sorry," Aunt Nola said, wagging her head, "but I don't buy it."

"I told you before that we have virtually nothing in common. Not likes or dislikes, certainly not the way we were raised."

"Ah, now we're getting somewhere. What's wrong with the way you were raised?"

"Oh, for heaven's sake, Aunt Nola." Several days' lack of sleep put an edge on Annie's tongue. And made her unwary. "His mother all but laid it out for me." Annie gasped, appalled at her lapse. Recovering, she shrugged. "Mrs. Carlyle simply stated what I'd already said to Ted. Only she was more candid about it."

Momentary silence greeted her words, and Annie dared to hope she'd pulled it off. A shuffling sound made her glance up. Aunt Nola pulled out another chair, raised her feet, and settled herself more comfortably. "I've got all the rest of the afternoon, missy. Take your time."

Maybe her aunt had time, Annie fumed, but she certainly didn't. Wearily, she pushed back her hair from her face. Why fight it? Aunt Nola was perfectly capable of wearing her down now that she had caught a whiff of the underlying reason for her decision. As succinctly as possible, she repeated Mrs. Carlyle's conversation at the brunch. When she finished, she propped her elbow on the table, resting her chin upon her hand. And Aunt Nola said *her* face was an open book.

After a few moments, her aunt's expression of outrage was replaced by a frown. She studied Annie from under lowered brows, her mouth turning down at the corners more every second. Straightening finally, she removed her feet from the chair and faced Annie squarely, her frown deepening.

"To think I'd live to see the day!"

"What?" Annie said, mystified.

"That a niece of mine—I know you think you're being noble, but you're just being a coward, girl."

"What!"

"Look, you're brave and fearless in every other part of your life. You start a business when you're sixteen and none of us believes you know what you're doing. Not only do you make a success of it, you're such a blooming success that you open a restaurant! You've faced down doubting Thomases, irate teachers, and downright angry parents over the years." Aunt Nola paused to draw a breath and looked at Annie, her eyes pleading for understanding. "Don't you see? You fight for everyone but yourself."

Annie shook her head, but her aunt persisted. "They won't thank you for it, you know." Confused, Annie stared at her. "Celia and the others. You've hid behind them for years, putting their interests before yours. That's why you never really cottoned on to any of those other men, only I never said anything because I didn't believe you'd lost your heart to any of them. But this time it's different. So why not fight for what you want?"

Why not indeed? If only it was that simple. Annie sighed. "What you don't know, Aunt Nola, because I didn't tell you, is that Mrs. Carlyle had something else to say as well. Sort of the coup de grace. She told me she had arranged a little reconciliation weekend for Ted and Veronica. That's why he wasn't here." Annie tried to smile. "He made his choice and obviously it wasn't me."

"Well, how could he do otherwise when you all but shut him out last week? What did you expect him to do, stay where he wasn't wanted?"

Annie pressed both sides of her throbbing head with her palms. "It wasn't like that." She explained about feeling she had to give Ted some space to make up his mind, but her aunt stared at her like she'd lost her mind. With the way her head hurt, maybe she had.

"Now you listen to me, my girl." Aunt Nola leaned toward her, emphasizing each word. "Did it ever occur to you that Ted had already had his chance with Veronica, *if* that's what he wanted? And did he take it? No!" Drawing herself up to her full diminutive height, her aunt glared at her. "And why not, you ask? Because he obviously didn't like the package deal, in spite of what his mother might say. And you all but push him back into the lion's mouth again!"

Thrusting her chair under the table, Aunt Nola studied her silently. Annie was suddenly reminded of a similar scene fifteen years ago in another kitchen after her father had died. Uncle Tully, Uncle Duke, and their wives had sat around this same table trying to convince Aunt Nola of the wisdom of letting them split the family up, each taking two children. Aunt Nola had faced them as decisively then as she faced Annie now, vibrating sheer determination to win. And she had. They all—she, Celia, Lynn, and Kit—had won in the long run because of Aunt Nola and her determination that they could do it.

Annie frowned. Was it that simple, that you just made up your mind about what you wanted and went after it? Sighing, she answered her own question. No, of course not. Not if it interfered with what someone else involved wanted.

But, a little voice of hope whispered, what if Aunt Nola was right? Mrs. Carlyle and Veronica had already had their chance and still Ted had turned to her.

Oh, God. What had she done?

She looked to Aunt Nola for reassurance, but her aunt seemed lost in a brown study. Uncertainly, Annie asked, "Do you think it's too late?"

Shaking her head, her aunt muttered, "Him being gone this weekend doesn't look good. It's worrying. And he should have been back yesterday, only he wasn't." She continued to shake her head. Slowly though, a grin replaced her concentrating frown. "But you know my motto," she said with a gleam in her eye. "Never give up."

How could she have forgotten? It had long been Annie's motto, too. And would be again, she vowed.

Standing on the sidewalk before the front entrance to his building and Apple Annie's, Ted looked after the retreating figure of Annie's Uncle Marmaduke. He shook his head in disbelief. He'd just been given a social cut. Unless Annie's uncle really hadn't recognized him in the early evening gloom, the big burly Irishman had completely ignored Ted's greeting and walked by him like a stranger.

He shrugged and paid the cab driver, then turned, frowning down at his briefcase, suit bag, and travel case on the sidewalk. He'd been in such a hurry to get here that he hadn't thought to direct the cabbie to the rear entrance where he could simply have deposited his luggage discreetly inside the back hallway. He couldn't carry all this into the front door of Annie's. Now he'd have to lug it upstairs before making an appearance.

Ten minutes later, Ted felt he had made himself as presentable as he could under the circumstances. His one-day trip to New York had expanded into two, and he'd already been on the road four days prior to that. He grimaced at his rumpled suit and longed for a shower. Only the thought of seeing Annie, holding her in his arms, and finally claiming her as his had brought him directly here rather than to his apartment first.

Patting his pocket, he started down the back stairs, whistling in anticipation. About halfway down, he caught a glimpse of a face turned up to his in surprise. Annie's cousin Maureen blinked, then disappeared, he supposed in the direction of the kitchen. What, he thought, no greeting? He was beginning to feel like he'd entered a time warp where everything was a little off center.

Charlie meowed at him as he came around the corner of the stairs, and Ted leaned over to scratch her behind the ears. Straightening, he turned toward the open back door of the restaurant and took two steps. And halted.

Everyone in the kitchen faced him, frozen in a tableau. His sense of a time warp deepened as he registered the fact that every single face looked decidedly unfriendly. What in the world was going on?

A glance showed him that Annie's office was dark and empty, and he'd already noted her absence among those gathered in the kitchen. The graying Frenchman Annie had hired as assistant manager looked disapproving, and Dora was positively menacing as she picked up a long wooden spoon and folded her massive arms. He spotted Maureen at the far end of the kitchen before she scuttled away to the restaurant's interior. A sense of unease crept up Ted's spine, and he began to wonder if something had happened to Annie.

"Where's Annie?" he asked sharply, his gaze flying from one to another of the staff. The memory of Annie's physical condition the day he'd left added a further jarring note. "Is she sick?"

Sompong frowned and turned his back, once again spraying dishes, while Dora simply harumphed in displeasure.

"What is it?" he demanded, striding into the kitchen opposite the stove from Dora. "What's wrong with Annie?"

The towering black woman looked down her nose at him. "And why should you care, coming 'round here after all this time? Ain't you done enough harm to that poor girl?"

Ted shook his head. His time warp had slipped entirely into the Twilight Zone. The rumble of feet at the entrance of the kitchen brought Ted around, and he sighed in relief. The bulk of Annie's Uncle Tully filled the entrance, backed up by Uncle Marmaduke. Now he'd get to the bottom of whatever nightmare was going on.

He'd taken only a couple of steps before Annie's uncles moved into the kitchen to confront him. That was the only word Ted could think of as he looked from their unsmiling faces to the unblinking gaze of Annie's cousins crowding through the kitchen door behind the bulk of her uncles.

Uncle Tully hitched up his pants, straightening until he loomed over Ted. "And just what might you be wanting here, bucko?"

Ted's anxiety over Annie's health diminished at her uncle's words, but there was obviously something amiss. "Okay," he said, leaning back against the chopping block and folding his arms, "I give up. What's going on? And where's Annie?"

· Uncle Marmaduke moved up beside Uncle Tully. "You just leave Annie out of it. In fact,"—the graying Irishman's mustache fairly bristled with indignation—"we've decided it would be best if you just up and moved your offices from here. That way Annie won't have to worry about continually running into you."

"Move my offices?" Ted looked at them as if they'd gone crazy. Or he had. His tired brain beginning to click, he put Dora's earlier comment together with the challenging stance of Annie's uncles, and the whole thing began to take on the color of a farce. Just as a smile began to form, the back door slammed. Everyone turned to see Kit slide to a halt in the doorway as he took in the scene. His surprise changed to the now familiar thrown-gauntlet look as his gaze collided with Ted's. Ted laughed and said, "It needed only this."

But he was proved wrong immediately as more of Annie's relatives crowded into the kitchen, bombarding him with questions. From somewhere, various aunts joined the throng around Ted.

"Where have you been for a week?"

"You don't lead a girl on, then disappear like Houdini."

"What's the big idea, making Annie unhappy?"

"Why did you treat Annie like that!"

At first Ted tried to answer the questions flying at him from all quarters, then threw up his hands in defeat. There was only one way to halt this flood of indignation. Reaching into his jacket pocket, he brought out the velvet jeweler's box and flipped open the lid.

Those closest to him saw what was in his hand, and their voices stumbled to a halt. But those on the perimeter only chattered more loudly, trying to figure out what was going on. Holding the box high in the air over his head, Ted waved it around for everyone to see. Their questions died away. Except for a couple of whistles, silence reigned as everyone gazed at the sparkling prisms of light thrown off by the diamond ring.

Into the quiet, Annie said, "If that's for me, I accept."

Ted spun around. His gaze riveted on Annie, he didn't remember wading through people three bodies deep to reach her side. Gathering her to him, he breathed in her familiar sweet essence and murmured a heartfelt, "Thank God."

Annie clung to him, her face pressed to his chest, and knew she had made the right decision. "I've missed you," she said, running her hands up to his shoulders and reveling in the ripple of well-defined muscles as his arms tightened around her. She murmured, "Six long days."

"Forever," Ted said. Loosening his hold, he dipped his head until his lips nuzzled the delicate skin beneath her ear.

Annie arched her neck as his lips traveled around the perimeter of her chin to settle firmly over hers. Her very bones seemed to dissolve as she melted against his strength.

"Well," Aunt Nola said in the hush of expectancy as everyone watched Annie and Ted's reunion, "I'd say this kitchen's got too many cooks. Shoo!" She flapped her hands. "Everyone out."

At the first grumbling murmurs, Aunt Nola looked beyond Annie, still locked in Ted's embrace, to the mulish expressions of those gathered around the couple. Raising her voice, she demanded, "And how do I get to the champagne if you don't clear out?"

As though from afar, Ted heard Aunt Nola's order and the babble of laughing voices retreating. He drew a ragged breath and leaned his forehead against Annie's. "They scared the daylights out of me, you know."

Annie chuckled. "I like your method of crowd control."

"I mean it." He slid his hands to Annie's shoulders and held her away from him to study her face, now smiling up at him. Dark shadows bruised the area under her eyes, and her face seemed more finely drawn to him. "I thought at first something had happened to you. Are you sure you're all right?''

Annie snuggled back into his arms again and raised her lips to Ted's throat, still tanned against the whiteness of his starched collar. "Hmmm. Now I am."

"That was some reception committee. Now, I know how your dates must have felt being given the third degree by your family. What on earth was going on?" As she went still in his arms, Ted looked down her. "Annie, what made them think I'd walked out on you?"

When she didn't respond, Ted led her over to a high kitchen stool before the chopping block. Leaning against it, he pulled Annie between his spread legs and tilted her chin up so he could see her expression. "Did *you* think I'd walked out on you?"

"Yes. And you only get to do it once."

Ted frowned. "Why? Didn't Casey give you my message?"

At that, Annie stared at him. "Message?"

He held her face between his palms, his thumbs grazing the hollows of her cheeks, and couldn't resist brushing her lips with his. "I tried to find you Wednesday afternoon to tell you I was going out of town. Failing that, I tried to write you a note, but couldn't find any scraps of paper on your desk. I did find Bryce and Casey playing in your office though and had the bright idea of leaving the message with Casey. I told him it was a secret and to—"

"Oh, no!" Her expressive features crumpled in dismay.

Stricken, Annie remembered hurrying into her office to grab her purse before leaving to keep an appointment with her old college professor. Casey had danced around her chanting his I've-got-a-secret theme, but Annie was running late and brushed him off with "That's nice, Casey."

Her guilt deepened as she also recalled that Casey had tried to get her attention on Sunday when Shelia stopped by after mass, but again Annie had not paid any attention to him, this time because she was too sunk in misery. That poor child.

"Oh!" Annie said as another thought occurred to her and she gazed at Ted in consternation. The full import of the situation sunk in, and she realized her assumptions about Ted's whereabouts had been all wrong.

Ted watched a flush rise and stain Annie's face. His thumb brushing her intriguing dimple, he said, "As much as I'm glad to see some color back in your cheeks, I have a feeling there's a tale behind that rosy glow." He arched an eyebrow in inquiry.

Annie burrowed close to him, needing to feel his arms around her. "Oh, Ted. I've been such a fool." Haltingly, she told him about her erroneous conclusions. His expression darkened when she mentioned his mother's part in her misconception, but he didn't interrupt her. "I'm sorry for doubting you," she said at last.

Ted hugged her to him. "You have no reason to be sorry," he said, his hands busy exploring the dips and curves of Annie's back. His hand slid from her hip to the delicious roundness of her bottom and pulled her closer yet. "If a mistake was made, we both made the same one. We erred on the side of generosity in giving the other the space to wrestle with our own demons. There's nothing wrong in that, love."

Remembering his mother's contribution to the confusion, he added, "My mother, however, has much to answer for."

"Don't be too hard on her. She loves you and only wants to see you reach your full potential."

Ted leaned back and waggled his eyebrows suggestively. "You can accomplish that . . . in more ways than one." Annie responded with a smile, but he could see she was worried. "Look, I put my family on notice a long time ago that I wasn't going to tread the path laid out for me. My dad accepted my decision. My mother . . . well, as you saw, she never gives up. I don't quite know when I became a black sheep, but it had something to do with the way I saw life at Jim's during all those vacations I spent with his family." He smiled down at Annie. "I think the operative word here is *family*. I get the same sense of relationship with your relatives. With mine"— Ted's smile faltered as he searched for words to explain the difference to Annie—"I think the best way to describe my family is that they lead parallel lives. They each live in a separate world that intersects at certain points, otherwise they go merrily along their way . . . alone.

"I don't think my dad minded when I decided to kick over the traces. He said my mother still had Geoff to mold. And she did. Geoff joined the family law firm, married my mother's choice, and settled in an adjacent community almost as insular as that of our parents. Their lives are a round of business dinners, being seen at the right charitable functions, and attending the correct parties where all the supposedly best people are."

Annie's heart felt lighter, but still she looked at him doubtfully. "And that's not what you want?"

"Good God, no!" Then Ted's expression turned rueful. "But I can see I was well on my way to being engineered into that life. I guess that's what Jim meant when he said I was becoming so predictable. However,"—he leaned down and kissed the tip of her nose—"that's before an Irish maiden made me see the error of my ways. A beautiful, full-of-life sprite whose energy expands to encompass and bewitch everyone . . . especially me."

It was hard to think with Ted feathering kisses across her face, but Annie strove to clarify one last point. "Politics? Do you want to run for office one day?"

"There's no way I'll ever consider politics."

"Oh, I don't know." Annie raised her arms to twine them about his neck, nestling against him. "It might be nice to have a senator or governor in the family."

Ted groaned as her breasts flattened against his chest, and he fought his instinct to drag Annie up to his office. With his luck, her family would send out a search party.

A rumble deep in Ted's chest alerted Annie to the change in his demeanor at the same time his hold on her loosened. At his laugh, she looked up in question.

"I just realized that your Uncle Duke must have sent out for reinforcements." He explained about being cut by him on the sidewalk earlier. "Your family has an amazing telegraph system."

"You don't know the half of it," Annie warned, leaning against Ted once more. Her lips unerringly found the side of his neck, and she traced a pattern up to his ear and across his face. At the same time, she dipped into his jacket pocket, retrieved the jeweler's box, and reaching behind her back, slipped it into Ted's hands. Against his mouth, she murmured, "Don't you have something that belongs to me?"

"Yes," came Aunt Nola's voice from the doorway, "will you get a move on? You're holding up the celebration."

ELEVEN

Because of her hectic schedule, Annie still had a few last minute things to move into Ted's apartment the morning of their wedding day. It was a little after ten as she tipped the doorman who had helped her carry the stack of boxes and honeymoon luggage upstairs to the foyer of her new home. She and Ted had decided to live there for the time being.

She sagged against the door and sighed with relief. This was the last thing she had to do before she could relax in a bubble bath and begin the long preparations for their late afternoon wedding. She unbuttoned and shrugged out of the blouse that had been tied at her waist and hung it on the doorknob. Dressed now only in a sleeveless tank top and matching shorts, she could work faster without working up a sweat. The weatherman had promised a wind shift out of the north by noon and she was keeping her fingers crossed. After their cool spring, whoever would have guessed it would turn so warm this early in June?

Leaving her luggage by the door for their departure tomorrow, she carried two boxes back toward Ted's bedroom. Their bedroom, she reminded herself as she brushed against the partially closed door with her hip. It swung open and she turned, took two steps, and stopped as Ted emerged from the bathroom with a towel wrapped about his waist.

He halted mid-stride and the towel he had been rubbing his head with fell unheeded to his shoulder. Annie's mouth went dry as she focused on the loose end of that towel against his suntanned chest. Drops of water still glistened in the golden hair that lightly furred his upper torso and tapered to his midsection where it disappeared under another towel.

"I—I thought you and Alex would be out on errands already." Annie's voice was faint and she could hardly get her thoughts to connect, especially with Ted staring at her so strangely. "Don't you know it's bad luck to see the bride before the wedding ceremony? What are you doing here?"

At that, Ted came toward her. "Right now, thanking my lucky stars that Alex and I stayed up so late talking last night."

She relaxed fractionally as he took the boxes from her and dropped them on the floor, then gasped as he took her rather roughly into his arms. Holding her tightly next to him, his tongue plundered her open mouth and after a second of surprise, Annie sighed and leaned into his embrace. The warmth she had begun to associate with kissing Ted seeped through her, and she struggled to raise her arms to draw him closer. Effectively trapped by his hold on her, she simply slipped her arms around him and discovered in reward that her fingers had acres of muscled skin to play with.

Ted tore his mouth away from hers and inhaled a ragged breath. "You don't play fair," he said, holding her slightly away from his body by her upper arms.

Annie dropped her head to his chest and, turning her face into the fresh herb-scented hair there, discovered his thundering heartbeat matched her own. She rubbed her cheek downward against his pelt's sleekness. She heard his quick indrawn breath at the same time she drew her hands lightly from his broad back to the hard planes of muscle over the ribs at his sides. "I don't think," she murmured and heard her own voice as from a great distance, "that I'm playing at all." She trailed quick, fluttering kisses across his still damp skin.

Once again she found herself caught up in a rough embrace. Ted's searching lips found hers, and she had no trouble at all deciphering the message his tongue sent with its movement in and out of her mouth. The increasing bulge of his arousal as her hips swayed as of their own volition against him echoed the thought. Conscious thought ceased to exist as need blossomed and grew.

Once again she struggled to free her arms and this time succeeded. As Ted's arms relaxed their hold, she slid down the length of his body and heard him groaning as he greedily nuzzled her neck. Annie only slowly realized she had exchanged one prison for another as his hands came round her sides, cupping her breasts. She went still. Her own breathing became audible to her as his thumbs explored her nipples, turning them into hard nubs.

Seeping warmth exploded into a lava flow. Her legs suddenly weak, trembling, Annie clutched at Ted's shoulders and dropped her head to his chest. With her nose nestled in the fine hair of his chest, his scent clogging her senses, she tasted his skin. Ted jerked at her touch, moving her mouth, then went rigid as she found his nipple and ran her tongue around it.

Annie felt the muscles of Ted's shoulders bunch, then herself being lifted with his hands spread wide across her bottom and forcing her legs to straddle him as he pulled her to him intimately. She continued her tasting expedition as he hoisted her up, her lips trailing from the fine, tickling hair of his chest, to the corded column of his neck. Her mouth grazed his ear, tasted his after-shave, the arch of his eyebrow, until she was too high and laid her face against the top of his head and, still open, filled her mouth with the taste of his clean, wet hair.

The warmth of Ted's mouth traveled from her neck to the top of her breasts. With a hungry sound, he fastened on a nipple through the thin cotton of her tank top and since she wasn't wearing a bra, it was as if the material didn't exist. At the exquisite heat of his mouth, she arched against him, holding his head to her, then began to squirm as his fingertips crept lower and began a magical motion on the insides of her thighs near their apex.

The sweet torture went on and on as he switched from one nipple to the other and maneuvered her body until he lodged his erection fully against her. They wavered while shudders ripped through both of them.

Chafing at the restriction of not being able to move freely, Annie opened her eyes. The thought uppermost in her mind was to get out of her clothes as quickly as possible. She burned from the heat spiraling through her and wanted to feel the hardness of Ted's body next to hers, to become his in the fullest sense of the word. Her dazed gaze swung from the ceiling to his bed and she seized on it, knowing the time for fulfillment had come.

"The bed." Annie hardly recognized the husky, breathless voice as her own as she pushed down on Ted's shoulders to get his attention. "The bed."

He turned and, letting Annie slide down his body once more, fell back across it. Hardly had her body come to rest, her breasts flattened against his chest, her legs trapped between his, than Annie reached for the tail of his shirt. At the same time Ted reared up and, twisting, flipped their positions so that Annie lay beneath him.

"Shhh, wait," he soothed. He grasped her hands in his and lowered his forehead until it touched hers. Annie lay buried in the bedclothes by his weight, her blood percolating to the heavy beat that drummed through her entire body, until she could stand it no longer and began to move against him. "Annie," he said and she opened her eyes to see that he spoke through clenched teeth, "if you don't stop moving, I'm going to forget my good intentions and take you here and now."

Responding with a frankness that surprised her, she whispered, "I thought that was the general idea."

Ted groaned. "Don't think I don't want to. I do."

"I know," she replied still breathless and wiggled against him. "I got that impression." She grinned at him unrepentantly.

Ted laughed but shifted his body so that they lay almost side by side and, kissing her hands, laced their fingers together. He held them safely between their upper bodies, their legs still tangled but with a whisper of space separating their hips. "What you don't know, minx, and what I shouldn't have forgotten, is that Alex should be here any minute."

At the reminder of his best man and the outside world, Annie jerked and would have fled from the bed except that Ted held her in place. Heat still suffused her body, but now it was embarrassment that stained her cheeks. She squeezed her eyes shut.

"Hey, look at me." Stubbornly, Annie kept her eyes closed and tried to block out the sound of Ted's command. But she couldn't ignore the soft kisses he pressed to her eyelids, her nose, her chin. "When I make love to you," he said gently, planting a kiss first at one corner of her mouth, then the other as she peeked at him, "I want to have all the time in the world. I don't want any interruptions because I plan to kiss every inch of you as I explore your delectable body."

Annie looked into his loving gaze and gulped. "Every inch?" she whispered.

He chuckled and pulled her to a sitting position as he

wrapped his arms about her. "Every square inch. We've waited this long. We can wait a few hours more."

Reluctantly, she scooted to the edge of the bed and struggled to rise to her feet. As she did so, Ted playfully swatted her on her bottom. She glanced back at him over her shoulder with a wicked grin. "Why not? Aunt Nola always says that a thing worth doing is worth doing well."

Annie, enveloped in another congratulatory hug, peeked over her great aunt's shoulder. Only about ten people remained in the bridal receiving line. She sighed and passed her great aunt on to Kit and Aunt Nola. Taking advantage of the fact that the next couple in line was engaged in conversation with someone behind them, she fluffed out the tulle of her gown and straightened the double veil crushed by the myriad of people who had already passed through the line.

Ted slipped his arm around her, drawing her close to whisper in her ear. "Hold on, darling. We'll get this show on the road in just a few minutes."

She closed her eyes momentarily, her fatigue dissolving as Ted's lips moved in a caress. His lips lingered, tracing the rim of her ear with his tongue. To combat the sudden weakness caused by his touch, she drew in a deep breath and tried for a light note. "The joys of having a large Irish family."

"I've been meaning to talk to you about that."

Annie wrinkled her brow at the serious note in Ted's voice and glanced up at him. Had the onslaught of her numerous family members been too much for him today? "What is it?"

His fingers encircling her wrist skimmed up the inside of her arm as he said, "How soon do you think we can escape and start on our own addition to this family?" The back of Ted's hand brushed the swell of her breast as he continued to trace the intricate lace pattern on the inside of her arm. She caught her breath and held it as an exquisite spasm tightened her chest. His other hand drifted south from the back of her waist and, cupping her bottom, caressed her through the layers of her bridal gown.

Since they stood in a corner by the door, Annie knew no one could see what Ted was doing. But she also realized, as a now familiar heavy warmth moved through her, that the expression on her face would probably give them away. "If you don't stop," she whispered through a suddenly constricted throat, "you're going to have to explain to everyone why the bride is in a puddle on the floor."

Ted laughed and brought his errant hand back to her waist, turning her for a quick kiss.

"Now hold on," a hearty voice boomed before them. With an effort, Annie opened heavy lids to see Uncle Garret grinning at her. "You've got the rest of your life, young fella, to cuddle Annie. Move over. Right now, it's our turn."

She found herself embraced in a bone-crushing hug that lifted her off her feet. Laughing, she introduced Ted to her uncle and Aunt Delia and delighted in the fact that the years had not dimmed their exuberance.

"Kit, Aunt Nola. See who's here," she said at last, before turning to the next people waiting to congratulate them. Annie bent closer, trying to hear Ted's introductions over the blare of a saxophone as the band started warming up.

"Dottie?" At her Aunt Delia's loud exclamation, Annie turned toward the length of the receiving line. "It is!" her aunt squealed. "As I live and breathe!"

Aunt Delia stood before Annie's new mother-in-law, her face wreathed in a big smile. As her arms stretched toward Mrs. Carlyle, Annie recognized the look of distaste on the face of Ted's mother. Less than two months ago, that withering look had been directed at her.

The throaty brass notes died away, to be replaced by

the strains of a violin. In the lull, Mrs. Carlyle's voice carried distinctly to Annie as she said, "I see you haven't changed at all, Cordelia."

Her aunt engulfed Ted's mother in an enthusiastic hug. "Dottie! Where have you been all these years?"

Annie blinked and turned to Ted. "Dottie?" she said, awed by her aunt's familiarity. His mother had finally consented to being called Dorothea by Annie and her family after Ted had lost his patience with her imperious snubs. "Dottie?" she repeated in wicked delight. Ted shrugged, apparently as mystified as she.

"We grew up together," Aunt Delia said, her piercing voice rising with excitement.

Annie glanced back to see Ted's mother surrounded by Kit and Aunt Nola, who was demanding an explanation, as well as Aunt Delia and Uncle Garret. She could even feel a little sorry for his mother, surrounded by the clamorous joviality of her Irish clan. A movement beyond Ted's mother drew Annie's eyes further down the receiving line. Celia leaned away from her dark escort and sent Annie a triumphant grin before a hand on her arm reclaimed her attention. Celia's expression became mutinous as she faced her partner, the best man and a close friend of Ted's.

Ted's touch brought Annie back to their interrupted introductions, but she sighed inwardly. With Jim Linden expecting his wife to deliver near the wedding date, Ted had chosen another friend to be his best man. Alex Devlin had arrived late yesterday from somewhere back east just in time for the dress rehearsal. Instead of being entranced with his dark good looks, Celia had an adverse reaction to his polished charm. Her acerbic tongue and withering looks, however, had not deterred Alex one whit. After one look at Celia, Ted's friend had stayed glued to her side. And Annie couldn't find it within herself to be sorry. Celia had to break out of her self-imposed prison sometime, and it would take a strong man to breach her defenses. Alex looked like he could handle the job with no strain. Since Celia in her role as maid of honor would be required to be his partner all evening, she couldn't avoid him.

Annie's thoughts were still distracted as Ted led her into the opening waltz. It didn't take more than a few heartbeats though for his touch to penetrate her awareness. She realized with sudden clarity that since their surprise meeting that morning, touch was no longer necessary to turn her already vibrating nerves into an exploding mass of expectation. One look from his expressive eyes promised a return to that state of bliss so abruptly interrupted.

His gaze held hers as they circled the room, moving in perfect harmony. "I didn't know you were such a good dancer," she said, smiling up at him.

A slow smile stretched his finely etched lips, and his eyelids dropped to half mast. "There are lots of things you don't know about me." He drew her fractionally closer. "And that I don't know about you. But as I've said before, discovery is going to be half the fun."

"Promises, promises," Annie said, surprised at her own brazenness but not the resultant heat suffusing her cheeks. The six weeks of their engagement had passed in a blur. What with Ted working like a demon trying to get through most of his caseload while training a new junior partner and Annie getting the gourmet show off the ground, as well as getting the restaurant onto a firm footing, there had been little time for privacy. And if this morning was an example of the fireworks touched off by closer intimacy, she thought the lack of being alone probably had been a good thing. Remembering, her lips parted and she glanced up with longing.

Muttering a curse under his breath, Ted tightened his hold on Annie and swung her into a series of spiraling circles that somehow brought them even closer. "If you keep looking at me like that, I'm likely to throw you over my shoulder and leave the wedding feast to feast on you instead.''

She rested her forehead against his chest. "If you don't stop making me dizzy, we'll have to leave anyway—and not for fun and games."

Instantly, he slowed his steps. "Are you all right?"

She opened her eyes to smile up at him. "Yes. Or I will be," she amended, "if I can keep my mind on more mundane matters like getting through this evening."

"You're not worried about this evening, are you?" Ted was studying her with a frown contracting his brows. "I don't mean the reception. I mean—well, afterward?"

Annie felt her heartbeat pick up its tempo. Worried? No, but she was certainly working herself up into a state of heightened expectancy. Should she tell him that? Could she tell him that she longed for that final intimacy? She opened her mouth to try and was forestalled by Kit tapping Ted on the shoulder and grinning at her.

"My turn." As Ted scowled at him, Kit took Annie in his arms and reminded his brother-in-law, "You're supposed to claim Aunt Nola now. Remember?"

He watched Annie until she smiled reassuringly and blew him a kiss over Kit's shoulder. Still distracted, he turned to scan the tables around the dance floor for Annie's aunt. She finally made things easier for him by standing so he could find her.

"None of those fancy steps for me," she told him as he led her onto the dance floor. He looked down at her in confusion. "You know, those circles you were spinning Annie in. I'm too old for that nonsense."

"I have a feeling," he told her, "that you're never going to be old. You'll probably be dancing at our children's wedding."

"Speaking of dancing at children's weddings, I must say that your mother continues to surprise me." She glanced to his left as the rest of the wedding party found their partners and swung into the waltz.

Ted followed her gaze and was struck dumb at the sight of his mother dancing with Annie's Uncle Marmaduke.

"Did you know about your mother's humble beginnings on the west side?"

He brought his attention back to Aunt Nola with an effort, struggling to marshal his thoughts. "No. That is, all my brother and I were told was that my grandparents moved to the North Shore area when she was fourteen. Apparently my grandfather's business had taken off like a shot, and he felt he could provide a . . . more elaborate setting for his daughter."

"Ah, so she's not entirely to blame for those airs she gives herself. No offense," she added, looking up at him, "but somebody has much to answer for. Look, the others are searching for new partners. I'm going to see if I can find Marmaduke. Maybe she told him some more."

Bemused, Ted watched her threading her way through the multiplying dancers as members of the wedding party separated to draw others onto the floor. His gaze wandered till he again found his mother dancing with Marmaduke. He felt he was due a long explanation.

But his mother proved almost as elusive as privacy with Annie did. The dance floor became jammed and he lost track of Marmaduke's massive figure. No sooner had he reclaimed Annie and extricated them from the whirling figures than the photographer had to take more pictures of them, this time posed beneath the flowering arch where he had lights and other equipment set up, he explained, for best results.

Swathed in yards of filmy material, Annie had never seemed so fragile to him as he stood behind her at the photographer's direction. His dark-clad arms encircled her and seemed enormous to him in comparison to hers in white lace. Annie moved her left hand on top of his as

directed by the photographer and again Ted marveled at
the contrast of size, as well as light and dark. Fine-boned
and delicate, her pale hand seemed that of a child in comparison to his. Something moved inside him and all his
protective instincts rose like sentinels. He swore that nothing would ever harm her if he could prevent it. Especially
not him on their wedding night. He would have to remember to go slowly in initiating Annie into the delights of
making love so as not to frighten her. And he would start
now by reassuring her and keep his baser comments for
another time, much later, when she was more accustomed
to him.

When the photographer had snapped off several shots,
Ted turned Annie. His gaze held hers as he raised her
hands to his mouth and placed a kiss on each one. And
since her lips were so tantalizingly close, he leaned down
and placed a gentle kiss there, too. "Everything is going
to be fine," he whispered. "I promise."

"Great shot," said the photographer coming up to
them. "Couldn't have planned it better myself. Now," he
said, effectively wedging his body between them, "it's
time for the toasts." Leading each by a hand at their
elbows, he hustled them toward the head table. "The rest
of the bridal party is in place. We just need the bride and
groom."

Ted pulled his arm free and pointedly removed the
man's hand from Annie's elbow, placing her arm protectively under his. "If you want to move us around like
mannequins, just say so. Don't touch."

Annie gazed at him in wonder as he settled her tenderly
in place, helping her to free her veil before he took his
place beside her. His solicitous and proprietary air continued through the long evening. When the toasts turned too
broad, a glance from Ted to Alex had the best man rising
to propose another one of his own. When she complained
during dinner of being thirsty, his searching look had a

waiter immediately refilling her water glass. When she sank back at his side after a round of dances with her uncles and confessed her feet were killing her, he leaned down and, despite her protests, drew her legs toward him until she was sitting sideways in her chair. Leaning his forehead against hers, he removed her shoes and calmly massaged her red toes, all the while talking to her in a low, soothing voice so that others left them alone and gave her a chance to recuperate.

"Oh, this is heavenly," Annie whispered after a time, her eyes closed in bliss. "It's almost like being a queen for a day."

Ted chuckled, then she felt him shifting and his lips grazed the side of her jaw. His breath tickled her ear as he said, "You deserve to be treated like a queen and not for just a day. I intend to see that you're pampered, protected and . . ." His voice trailed off as Annie, off balance since he moved his forehead from hers, tilted forward and his hand slid from her ankle up the back of her calf. "And well loved."

Annie was not surprised his voice ended in a guttural growl since she was having trouble breathing normally herself.

"I think," he said, his hands firm on her ankles once more, "we'd better circulate."

At that moment, Annie heard booming laughter and turned her head toward the infectious ripples of delight as feminine voices joined in. At the unusual sight of Mrs. Carlyle laughing unrestrainedly, Annie nudged Ted.

His glance followed hers. "Let's go investigate."

Annie halted his headlong rush and instead pulled him around, passing Celia sitting with Alex's arm looped over her shoulders as he leaned in close to say something to her. They approached behind Ted's mother, seated at a table with several of Annie's aunts and uncles.

"You make it sound," Uncle Marmaduke complained

to Mrs. Carlyle, "as though I didn't treat you any differently than I did my cousins. What about that time, right before you moved, when I asked you to the Valentine dance?"

"That's because you were scared to death of Rowena. I"—Mrs. Carlyle slanted him an arch look—"was too well-bred to do the pursuing and you knew you were safe with me."

Uncle Tully let loose a whoop, and the others joined in the laughter. Wiping his eyes, he said, "She's got you there, Duke."

Uncle Marmaduke hunched a massive shoulder and from his stubborn look, Annie knew he was far from giving up. "Well, I always protected you from the boys' roughhousing and included you in our games."

Seated next to him, Mrs. Carlyle nodded. "Yes, you did."

Several of those gathered around teasingly sighed, "Ahhh."

"But in hindsight," she added, "I think you protected me simply to protect yourself. If I went home crying it wasn't long before your mothers appeared"—Ted's mother glanced at Tully, Duke, and Garret—"to lead you each home by the ear."

When their laughter quieted down, she said, "And as for playing games, the last time we played hide-and-seek I was the first one in Delia's gardening shed at the back of their property. It had taken me all summer to work up my courage to hide in those dark depths and it was the perfect place. Imagine my surprise, then, to be rudely pulled through the door at the last moment and be left standing on the outside when someone—Jeremy, I think—came seeking."

"That was my favorite hiding place," Duke explained amid the laughter, "and I was a great hulking boy. Where else was I going to hide?"

A trace of a smile lingered on Mrs. Carlyle's lips. "I'm sure I don't know, but it was hardly chivalrous of you."

"Oh, well, chivalry," muttered Duke. "What were we, thirteen? What thirteen year old thinks of chivalry?"

"We did," chimed in Aunt Delia. "That was the summer we discovered *Ivanhoe* and the knights of the Round Table. You lugs were simply too dense to take our hints."

Duke laughed with everyone else, but Annie saw the deepening tinge to his ruddy complexion. So did Uncle Tully. He rose and clapped him on the shoulder. "Methinks you need some fresh air, Sir Knight. Ladies"—he bowed to the table—"your servant."

Duke lumbered to his feet and gave a jerky bow before being led away by Tully. Mrs. Carlyle's gaze followed them briefly. Garret half rose as Annie approached the table, and she sighed in relief as Aunt Delia studied her shrewdly.

Taking her husband's arm, her aunt prevented him from sitting again. "Come on, Sir Garret. You can be chivalrous and lead me around the dance floor some more." Without being too obvious, Aunt Delia was able to hint the others away from the table, all except Aunt Nola at the end who ignored her.

Pulling out Duke's vacated chair next to his mother, Ted settled Annie there, then sat between her and Aunt Nola. Annie glanced uncertainly at her mother-in-law. She wanted to say something to retain the warm feeling left from the others' discussion, but she was unsure how to bridge the gap without trespassing in a personal area and thought interfering.

Mrs. Carlyle solved the problem for her. She left the careful study of her wedding ring, glanced at each of them in turn, and sighed. "It was a long time ago."

After a moment, Aunt Nola prompted, "Meaning what?" Annie's and Ted's gazes swung to her.

"Meaning . . ." his mother's voice drew Annie's and

Ted's eyes back as her hands fluttered helplessly a moment. Then she clenched them into fists and straightened in her chair. "Meaning the girl was vastly different from the woman. I know what you're thinking, but it's too late."

"Oh, posh!" Annie's and Ted's heads turned once more to Aunt Nola. "A tiger may age, but it doesn't change the pattern of its stripes."

Silently, Annie and Ted swung their gazes back toward his mother. She smiled at them wryly. "You two look like you're at a tennis match." She glanced beyond them to Aunt Nola. "I know you mean well," she said gently, "but I think—I really think you're going to have to accept my word as to how I feel about this . . . reunion."

Once more Annie and Ted turned their heads toward her aunt. She had propped her chin on one hand while the other beat an absent tattoo on the tablecloth. "If you don't mind some plain speaking," she said at last, gathering up her evening bag, "I'll admit I've had some uneasy moments about your starchy ways. But after this evening"—she pushed back her chair and Ted stood to help her up—"I'm a whole lot easier in my mind." She walked around to Mrs. Carlyle's chair and put a hand on her shoulder.

Smiling down at Ted's mother, she said, "Any time you get lonely, you just give me a ring. You saw them. They were genuinely pleased to see you again. Wouldn't take but a couple of phone calls and by the time you reached the restaurant, I could have the whole kit and kaboodle assembled for a gabfest." She patted Mrs. Carlyle's shoulder. "You think about it."

After Aunt Nola left them, they all remained caught up in their own thoughts. After a few moments, Ted's mother said, "Don't hold out too much hope. Despite what your aunt said about tigers not changing their stripes, there's another old adage about teaching an old dog new tricks."

Her gaze flicked around the crowded hotel ballroom, and they heard her sigh. "After insisting that certain important personages be invited, I've spent almost the entire evening with my . . . old friends. I should go see if the others have all melted away."

Mrs. Carlyle picked up her cigarettes and lighter and dropped them into her evening bag. She fiddled with the clasp, then turned to Annie. For the first time, Annie saw beyond the polite social mask to the woman below as Ted's mother held her gaze. A slight smile touched her lips. "Honesty forces me to admit that Ted could have done a great deal worse by marrying elsewhere. I hope you'll both be very happy." She briefly laid her scented cheek alongside Annie's, kissed Ted, and left.

Ted dropped back down beside Annie, staring after his mother. "Well, I'll be damned. My mother and Marmaduke!"

Annie put her hand on his knee. "We should be very grateful that your grandfather's business prospered."

"Why's that?" Ted's expression was distracted as he finally turned to her and covered her hand with his own.

"Because, silly, if it hadn't, he wouldn't have moved. And if he hadn't moved, your mother and father wouldn't have met. And if your mother had stayed in the old neighborhood, you might have turned out to be one of my first cousins." Annie giggled at his stunned expression. "But he did, they did, she didn't, and you aren't."

TWELVE

"I'll be forever grateful for only being related to you through marriage," Ted said with a grin. He looped an arm around Annie and drew her close. "Speaking of which, don't you think it's about time we get it underway? Isn't there something about throwing the bridal bouquet?"

"Yes, but there's one *tiny* thing you have to do first."

"Me?"

"Umm-hmm. And I think you have to do it with your teeth."

"My—Oh!" His confusion ended with a wicked laugh. "The garter. Somehow I'll find the strength. Come on, Mrs. Carlyle," he said, helping her up, "let's tantalize everyone with a flash of your pretty legs."

Faster than she believed possible, Annie found herself sitting on a chair in middle of all the groomsmen. The whistles and comments started as soon as the band struck up "The Stripper," while Alex laughingly helped Ted to his knees.

"Allow me," Ted said, reaching for her foot. Removing her shoe, he bent and kissed her instep.

Shrill whistles split the air, as well as laughter and applause.

"No hands, no hands," several insisted, and Ted put his hands behind his back.

To the heavy drumbeat of the music, Annie raised the hem of her bridal gown by inches, then lowered it before raising it again. Ted planted several kisses in a row on her exposed leg, clownishly waiting for her to raise her gown again. By the time Annie had raised it above her knee to show the garter, she and Ted were laughing so hard neither could help the other. Her whole body shook, and he couldn't stop laughing long enough to grab the garter with his teeth. And because he kept missing, it tickled her even more. Eventually, Ted managed to grab the rosette in his teeth and start tugging the garter down. Halfway, he started pulling it back up again.

Annie leaned over and said next to his ear, "I thought you were in a hurry!"

With an arched brow, he turned a roguish look at her, then motioned upward with his chin. He did it again, pulling up with the rosette in his teeth, till she got the drift of his message and raised her leg. The garter slid off, with Ted nipping at Annie's arch as it passed over the top of her foot. Waving it triumphantly in the air, Ted stood and turned, then tossed it over his shoulder. Annie held her breath when it looked as if Kit would grab it, then Alex made a lunging dive in front of him to come up the winner. Ted clapped him on the back.

He had barely drawn Annie to her feet when Celia came up to her with the bridal bouquet. The bridesmaids and single women chased the men from the floor, except for Ted who held Annie's free hand. Holding tightly to the bouquet, she made a production of swinging it from in front of her to the top of her head.

Those gathered around counted out loud. "One."

Annie glanced to her right as she lowered the bouquet for the count of two. Celia stood to that side rather than in back of her. It didn't look as if her sister planned to try to be the next bride.

On the count of three, Annie brought her arm up to the top of the arch, then loosened her grip at an angle. The bouquet flew through the air and hit Celia squarely in the chest before she realized it was coming in her direction.

"Beautiful hook shot," Ted said laughingly as she turned toward her stunned sister.

They watched Celia surrounded by a swarm of congratulating women and Alex approaching her as he swung Annie's garter on his index finger like a lasso. He leaned in close to say something to Celia and while a slight smile remained frozen on her sister's face, Annie knew her well enough to know she was spitting mad. Celia answered Alex and although the laughter and music prevented her from actually hearing her sister's reply, Annie knew she had said no.

Celia politely but forcefully made her way to Annie's side. Alex watched her with a perplexed expression but made no effort to follow. "Come on," she said, ignoring the congratulations being offered for catching the bouquet. "Aunt Nola is waiting in our room to help you change."

Meekly Annie turned, whispered to Ted that she wouldn't be long, and followed Celia out of the ballroom. Walking down the long corridor to a rear elevator, Annie allowed the *swish, swish* of her gown to fill the silence. She hadn't grown up with Celia without learning when to be quiet. The music to "The Stripper" kept running through her mind, as well as the teasing glint in Ted's eye as he playfully removed her garter.

Aunt Nola answered their knock at the door of the room she and the girls would stay in that evening. "Your clothes are all laid out, Annie. With the two of us to help you, you can be ready in under fifteen minutes." Her aunt was already reaching for the row of buttons down her back when she noticed the flowers Celia carried. "*You* caught the bouquet?" she asked on a high note of surprise.

Laying it aside, Celia reached up to remove Annie's veil. "Yes. The best man and I remain a matched set. He caught the garter." Her lovely face remained perfectly smooth, as did her voice with no intonation.

Out of the corner of her eye, Annie caught her aunt's arrested expression before she shrugged eloquently. "Well, you can both tell me all about it over a late supper." At Celia's start of surprise, Aunt Nola said, "Oh, did I forget to tell you?" She returned to the buttons and spoke from behind Annie's back. "Alex invited the bridal party to a light meal here at the hotel later, after Annie and Ted are off. He said we'd all be hungry again after everything was over." Aunt Nola bent lower as she reached the end of the row. "Such a nice young man. Too bad he lives back east, but he told me he travels here a lot."

Surreptitiously, Annie waggled her fingers at Aunt Nola out of Celia's line of sight. By the tightening of her sister's lips, it wouldn't take much more to goad her into a full revolt. Fortunately, her aunt held her tongue except for exclaiming over how beautiful Annie looked and how well everything had gone. They made it down to a side entrance near the ballroom only five minutes late.

Ted watched Annie hurry toward him and thanked the fates that had delivered her to his building in search of a home for her restaurant. He felt someone stir at his elbow and, turning his head, saw that Alex looked as enthralled as he felt. Laughter shook him gently, but he stilled it immediately.

If his friend hadn't caught on yet that he was hooked, Ted wasn't going to put him on the alert. Alex, who when asked to be his best man, had said, "Now, why would you want to go and do a thing like that? Couldn't you just live with her, you know, to see if it takes?"

Ted had replied obliquely that his boxing form wasn't

up to that kind of weight and insinuated that one day Alex too would fall prey to the parson's mousetrap. "Not me," his friend had insisted. "I'm not cut out for marriage. I'm like a gourmet, constantly searching and testing, but sure I'll never find the perfect meal."

Ted let his gaze rest on Celia a moment. Her similarity to Annie was strong in cast of feature and frame, and although he had found her to be pleasant enough, she didn't seem to have Annie's exuberance or zest or whatever it was that made his Annie particularly right for him.

He grasped her hands and held them wide as he whistled in approval. "Very chic," he said, admiring the cherry red of her coat dress against the creaminess of her complexion.

"Raw silk which is guaranteed to be virtually crush proof," Annie explained. "So no matter what our destination tomorrow, I should arrive looking like I do now. Won't you tell me where we're going?"

"No, it's to be a surprise." Annie's dimple deepened as she pretended to pout, and he leaned down to kiss it. Soft, fragrant, and his. "Kiss your aunt good-bye. It's time to go."

The bridal party followed them through the revolving door out to the sidewalk. To Ted's amazement, it looked as if the entire wedding party had moved outdoors. Rice began pelting them halfway to the curb. As those in front parted to make way for them, he could see for the first time that the limo had been decorated in traditional style.

Amid the shower of rice and calls for happiness, he escorted Annie to the car where Alex stood waiting to open the door. He had clued his best man in on the surprise awaiting Annie inside, but he didn't want everyone else to know about it. At the last possible moment, Alex opened the door and Ted quickly followed Annie into the interior. As soon as the door closed, the car pulled away.

She had stopped midway across the rear seat and stared at the sprays of tiny white flowers which festooned the other seat of the limo. She finally slid over, picking up a bouquet prepared for her, and buried her face in the drift of white. After a moment, she whispered, "Oh, Ted. Apple blossoms!" And sniffed. The face she turned to him was dewy with unshed tears in juxtaposition with a heartbreaking smile.

"If you tell me you're allergic to them, I'm going to feel like an idiot."

"No, silly. I'm just so h-happy."

"Well, thank goodness for that," he said, handing her his handkerchief. "I'd hate for everyone at the hotel to think you were regretting your marriage already."

"H-hotel? Aren't we going to the apartment?"

"We are not." He tucked her head on his shoulder. "As of now, Mrs. Carlyle, you will live in the lap of luxury. For the next two weeks of our honeymoon anyway. After that, I promise to do my best to provide well for you."

"What about our luggage?"

"Waiting for us at the hotel."

"Oh, my toiletry bag—"

"On the front seat of the car." When she was quiet for a few moments, Ted said, "What, no more questions?"

"Yes, one. Where on earth did you find apple blossoms in June?"

"It wasn't easy." He chuckled. "The florists thought I was nuts, but I finally found one who suggested putting branches just budding into cold storage."

Annie snuggled closer. "It was sweet of you to think of it." Her head moved a little until her face slanted up toward his. "Funny, but I find it hard to reconcile this romantic side of you to the rather stuffy business-is-all man I met barely three months ago." Her breath was warm on the side of Ted's neck.

"One of those little discoveries I mentioned it was going to be so much fun finding out." He lowered his head, intending only to drop a light kiss on her tantalizingly close lips. But gentleness disappeared in the heat that blazed to life between them, until Ted unwillingly tore his mouth away. "This ride needs to be either shorter or longer," he said, shifting on the seat and ducking his head to peer through the window.

Annie peeked at him through her lashes. The planes of his face appeared taut and made him look forbidding. As she knew from resting against his side, his body had gone from its familiar hardness to rigidity. What had happened?

Fortunately for her peace of mind, the car pulled to the curb within a matter of minutes. From there, as far as she was concerned, it was like entering Aladdin's cave. Vases were produced, the sprays of apple blossom gathered and conveyed, along with Annie's case and themselves, into the hotel in the tender care of a gloved bellman. Nice technique: no waiting in line for registration, no hanging out till someone could help them with their possessions, few though they were. They were conducted through an ornate lobby to a glass elevator from which they could watch the play of lights and people. Their own personal genie supplied the magic password and ushered them into a beautifully luxurious suite where a cold supper had been left for their enjoyment. Silky fabrics and beautiful woods gleamed in the low lights throughout the suite which had been prepared for them.

Finally left to themselves, Ted joined Annie at the floor-to-ceiling windows overlooking the city. Slowly, he reminded himself. Slowly. Careful not to let his body brush hers, he put his hands at her waist, then leaned over and kissed her on the side of her neck. Her sweet fragrance filled his senses and his lips softened and opened, tasting as they had that morning the particular scent that was hers alone. His mouth trailed from one side to the other, pausing along the way to savor the exposed delicate stem of her neck, bared by Annie's still upswept hair.

When he realized his fingers were moving in a circular pattern on the trim hollows of her hips, he used the pressure of his mouth alongside her neck to turn her to him. "Are you hungry?" he asked against her throat. He felt the slight movement of her chin as she shook her head. "Thirsty?" His tongue flirted with the tiny dip of her collarbone.

Again that small movement, but this time a "no" sighed between her parted lips. He raised his hands from her hips, up past the flat planes of her midriff, and filled them with the heavy warmth of her breasts. His mouth found hers the same instant his thumbs began to circle her nipples, trapping Annie's gasp as his tongue dueled lightly with her own.

Her arms twined around his waist and she closed the distance between them. She rose slightly until her body fitted against his. At the touch of her hips on his engorged flesh, Ted slipped his arms around her. His hands raced over the curve of her bottom and, lifting her, brought her fully against him. She tilted her hips and he ground himself at her through their clothes. In her innocence, Annie inflamed him, weakening his control and his plan to proceed slowly. The urge to bury himself in her warmth made him ache. With an audible groan, he wrenched his thoughts to Annie and making this first time perfect for her.

It had been bad enough being tantalized by her for the past month and a half and knowing there wasn't a damned thing he was going to do about it. It may have been an old-fashioned idea, but it seemed right for Annie. To seal his determination, Ted had carefully orchestrated their time alone to eliminate temptation. Even so, Annie had come damned close a couple of times to losing her virginity before the wedding. Especially this morning. Remembering the feel of her nearly naked body in his arms, he gritted his teeth and buried his face against her neck, focusing his attention on fighting down his soaring desire to strip her where they stood. Annie moved against him again as she rained kisses along the only area of his body she could reach, the side of his face and neck. He shifted his hold on her and, dropping one shoulder, slid an arm around her legs and lifted her. He couldn't wait any longer. And he didn't think she wanted to either.

"Where are we going?" Annie's voice was barely a whisper.

He glanced down at her as she looped her arms around his neck. "Some place infinitely more comfortable than the sitting room floor—or couch."

She smiled at him through heavy-lidded eyes. "The floor? Really?"

He laughed and strode into the dimly lit bedroom. "You'd be surprised at the varied places that can be put to a useful purpose."

"Ah," Annie said against his neck, "another of those delightful discoveries you mentioned."

He loosened his hold and let her slide against his body to the floor. Kissing her on the tip of her nose, he said, "Don't go away."

He removed his tuxedo jacket and hung it on the back of the desk chair. The formal tie followed. He heel-and-toed one shoe against the other until he pried one loose, then the other, while pulling his shirttail out and unbuttoning his cuffs and collar. Starting on the line of buttons down the front of his shirt, he walked back to Annie. A step for each button of his shirt undone. She reached out and helped him finish, then stood grasping a side of his shirt in each hand and looking at him uncertainly.

"Come here." He took her by the hand and led her over to the closet. "I know you want to wear this dress tomorrow, so I'm very helpfully going to relieve you of it." A small smile appeared, deepening her dimple. He undid the few ornate buttons quickly. "Of course," he added, turning Annie so her back was to him as he eased it off her shoulders, "the fact that it also greatly enhances what I have in mind doesn't enter into it. No," he said when she would have turned back around, "stay as you are just a moment."

He put her dress on a hanger and hung it in the closet. "Now, where were we?" He placed his palms against the sides of her arms at the shoulder, holding her in place. She wore a wisp of a slip with tiny straps that did nothing to hide the curve of her hips. He slipped his arms over her shoulder and filled his hands with her while nuzzling her neck. "God, you're so soft."

She arched into his hands and reached behind her, pulled him against her. He chuckled against her hair. "You're a fast learner." Then his breath caught in his throat as she swiveled her hips, all the while pressing back against him. He moved one hand down the satiny smoothness of her abdomen and caressed her through her slip. She jerked against his fingers, and he whispered, "Easy," in her ear. He stroked her gently, letting her learn his touch. When her hips started to move against him once more, he turned her, feasting his eyes on her loveliness.

"So beautiful."

He pulled pins from her hair, releasing it to cascade over her shoulders. Holding her by her waist once more, he traced with his tongue the lace of her slip where it met the creamy rise of her breasts. He lowered his head and traced the curve of one breast, opening his mouth and tasting her as he traveled back to the valley between them, and repeated the action on the other side. This time though, his open mouth sought her nipple and closed on it through the filmy fabric of her slip.

Annie couldn't block her cry of pleasure as he sucked at her through the thin silk. His mouth was so hot, yet she shivered from the exquisite shock that rippled through her. From within, a tightening grew, and it deepened as Ted's mouth moved to her other breast. She strained against him, wanting she knew not what, but as her breath quickened to the beat of her blood, her hands searched blindly to bring him against her to help assuage some of the pressure she felt building inside her.

"Not yet," he said, moving his hands down her arms and effectively blocking her search as he held them at her sides and knelt before her. "Not yet, my sweet."

His mouth moved down her body, scorching her through the silk, then leaving her shivering in its damp coolness as he moved on, ever lower. She gasped as his mouth fastened on her at the apex of her thighs and felt a rush of liquid heat pouring through her. Her flailing hands found his head, and she slid her fingers through his hair and held on as he worked his magic on her.

Ted felt her begin to tremble and ran his hands down the outside length of her long legs in a circular, warming motion. As he raised his hands against the silkiness of her nylons, her slip caught in his fingers and he raised that, too. His questing fingers found bare skin and the elastic of a garter belt, then another wisp of thin material. He slid the slip up to her waist and held it there, nudging aside the fold of fabric that blocked his goal. He let his teeth graze her femininity through the final layer of her panties, then soothed her with his tongue.

Her moan and the whisper of his name enflamed him. "Now, baby," he said, standing to release the button and zipper of his pants. "Now I'll teach you real pleasure."

As Ted bent to step out of his pants, Annie leaned on him. There was no strength left in her legs. Her entire body seemed suffused with languor, yet tremors that seemed to start on the inside shook her. She thought at first that her legs had given way, then Ted's mouth found hers and she was crushed against his chest as he lifted her. He placed her on the bed and followed her down, his weight pinning her and at the same time releasing another flood of liquid heat as she felt his hot skin along her body.

He lifted away from her, and she felt him pulling her up. When she realized he was trying to remove her slip, she helped him, frantic to feel her breasts against the hard planes of his chest. She reached for him as she fell back on the bed, but again Ted fended off her questing hands and held them above her head.

"Easy, love, easy. We've got all night," he said in a guttural voice Annie hardly recognized. "I want to see you in all your glory."

His lips trailed down her arms, her neck, around the perimeter of her breasts, planting fleeting kisses while his fingers followed behind. He worked his way down her body, turning her slightly to release the fastening of her garter belt. He laved the hollow of her belly button and her abdomen, his hands holding her hips still. Now it was his tantalizing fingers that devised a path for his mouth. He released her nylons and peeled one down, his fingers grazing her skin lightly and setting her aflame, then quenching the fire with his mouth. He repeated the same benediction on her other leg, then turned her over and began the magic again from her neck down.

Annie had ceased to think. She could only feel. An inferno raged within, and she squirmed and twisted against Ted and the sensations he caused to rocket through her. At last he turned her and her mouth sought his greedily. He nipped at her lips, and her tongue scraped across his teeth before his tongue plunged into her mouth. She started as his fingers tangled in her triangle of hair, but as they began a magical dance there she strained against his hand, wanting, seeking more.

His fingers entered her and she felt a measure of release with the motion of his hand. Then the pressure began to mount again and she became aware of a low keening sound. She choked it off when she realized the sounds came from her own throat, but Ted kissed her again and said, "Let it out, baby. Tell me if it feels good."

He lowered his head until he was sucking and pulling hard at her breast, his fingers dancing away below. "Do you like this?" he asked and not waiting for her answer, took her other nipple into his mouth, grazing it with his teeth and pulling at her.

His mouth left her breast and she cried out, "No, don't stop." The inner tightening had reached a pitch where Annie felt she was on the edge of a precipice, but it faded as his lips moved down her body. "No," she repeated in disappointment, her hands curled into fists.

"Don't worry, love. I'm not going to stop."

His tongue traced a path from her hip, across where it joined her leg, and rose in a curve over her abdomen to her other hip before tracing the seam of that leg. Then the warmth of his mouth was full on her and she tried to protest, but his hands held her hips prisoner and his tongue was in her and she had no breath except to pant as the upward spiral began again.

His mouth moved on her, his tongue flicking wildly, and Annie bent her head back into the bed until she was bent like a bow. The spark of warmth begun by his mouth grew until it exploded like a volcano, and the tremors that shook her gushed like fire through her veins. The spasms were still echoing when he moved up her body and found her mouth.

Ted positioned himself between her legs and began to ease into her. He stopped when he reached the barrier of her virginity and felt Annie tensing under him. "It's going to hurt for a moment, love, but only for a moment."

Before she had a chance to react, Ted plunged into her, stopping her cry with his mouth. Beyond that first penetration, he halted and began again to love her with his mouth and hands. He didn't know how long he could hold out before his body took over for its own release, but he focused on bringing Annie pleasure and that could only happen if she relaxed. Before he believed possible, she began to move against him in a dance as old as time. Her response delighted him and at the same time increased his dilemma, for every motion enflamed him more.

Bracing himself above her, he began to move within her. The pleasure was so exquisite it hurt. But he prolonged the agony with slow thrusts, straining for control, until Annie was meeting him with thrusts of her own. His entire body throbbed and gleamed with sweat, but still he watched her face in the lamplight. At last her expression became taut, expectant, and as he felt the first quiver within her, his control broke. His thrusts became powerful and he drove into her hard, seeking his own release. Her sobs of fulfillment sent him over the edge with a cry of love.

Although Ted lay upon her, his head resting against her throat and shoulder, Annie didn't feel crushed by his weight. How could she? She was completely boneless, her body reduced to a mass of tingling nerve endings. A wave of tenderness swept her and her arms tightened on Ted, her fingers stroking his damp skin.

As though her movement had wakened him, he stirred and started to move away. "No," she said, tightening her hold even more, "please don't go."

He chuckled next to her ear. "I wasn't planning to go anywhere. I don't have the strength." His lips moved over hers gently. "How about you? Are you all right?"

"Ummm-hmmm. Very all right, if the object was to make me feel complete, replete, to use your words, 'well loved.' " Then she smiled up at him. "I feel like a bowl of Jell-O." Kissing him, she said, "I love you."

"I love you, too, Mrs. Carlyle." He shifted his weight to the side, pulling her with him, and found a pillow. Idly, his fingers trailed up and down her hip. After a few moments he said, "Jell-O?"

"Hmmm. Describes it exactly."

"Your analogies amaze me. Do you know how often you say something that refers to food?"

She yawned. "Well, after all, I'm not a lawyer. I'm a cook."

He squeezed her to him. "And a very good one, too."

A few moments passed, and Annie heard and felt him yawning as well. She snuggled closer. Her eyelids were getting heavy when she thought of something. "Ted?"

"Hmmm?"

"Are people like Jell-O?"

"What?" His voice sounded foggy next to her ear.

She struggled to keep her eyes open. "When you make Jell-O, it's all soft and . . . mushy, like we are now. But you put it in the fridge for a while to set and, presto, it's firm." She heard the rumble in his chest before his laughter erupted.

Still chuckling, Ted hugged her to him. He was going to love being married to this woman. He brought his chin up and smiled into her heavy eyes. "The answer is yes. But like Jell-O, we have to *set* for a while." He laughed again. "Give me a while and I'll show you."

EPILOGUE

"It's my turn," Kit said, trying to relieve Ted of his burden.

"No, it's not. I just took her from Aunt Nola." Ted shifted his infant daughter to the opposite shoulder, away from his brother-in-law.

"Look, you're her father. I'm just a visiting uncle. You get to hold her whenever you want."

"You'd think so, wouldn't you?" Ted said, his air one of a man with a grievance. "A man works, slaving to make life more comfortable for his wife and child. When he comes home at the end of a long day, does he get to kiss his wife hello? Does he get to hold his only child? No, he doesn't," he told an amused Kit.

"No, he doesn't," agreed Annie, coming up behind him. She put her arms around him and kissed her daughter's head where it lay on his shoulder. "Not when the house is full of company and his wife is busy cooking dinner. If you think it's crowded out here, you should come into the kitchen."

Ted pulled her around with his free arm, drew her to him, and kissed her thoroughly. Still holding Annie next

217

to him, he cocked an eyebrow at Kit and said, "Any objection?"

"When I can see how happy it makes her?" Kit shook his head, then added, "You must teach me your technique sometime."

Annie broke from his embrace to welcome her brother. "Not for sometime yet. Don't you have another two years to run on your contract?" At his nod, Annie said to Ted, "No instructions until he's home for good. Otherwise we might wind up with a lovely senorita as part of the family."

"Would that be bad?" Ted asked, relenting and letting Kit hold his sleeping niece.

"Only if it meant he was tempted to make his home south of the border." Annie tucked the end of the baby's blanket in tighter. "If he did that, when would Catherine Ann Carlyle ever see her uncle?"

"Isn't that name rather a mouthful for such a little bundle?" Kit rubbed his chin against the downy hair of the sleeping infant.

Annie laughed. "She'll grow into it. Dinner in thirty minutes," she added over her shoulder as she left them.

Ted's gaze followed her trim shape down the hall. She was wearing one of the dresses he had bought her in Italy on their honeymoon. He smiled, remembering, but then his body did some remembering of its own. He swore under his breath, impatient with the delay in making love to her. Another two weeks seemed like a century, he thought, turning to take drink orders from his guests.

Presiding later at the head of the table, Ted gazed with pleasure at his assembled family. Aunt Nola, of course, and Annie's two sisters. Since Catherine and Annie had come home from the hospital, the three of them were in his house almost as much as they were in their own. Which was no hardship since he and Annie had found a lovely brownstone at the end of one of the streets opening on to Lincoln Park only a few blocks from her former home.

He hadn't thought there could be greater happiness than being married to Annie and living in their own home, with family to drop in from time to time. That was before the advent of his daughter, Catherine, and the steady stream of visitors occasioned by her arrival. Life was good and he was a very lucky man.

Kit was at the end of the table near Annie, home from Peru for a month's leave and the reason why their home was jammed with welcoming relatives. Their daughter's baptism in two days had been planned to coincide with his return.

Uncle Tully was there with his wife. Next to them were Duke's twins Trevor and Trudy. Both had done well in their first year of college and neither had changed the plan of becoming a lawyer and a policeman, respectively. Across from Tully sat Uncle Marmaduke with Ted's mother. The courtship, if it could be called that, hadn't changed in tempo much that he could see during the past year. Annie thought differently. Next to him sat Consuela, and he realized with a start she was talking about the date of her daughter's discharge from the hospital.

"No more problems with Immigration?" Kit called from his end of the table.

"Certainly not," Annie answered. Her heart swelled as she saw Ted was in what she called his counting mode: enumerating their blessings like totems. Only the number kept changing, depending upon who happened to drop in at the end of the day. "But they're returning to Mexico for a long visit once Maria is up to it."

"Speaking of returns," Ted spoke up, "I heard from Alex today. He's being transferred here to his company's headquarters."

Annie's gaze immediately shifted to her sister Celia, whose only reaction was a slight pause in raising a cup to her lips. Alex had visited them twice during the past year, but Annie didn't think the visits could be called much of a success from Celia's reactions at the time. But if Alex was going to be around permanently . . .

She came back to the present with Aunt Nola's question about when Alex would arrive.

"Within a month if things go as planned," Ted said.

"Such a nice young man." Aunt Nola's head turned toward Celia as she said, "We'll have to do what we can to help him settle in."

Annie's gaze met Ted's down the length of the table, and they shared a secret smile. Aunt Nola had obviously decided to play matchmaker again.

SHARE THE FUN . . .
SHARE YOUR NEW-FOUND TREASURE!!

You don't want to let your new books out of your sight? That's okay. Your friends can get their own. Order below.

No. 33 A TOUCH OF LOVE by Patricia Hagan
Kelly seeks peace and quiet and finds paradise in Mike's arms.

No. 34 NO EASY TASK by Chloe Summers
Hunter is wary when Doone delivers a package that will change his life.

No. 35 DIAMOND ON ICE by Lacey Dancer
Diana could melt even the coldest of hearts. Jason hasn't a chance.

No. 36 DADDY'S GIRL by Janice Kaiser
Slade wants more than Andrea is willing to give. Who wins?

No. 37 ROSES by Caitlin Randall
It's an inside job & K.C. helps Brett find more than the thief!

No. 38 HEARTS COLLIDE by Ann Patrick
Matthew finds big trouble and it's spelled P-a-u-l-a.

No. 39 QUINN'S INHERITANCE by Judi Lind
Gabe and Quinn share an inheritance and find an even greater fortune.

No. 40 CATCH A RISING STAR by Laura Phillips
Justin is seeking fame; Beth helps him find something more important.

No. 41 SPIDER'S WEB by Allie Jordan
Silvia's quiet life explodes when Fletcher shows up on her doorstep.

No. 42 TRUE COLORS by Dixie DuBois
Julian helps Nikki find herself again but will she have room for him?

No. 43 DUET by Patricia Collinge
Adam & Marina fit together like two perfect parts of a puzzle!

No. 44 DEADLY COINCIDENCE by Denise Richards
J.D.'s instincts tell him he's not wrong; Laurie's heart says trust him.

No. 45 PERSONAL BEST by Margaret Watson
Nick is a cynic; Tess, an optimist. Where does love fit in?

No. 46 ONE ON ONE by JoAnn Barbour
Vincent's no saint but Loie's attracted to the devil in him anyway.

No. 47 STERLING'S REASONS by Joey Light
Joe is running from his conscience; Sterling helps him find peace.

No. 48 SNOW SOUNDS by Heather Williams
In the quiet of the mountain, Tanner and Melaine find each other again.

No. 49 SUNLIGHT ON SHADOWS by Lacey Dancer
Matt and Miranda bring out the sunlight in each other's lives.

No. 50 RENEGADE TEXAN by Becky Barker
Rane lives only for himself—that is, until he meets Tamara.

No. 51 RISKY BUSINESS by Jane Kidwell
Blair goes undercover but finds more than she bargained for with Logan.

No. 52 CAROLINA COMPROMISE by Nancy Knight
Richard falls for Dee and the glorious Old South. Can he have both?

No. 53 GOLDEN GAMBLE by Patrice Lindsey
The stakes are high! Who has the winning hand—Jessie or Bart?

No. 54 DAYDREAMS by Marina Palmieri
Kathy's life is far from a fairy tale. Is Jake her Prince Charming?

No. 55 A FOREVER MAN by Sally Falcon
Max is trouble and Sandi wants no part of him. She *must* resist!

No. 56 A QUESTION OF VIRTUE by Carolyn Davidson
Neither Sara nor Cal can ignore their almost magical attraction.

Meteor Publishing Corporation
Dept. 192, P. O. Box 41820, Philadelphia, PA 19101-9828

Please send the books I've indicated below. Check or money order only—no cash, stamps or C.O.D.s (PA residents, add 6% sales tax). I am enclosing $2.95 plus 75¢ handling fee for *each* book ordered.

Total Amount Enclosed: $_____.

____ No. 33	____ No. 39	____ No. 45	____ No. 51
____ No. 34	____ No. 40	____ No. 46	____ No. 52
____ No. 35	____ No. 41	____ No. 47	____ No. 53
____ No. 36	____ No. 42	____ No. 48	____ No. 54
____ No. 37	____ No. 43	____ No. 49	____ No. 55
____ No. 38	____ No. 44	____ No. 50	____ No. 56

Please Print:
Name _____
Address _____ Apt. No. _____
City/State _____ Zip _____

Allow four to six weeks for delivery. Quantities limited.